Donald McCathern
2005

GERALD MCCATHERN

PALO DURO GOLD

Outlaw Books

OTHER READERS COMMENTS

My Great Uncle has a signed copy of *Dry Bones* and my Step Father picked it up and began reading and did not hardly set it down until he had finished. We must have the other two books, *Horns* and *Devil's Rope* -- Belinda Hohertz -- Abilene, TX

I purchased *Horns* from you while visiting your canyon and am now ready to read the next adventure of One arm Jim, Ned and the Ceebara ranch. I especially appreciated the irony of the buffalo hunters demise closing out your depiction, *Horns*. I enjoyed your story, writing style and your brand of Texas history and have a hunger for more! Please send the next book in your series. -- Jim Paul -- Ennis, Texas

---

I purchased the first book in your trilogy series, *Horns*. Being a rather picky reader, I really wasn't expecting very much from an "unknown writer". Boy, was I ever WRONG. I loved the book. Your character development and insight are magnificent. Through your descriptive verse, I can actually visualize what is happening and picture the surrounding landscapes. It is almost as if I have actually visited the characters on their ranch or made one of the rides across it with them. I am very anxious to have the final two books in the series, *Dry Bones* and *Devil's Rope*? I will continue to let my contacts in on my little secret of the wonderful writer I have discovered. -- Jacque Harris -- Ft. Worth, Texas

---

I could hardly lay your book down, but alas duty called. When I had a spare moment, I would once again delve into the captivating pages of *Quarantine*. I thoroughly enjoyed every moment of it. I wish to order the Trilogy, *Horns*, *Dry Bones* and *Devil's Rope*. -- Julie Jones - Oklahoma

First of all, let me tell you how much I have enjoyed the two books , *Horns* and *Dry Bones*. The best I have ever read! -- Gary Noblett, Pampa Texas

My wife, Lucy, and I were visiting Palo Duro Canyon and purchased your book Quarantine! I thoroughly enjoyed the book. It was all you promised it would be for a Robin Cook fan. Please write more like it. -- Rodney Thompson --Florida.

I have just completed reading Horns, and enjoyed every minute of it. It touched me so much that I haven't started Dry Bones for fear my red eyes will never disappear. -- Katherine Tinney, New York.

Author! Author! Author! Just this moment finished Dry Bones. Had to sit down and let you know how much I enjoyed this book. It is every bit as enjoyable as Horns and maybe more so! Earl J. Gorel -- Houston, Texas

Both my husband and I enjoyed your book Horns. We can't wait to receive Quarantine and Dry Bones. -- Darla Criswell -- Texas.

The first book, Horns, I thoroughly enjoyed, the second, Dry Bones, I couldn't put down. I can't wait for Quarantine. -- Richard Opperud -- Texas.

Palo Duro Gold

a Novel by

Gerald McCathern

Copyright 2005 by Gerald McCathern
First Printing 2005

ISBN 0-9656946-6-6

A work of fiction, with historical
references and documentation.

Published by
Outlaw Books
419 Centre Street
Hereford, Texas 79045

Phone 806-364-2838
Fax 806-364-5522
e-mail/ gmccath@wtrt.net
web page/ outlawbooks.net

Dedicated to the memory of Louis L'Amour, who gave me untold hours of reading pleasure with his tales about the west.

PALO DURO GOLD

Foreword

The *Llano Estacado*, Staked Plains, in far north Texas, is a geologic wonder -- rising four thousand feet above sea level, and a thousand feet above the surrounding lands. Geologists tell us that millions of years ago, an ancient sea covered this land, and as tectonic forces pushed the land above the sea, the water, in its rush to escape, carved huge canyons along its edges and through its heart.

Palo Duro is one of those canyons, carved by the head waters of the Red River. It is majestic in its size and beauty, one thousand feet deep and one hundred and twenty miles long -- second only to the Grand Canyon of the Colorado. Its steep walls reflect the multi-colors of the sandstones, shales, gypsums and clays which were deposited when God's handiwork was creating the world, eons of time ago.

This novel is set in time, 1875 to 1885, a mere blink of an eye in God's calender, and after the forces of nature created the canyon. For hundreds of years, the land of the Palo Duro was void of any kind of civilization, but was a home to the coyote, the bob cat, the deer, the antelope, the buzzard, the rattle snake, and the great herds of American Bison -- the buffalo.

Then came the wild and free red man -- discovering a place of refuge when the cold winter winds howled across the flat, grass covered prairies. A place swarming with the animals which were needed for his survival -- the meat of the animals for sustenance, the skins of the animals for clothing and shelter, and the bones of the animals for tools, utensils and weapons.

In a land of little moisture, the cool, clear, spring fed waters of the Red River gave him water to drink and in which to bathe. Its bounty of fish supplemented the red meat of the animals. Berries from the bushes, and beans from the trees were plentiful. It was truly a paradise for a people who had not yet developed the art of producing food from the soil. And he was very protective of the canyon which he called home. He was willing to fight and die for control of his utopia.

And fight he must, as the encroachment of civilization brought the white man -- the white eyes, the blue coats, the yellow legs, as he would know them -- to the edge of his domain.

His land was the last frontier in the state of Texas. Civilization had passed it by, believing the land to be a dry, treeless, wasteland -- unworthy and unable to support life. But the migrating herds of buffalo left a trail for the white man to follow, and he began to covet the red man's land. As he began to slaughter the red man's commissary, he moved ever closer to the canyon called Palo Duro. A five year war between the red man and the white man ended with the last battle being fought in the depths of the canyon, with the hapless Indians being forced from their land, and made to live on a desolate reservation, two hundred miles to the east.

The *Llano Estacado* and the Palo Duro Canyon, in 1876, became a white man's land -- and the great herds of buffalo were slaughtered and replaced by longhorn cattle. Huge ranches, some as large as a million acres, were born, and cowboys replaced the Indians and became the principal possessors of the land.

History records that with the cowboy and the longhorn cattle, came the outlaws, the gamblers, and the gun slingers. It was a land of men and few women. A wild and rough land, where the newly developed six shooter and repeating rifle was the law. For ten years, 1875 to 1885, the centers of civilization in a forty thousand square mile area, lay in two lawless towns, Mobeetie and Tascosa, and the principal residents of those two small communities were whiskey merchants and prostitutes.

With no newspapers, the early recorded history of the area is sparse, but many great historians such as J. Evetts Haley (Charles Goodnight)-- J. Frank Dobie (The Longhorns) -- Frederick Rathjen (The Texas Panhandle Frontier) -- Pauline and R.L. Robertson (Panhandle Pilgrimage), have filled in many of the historical holes and brought to life the interesting and almost unbelievable events which took place during this ten year period.

However, for lack of evidence, much of the history of the area has been ignored or lost through time, and speculation has led to fictionalized versions of unrecorded events. Where fact has ended, fiction has taken over.

I have been a resident of the Texas Panhandle all of my seventy eight years, as was my father who lived for ninety seven years. My grandfather, lived to be sixty, but his father -- my great grandfather --lived to be one hundred and six years old. He brought his family from Van Zandt County, Texas, in covered wagons, trailing a herd of longhorns across the Red River.

My father was foreman of the Figure 2 ranch in the eastern Texas Panhandle and met many of the old time cattle barons, including Charles Goodnight. As a child, growing up in Mobeetie, I heard many of their tales, versions which sometimes failed to follow the strict documented and recorded historical facts.

Many of the events which take place in *Palo Duro Gold* are based on documented history, however, many of the events are speculation on my part, based on some of the stories which were passed down to me by my ancestors -- and many of the events are strictly fictional, built *around* historical events and historical characters, and brought to you, hopefully, for your reading enjoyment.

Although many of the characters are actual, such as Charles Goodnight, Mary Goodnight, Tom Bugbee, Temple Houston, Deacon Bates, Senator Dorsey, Bat Masterson, Billy Dixon, Billy the Kid, and the vicious outlaw, Sostenes l'Archeveque -- many of the characters are fictional, such as the entire Ceebara ranch family, Chief Parker, Smokey Brown and many of the outlaw types, saloon keepers and painted ladies.

The Palo Duro gold was factual, as recorded by J.Evetts Haley, in his excellent book, *Charles Goodnight.* Pauline and R.L. Robertson record the event in their excellent book, *Panhandle Pilgrimage*, and an article in the September 25, 1966 issue of the *Amarillo Sunday News-Globe,* entitled *A Killer's Legacy of Terror,* relates the exciting story and is on file in the Panhandle Plains Museum.

No one, however, has discovered the location of the gold -- until now? I have tried to fill in the historical holes with my fictional ideas, consequently, I must designate this story as fictional, with this comment -- *if it didn't happen this way, it should have*!

Pleasant reading.

The author

1

The black racing stallion stretched his long legs across the rough terrain as the rider touched spurs lightly to his side. He had been running this way for nearly an hour, and the exertion was beginning to tell on his breathing.

"Hold up, boy," the rider said softly, speaking Spanish, as he pulled gently on the reins.

They stopped on the rim of a small knoll in the otherwise flat and deserted country of Eastern New Mexico Territory. The horse, dripping sweat, blew his breath noisily through his nostrils, as his master looked back down the trail from which they had come. A small dust cloud could be seen more than five miles to the west. The rider smiled and spoke once more to the stallion, "They will never catch us now, Diablo," as he dismounted and stretched his legs.

Tall, over six feet, his sweat-soaked, unruly blond hair curled below the large, Mexican sombrero which was tied securely below his chin. The sombrero was adorned with the skin of a huge rattlesnake which coiled menacingly around the crown.

Dust and blood covered the black, form-fitting suit of fine linen. The wide bottomed trousers were slashed up the side and laced with red and green ribbons. Buttons on the vest were silver as was the huge buckle on his belt. Twin pearl-handled revolvers hung from the belt which encircled his waist, and a bandoleer of rifle bullets was draped across his chest. A new Winchester repeating rifle was stuffed securely in the saddle boot.

Beneath the broad hat band, his long blond hair and blue eyes struck a strange contrast on the swarthy, olive-brown tint of his skin. He considered himself Mexican although his father was French and his mother was Mexican-Indian.

He hated *gringos*. He had killed twenty-one by the time he was twenty-one years of age -- one for each year. His viciousness and hatred, however, was not limited to *gringos*, ten Mexicans had fallen victim to his murderous rampages. Even though he was Mexican, himself, he felt no remorse for the killings of his own kind. He killed for the love of killing. Mexicans in Santa Fe called him *El Darse Loco* -- Mad Dog Sostenes.

His birth name was Sostenes L'Archeveque[1] . When he was only eight years old, he watched as his father was tortured and murdered by a *gringo* and he swore, as he watched the dirt being thrown on his grave, to kill every *gringo* he met.

Although he wore his pistols tied to his leg like most gunfighters of the day, and wore a bandoleer of bullets wrapped around his chest, his favorite weapon was the sharp, pointed, double-edged dagger which hung from the back of his belt. Sharp as a razor, he loved to see the blood flow from the wounds which he could inflict with the blade.

He gave his victims no quarter -- to him, a fair fight only invited disaster. His method of operation was knifing or shooting

---

[1] Charles Goodnight - J.E. Haley

them from the back in order that they could not defend themselves. Last night, *gringo* victims numbers nineteen, twenty and
twenty-one were murdered by his guns in Jose's Cantina in Las
Vegas. Slipping his pistol from its holster below the table, he
shot the three unsuspecting gamblers, who were playing poker
with him, because he believed that they were cheating. Not satisfied with just gunning them down, in anger, he pulled the
sharp dagger from his belt and quickly slit the throats of each
of his victims, and laughed as their blood covered his hand and
spotted his clothing. Although the Cantina was crowded with
drinkers and gamblers, no one was willing to interfere for fear
that they would meet the same fate as the three unfortunate
gringos.

He laughed and shouted *"Adios, amigos!"* as he grabbed
up the stakes from the table, bolted out the back door of the
Cantina, mounted his black stallion, and rode east toward the
Texas-New Mexico border. Once he crossed the border into the
unsettled, lawless Texas Panhandle, he knew he would be safe -
- he had made this trip several times before, with posses hot on
his trail.

Borregos Plaza was his destination, a sheep ranch owned
and occupied by his brother-in-law, Nicholas "Cola" Martinez.
In recent years, Mexican sheep herders had migrated down the
Canadian River and had established a small community, Atascosa Plaza, in the Texas Panhandle, only thirty miles from the New
Mexico border. Atascosa was surrounded by several Mexican
Plazas -- Borregos, Romero, Salinas, Trujillo, Sandoval and Cha-
vez[2]. Sostenes did not stop for rest until he reached Salinas Plaza on the Texas- New Mexico border, where he knew he would

_____
2Panhandle Pilgrimage - Robertson

be safe from the pursuing vigilantes.

Salinas Plaza, named for the huge salt lake nearby, was occupied by twenty-five Mexican families, who operated stores and
saloons, and was frequented by salt traders from the Santa Fe
and Las Vegas area. Everyone in New Mexico knew and feared
Sostenes, and the crowd quickly left the Cantina when he swag-
gered through the door.

"Tequila!" he shouted, pounding the bar with his fist.

The frightened bar tender, poured him a glass, spilling
some on the bar.

Drinking it down in one gulp, Sostenes pushed the glass
forward and demanded another. "A steak -- rare!" he ordered.
Picking up his glass and the half-empty bottle, he walked to a
dark corner of the saloon and sat down with his back to the
wall and his eyes on the door.

The bartender delivered the steak, rare and still dripping
blood, and nervously asked if there was anything else. "Yes,"
Sostenes replied, "I want my horse fed and watered and a room.
If anyone comes asking for me, you are to tell them that you
have not seen me. You will be the first to feel the steel of my
blade if they find me."

"*Si, senor* -- I will tell no one," the frightened bartender replied.

Sostenes need not have worried, the posse, realizing that
the outlaw had crossed into Texas, turned and headed back to
Las Vegas. The next morning, the residents of Salinas were
thankful when the Mexican outlaw mounted his black stallion
and rode eastward into Texas down the Canadian River.

2

One month earlier, James and Steve Casner -- sons of John Casner, an Anglo sheepman, who had struck it rich in the California gold fields -- had preceded Sostenes into the area and were even now, departing Atascosa with their flock of sheep, looking for new pastures where there were few people and free grass. They were being guided to the head waters of the Red River by a young sheep herder from Borregos Plaza, a nephew of Sostenes.

John, tired of the drudgery of mining, dreamed of owning a sheep ranch some day. Hearing about the huge unsettled grasslands of the Texas Panhandle and a deep canyon which cut through the middle, he decided that this was where he would set roots. He called his four sons together and spoke of his plans.

"Lew, you and I will remain in California until we can dispose of our mining interests. James and Steve will take our gold bullion to Carson City and have it minted into gold coins. Near as I can tell, we must have nigh onto thirty-thousand dollars worth. I want them to take the gold to New Mexico, buy some sheep and herd them across the Llano Estacado to the head waters of the Red River. I hear there is a deep canyon there with plenty of water and grass. Pick out a good site, and set up a headquarters -- we're going into the sheep business."

"What about the Indians, Pa?" James asked. "I thought the Texas Panhandle was a Comanche stronghold."

"They ain't no more," old John explained. "I hear the cavalry came in and chased 'em all back to the reservations. That country is wide open and free for any one with guts enough to go in and take it. New Mexico sheep men have already laid claim to the grass along the Canadian River, just inside the Texas border, we'll stake our claim on the Red River in that deep canyon."

"Why don't we just take our flocks down the Canadian, too, Pa?" Steve asked.

"Mexicans!" the old man replied. "I don't want our ranch to be anywhere's near a bunch of Mexican sheep herders. Can't trust them, wouldn't be no time 'till they stole us blind, and leave us with an empty poke."

"You want us to carry all that gold with us, Pa?" James asked.

"Yes, you'll need to use a couple thousand dollars to buy sheep and supplies. Me and Lew will be there before winter sets in. Just don't be broadcasting to any one that you're carrying that kind of cash around. Once in the canyon, find a good place to hide it."

....

After purchasing five thousand sheep in Trinidad, Colorado, the two brothers hired two herders, and trailed the flock over Raton Pass and down the Canadian River to Atascosa in the Texas Panhandle. In Atascosa they hired a young Mexican lad to guide them across the flat prairie to the lip of Palo Duro Canyon.

Reaching the canyon, James and Steve dismounted and

walked to the edge of the caprock and gazed with awe at the panorama which lay before them. The sun was still a couple of hours before setting behind a cloudless sky, and its rays cast a golden sheen to the rocks and cliffs below. A huge buck deer, grazing on the lush grass a few feet below the rim of the canyon, looked up at the two men in surprise, then bounded out of view, around a point in the canyon wall.

Breathless, James said, almost in a whisper, "Would you look at that, Steve! All the colors of the rainbow, sparkling in the rocks. Must be a thousand feet to the bottom."

His brother gazed on the sight without answering, allowing his eyes to move slowly from the small blue stream which wound along the canyon's floor. Huge cottonwood trees, appearing as small bushes in the distance, lined the banks of the stream. The dark forms of hundreds of buffalo were grazing on the carpet of knee-deep green grass which stretched from one side of the canyon floor to the other. His eyes followed the stream as it faded in the blue haze of the distance, finally disappearing around a bend in the canyon.

"A sheepman's paradise, James -- a damned sheepman's paradise!" he finally answered.

Behind them, grazing on the lush prairie grass, five thousand sheep, being herded by two large sheep dogs were moving slowly across the flat, treeless prairie. A small, canvas covered wagon, pulled by two mules, stopped a short distance from the rim of the canyon, and a young Indian herder stepped down.

"We'll make camp here for the night," James said, as he led his horse back toward the herd. He made a motion with his hand and the two dogs began to circle the sheep.

A small playa lake, no more than three hundred yards from

the canyon's rim, filled by recent rains, would supply them with water until they could find a way down the canyon's walls.

....

The next morning, with the sun barely breaking the horizon across the canyon's rim, the two brothers looked once more at the changing scene below them. The canyon appeared different than what they had observed the day before, with the dark shadows on the face of the canyon's east wall, hiding much of the brightness of the colors. As they watched, and as the sun slowly rose, the colors began to reappear, and the canyon became cloaked once again in the reds of the clays, the blues of the shale, the yellows of the sandstone, and the whites of the gypsums.

Pointing, Steve shouted with excitement, "Look, James. With the sun casting shadows on the west face, there is the faint outline of a trail winding from the top to the bottom. It may just be a game trail, but it appears to be too wide for that. I'm betting that's the way the Indians were able to pass from the top to the bottom."

"Let's have a look," James responded, as he mounted his bay and rode around the rim towards the trail which Steve had spotted.

As Steve had suspected, the trail had been used by the Indians, winding from a small break in the caprock, down through a growth of Juniper trees, through a jumble of large boulders which had caved from the canyon's rim, around a talus slope and finally dropping onto the canyon's floor.

Looking up from the bottom, James pointed to the white canvas of their wagon, which was no more than a white speck on the canyon's rim, "Our sheep will make it easily, but we will need to take the wagon apart and carry it down on the backs of the mules."

By nightfall, the sheep had been pushed down the narrow trail and the dogs had circled them next to the stream. Much of the supplies had been removed from the wagon, loaded on the backs of the mules, and carried to the canyon's floor. The Indian herders were dismantling the wagon.

Sitting next to a bright campfire, the two brothers were drinking coffee and discussing the days activities. "Pa is going to be pleased with our choice of a camp site," Steve said as he picked up the huge black coffee pot from the fire and poured himself another cup.

James, sitting on a flat rock, gazed at the flock of sheep, bedded down on the opposite side of the stream, nodded his head and replied, "He won't believe it, big brother. This is really a paradise -- fresh water, grass belly deep on the sheep, no neighbors to bother us, shade in the summer and the canyon walls to protect us from the winter winds and snows."

As darkness enfolded the canyon, the two brothers spread their blankets next to the fire and dropped off into a deep sleep, dreaming of their good fortune, unaware of the approaching danger.

....

Atascosa was changing, no longer was it limited to Mexican sheep herders. The Red River Indian wars had ended and the feared Comanche Indians had been relegated to the reservation in Oklahoma Territory. With the Indians gone, the white buffalo hunters now had free run on the huge buffalo herds that migrated across the plains and the hunters had found Atascosa to be a good place to dry their hides and ship them to the railroad at Dodge City. With them came the saloons, the gamblers and the prostitutes. The sleepy Mexican village was now a wild and lawless frontier town, with several saloons, cantinas and brothels to serve the increased population.

Casimiro Romero, Don of the Atascosa Plaza, was concerned. He had been the first to bring his family and his sheep into the area, wishing only for peace and privacy. These Anglo hunters would bring nothing but trouble. He didn't realize that trouble would come so soon - and from a different direction.

....

The black racing stallion mounted by the handsome Sostenes pulled up to the hitching rail of the Mexican cantina on the sandy main street of Atascosa. Sostenes looked around, smiled and dismounted. He intended to quench his thirst before proceeding to Borregos Plaza, a short distance down river. Buffalo hunters eyed him suspiciously as he elbowed up to the bar and ordered Tequila.

"Would you look at that, men," a huge, dirty, bewhiskered hunter shouted so all could hear, "ain't he about the prettiest thing you ever did see?"

The crowd guffawed their agreement. The antagonist walked over and felt of the fine linen shirt, then reached for Sostene's sombrero -- a move he should not have made. He failed to see the Mexican's hand as it pulled the sharp blade from his belt. His eyes bulged in disbelief as he felt the point of the dagger plunge deeply into his chest. Dropping his hand from the hat brim, he tried to speak but no sound came. His lips quivered, his knees buckled and he fell, face down, dead at Sostenes feet.

With the knife in his left hand, the Mexican outlaw quickly

drew his right pistol and slowly waved it at the surprised hunters. "I am Sostenes," he said, smiling, "and I have six bullets in my gun for any six of you who would like to take up this fight."

The hunters moved back, wanting no part of this yellow haired Mexican's threat. Two hunters, holding their hands out in a sign of peace, stepped forward and dragged the dead hunter from the room, trailing blood across the floor.

Sostenes wiped the blood from the knife on his trousers, replaced the knife in its sheath, as he kept the revolver pointed at the crowd, and turned to the bartender, "My Tequila, *senor*, if you please," as he placed a gold coin on the bar. Turning the glass up, he downed the drink and backed slowly to the door, stepped out, mounted the black and rode quickly out of town.

The outlaw Sostenes had arrived in Atascosa!

....

Shortly thereafter, the residents of Atascosa were surprised and upset when a herd of eighteen hundred head of longhorn cattle were driven down the sandy main street by a small group of cowboys, led by a huge bewhiskered cattleman. The startled residents of Atascosa watched from doorways as the herd moved slowly through town and stopped at the banks of the swollen Canadian River.

Casimiro Romero could not believe what he was seeing. He had learned long ago in New Mexico that cattlemen did not like sheepmen and feared the results if this cowboy intended to establish headquarters in Atascosa. He knew that Sostenes could be the spark which would start a bloody war between the cattlemen and sheepmen.

"*Buenos Dias, Senor*," he said as he approached the bewhiskered cowboy who sat stiffly on the back of the blue roan gelding in the middle of the street.

"Howdy," the cowboy replied as he stepped down from his horse. Holding out his huge gnarled hand, he said, "Name's Goodnight, from Pueblo, Colorado and Waxahatchie, Texas."

"Casimiro Romero," the Mexican *Don* replied, bowing slightly as he took Goodnight's hand.

Goodnight pulled the soiled bandana from around his neck and wiped the dust and sweat from his face as he looked a-round at the Mexicans and buffalo hunters who were starring at him from the doorways.

"Guess you're wondering what a bunch of mangy longhorns are doing, invading your town," Goodnight said, smiling. "Well, sir, it's my understanding that because of quicksand, Atascosa is the safest place to cross the Canadian River for many a mile. I've been summering my herd along the river over in New Mexi-co. Plan on wintering down river apiece. Didn't realize you sheep men had come this far east. We're taking this herd to the Palo Duro Canyon where I intend to set up headquarters for my ranch, and I don't want to lose half my herd in the quicksand of the river."

"Si, *Senor* Goodnight. I understand. I know the canyon you speak about. We have grazed our sheep in the area now for two years. It is a fine place for a ranch," Romero replied, then ad-ded, "You are wise to cross the river here."

"The hell you say. Been grazing sheep all the way from here to the canyon? That must be fifty or sixty miles. I don't know that I'm going to cotton to having sheep eating the grass in my canyon," Goodnight said with a note of anger in his voice.

"Why don't you join me at my *casa*, *Senor* Goodnight, and we can discuss this problem over a glass of wine," the Mexican

Don replied.

"Wouldn't care for the wine, Romero, I'm a teetotaler," the cattleman replied gruffly. "Don't touch anything that's got alcohol in it but I could use a hot cup of coffee if you've got one handy."

Romero smiled, "I have coffee,senor -- come."

Goodnight gave the reins of the roan to one of his cowboys and followed the small Mexican to the huge adobe *hacienda* at the end of the street.

They were met at the door by two ladies who Casimiro introduced as his wife, Carmilita and his daughter Piedad. "Bring hot coffee to the drawing room, please. My friend, *Senor* Goodnight and I have business to discuss." The ladies disappeared down the hallway as Romero led Goodnight into a large room furnished with sheep skin covered couch and chairs.

Goodnight was impressed with the comfort of such a home, built in the wilderness so far from civilization. It far surpassed in splendor the crude dug-out he intended to construct as a headquarters for his ranch in the Palo Duro. Some day, however, he vowed to construct an even greater mansion for his new wife, Miss Molly, who was waiting for him back in Pueblo.

"I have a proposition, Romero," Goodnight said, as he sipped the strong black coffee.

Suspiciously, Casimiro looked into the flashing eyes of the cattleman, then answered, "I wish to hear."

Leaning forward in his chair, Goodnight said, "There ain't no use in us bucking each other over a little grass. This prairie is large enough to feed all the cattle and sheep in the whole damned world. I'll leave the Canadian River and the adjoining ranges to you and the sheep men if you'll agree to keep your sheep away from the Red River and the Palo Duro Canyon."

Relaxing, Casimiro replied, "I have no problem with such an agreement, but I can only speak for myself. Other sheep men may not wish to limit their ranges. Even now, I understand that a new herd is being grazed in the vicinity of the Palo Duro."

Angrily, Goodnight asked, "Who would that be?"

"Two brothers, newly arrived from California. I know little about them, other than their names -- the Casner brothers. They have a fine flock of sheep, maybe five thousand. I suspect they are very wealthy, rumors are that they have brought more than twenty-five thousand dollars in gold coins from the gold fields of California."

"Mexicans?"

"No, *Senor* -- perhaps Castillians, from the sheep country in the mountains of Spain, but I am not certain. They may be Anglo."

"No matter, I will find them and convince them it will be better to keep our herds separated."

"I hope they will agree, *Senor* Goodnight -- I have seen wars between sheep men and cattle men in other areas. It is not a good thing."

"Like I said, Romero, there's enough grass for everyone. You pass the word among your friends along the Canadian and I will speak to the Casners."

3

Goodnight crossed the rain-swollen Canadian River at Atascosa with his herd of longhorns and continued his trek across the huge, flat, prairie lands. He allowed his cattle to graze leisurely as he moved slowly toward his canyon. Shortly after leaving Tascosa, he was surprised when two young cowboys approached the herd from the east.

Riding up and sticking out his hand, the taller of the two, who seemed to be the boss, said, "My name's Armstrong -- Ned Armstrong, and this here," pointing to the other cowboy, "is Billy Bonney."

"Goodnight -- Charles Goodnight," the huge cattleman said. "Most folks just call me Colonel," as he leaned from the saddle and took Ned's hand in a bone-crushing grip. "What you boys doing out here? If you've got in mind to steal a few of my cows you need to know that the last one who tried it is hanging from the limb of a cottonwood tree back in Colorado."

Ned smiled, "We was thinking the same thing, Colonel. See, me and Colonel Jim Cole have a ranch sixty or seventy miles to the east on Red Deer Creek -- that's a small tributary of the Canadian River -- and me and Billy were out looking for strays. We thought you might be rustlers until we saw your brand."

"Didn't know there was another ranch anywhere in the Panhandle," Goodnight said. What's your brand?"

"C bar A on the left hip, Colonel. We trailed up five thousand head from down around Waco and are stocking Colonel Cole's million acre land grant. Some day we plan to run a hundred thousand head."

"Well I be damned," Goodnight replied. "Looks like you got bigger plans than me. A million acres, you say? I hope it don't include the Palo Duro on the south fork of the Red River, that's where I plan to make my headquarters."

"No sir, it don't," Ned replied. "Our grant reaches from the Canadian River to the North Fork of the Red River. The Salt Fork of the Red lays in between the North and South forks. The Palo Duro is another fifty miles to the southwest of our south line."

"Sounds like you know the country pretty well, Ned," Goodnight said as he dismounted and took a plug of tobacco from his vest pocket.

Ned and Billy dismounted and stretched as the colonel handed the plug to Ned, who took a bite and gave it to Billy. They chewed without speaking, soaking the hard, sweet tobacco with their saliva until it was soft.

Spitting, Ned said, "Pretty well, I guess, Colonel. I rode as scout for Colonel Mackenzie during the Indian wars. We trailed Quanah Parker and his tribe all over hell and half of Texas and finally caught them down in Palo Duro Canyon. Wasn't much of a battle, the Indians escaped but we got their horse herd and burned their lodges so they had no alternative but to head for the reservation in Oklahoma."[1]

"Well, now ain't that something? Scout for Mackenzie! I was

---

[1] See Horns - McCathern

scout one time for Sul Ross and his Texas Rangers during the war. We chased the Indians but never this far north. We rescued that half-breed Quanah's ma, Cynthia Ann Parker, down on the Pease. You know the Comanches captured her when she was no more than seven or eight years old. When we found her, she weren't white no more -- turned into a redskin, and married to the Chief.

"Maybe you can help me, Ned. I been wondering how in hell I was going to get this herd down into the canyon. I hear it's a thousand feet deep with steep walls and a caprock all the way around."

"You heard right, Colonel. There's a few narrow Indian trails from the top to the bottom but they are hard to find. I guess me and Billy could go with you and point out the best one. They don't expect us back to headquarters for another week," Ned replied.

"I'd be much obliged, Ned," Goodnight said as he spit a brown stream of tobacco juice at a hapless horney toad which scurried under a buffalo chip.

....

While Ned and Billy were guiding Goodnight to the lip of the canyon, back in Tascosa, Sostenes was questioning his young nephew. "You are certain you saw the gold," he asked.

"Si, twenty-five thousand dollars in gold coins! I saw them. Mr. Casner showed them to me. They were in a chest in the sheep wagon," Pedro Martinez said, emphasizing the size of the pile of coins with his hands.

Pedro had guided the Casner brothers to the rim of the Palo Duro Canyon, then returned to Borregos Plaza.

"Do you think you can find their camp?" Sostenes asked.

"*Si*. Maybe for ten dollars in gold I will take you," the young Mexican replied, smiling.

"Get your pack, we leave at sunrise tomorrow," Sostenes ordered, with an evil glint in his eyes.

....

Goodnight gazed with awe at the huge chasm which lay below him. The grass was still wet from the previous night's storm and the sun's rays sparkled like diamonds from the wet leaves of the trees and the freshly washed rocks.

"That's a helluva sight, ain't it Ned," he said as they dismounted. "I've chased these mangy longhorns from South Texas clear up to Montana and I ain't never seen a more beautiful setting for a cow ranch."

"Yes, sir, it sure is," Ned replied. "Looks to me like the only problem you're going to have is keeping the buffalo from eating all your grass."

Goodnight cursed as he recognized the problem which Ned had referred to, thousands of buffalo which were grazing slowly along the stream's banks, appearing as small black ants in the distance.

"You're right, Ned. First thing I'm going to do after we get the herd down is have my cowboys chase those mangy shaggies out the lower end of the canyon. There must be ten thousand or more that we can see from here, probably a lot more down where the canyon widens," Goodnight agreed.

Pointing, Ned said, "There's your trail, Colonel. Ain't much but it will take a longhorn steer or a loaded mule. You'll need to dismantle those wagons and haul them down a piece at a time."

Some of the cowboys began dismantling the wagons and

loading the parts on the backs of the mules to be transported to the bottom, while others were heading Old Blue to the trails beginning. The herd of eighteen hundred head followed the big lead steer faithfully, and soon the canyon wall had a stream of multi-colored longhorns strung out down the narrow trail, from top to bottom.

The canyon echoed back the sounds of the bawling cattle, horns banging against rocks and trees, and the shouting and whistling of the cowboys as the herd flowed down the narrow trail. By the time the sun was high over head, all the cattle had reached the floor of the canyon and had begun grazing on the lush grass along the streams banks. Several longhorn bulls were challenging buffalo bulls, and fights between the animals were kicking up dust, tearing out grass and breaking down trees, as the two herds mixed. The sound of their battles was deafening as they struggled to establish dominion.

"Push those cattle up stream," Goodnight yelled as he kicked his blue roan into a gallop around the herd. "Keep them separated from the buffalo!"

Once the two herds had been separated, the cowboys turned their horses and began chasing the black shaggy beasts down stream, firing their pistols and shouting obscenities. The buffalo herd stampeded and headed for safety down stream. Quail and turkey took flight, and deer bounded through the rocks and trees in an effort to escape the stampeding buffalo. Sound of shots from the cowboy's pistols, being fired into the air, bounced off the canyons walls and echoed eerily up and down the length and breadth of the deep canyon, finally fading miles away from the ears of the shooters. The air was filled with fine red dust, kicked up by forty thousand stampeding hooves.

Hundreds of small black bears scurried out of plum thickets and sought shelter in the rocks along the canyon walls.[2] Trembling with fear, coyotes and bobcats ran for shelter in front of the stampeding herd, and many were trampled before they could escape.

Biscuit, the Colonel's cook, shot a young buffalo as it rushed by his camp fire, and soon had it skinned and hung in a nearby cottonwood tree. By late afternoon a make-shift camp had been constructed next to the stream, coffee was boiling over a warm fire and the cook was broiling fresh buffalo steaks over the coals. The cowboys, fatigued from the days efforts, were removing saddles and staking out their mounts in the lush grass. A storm cloud was sticking its ominous head above the canyon's rim and thunder could be heard in the distance.

Colonel Goodnight, Ned and Billy were sitting on logs next to the fire, discussing the successful days activities. "I'm much obliged, Ned, for your help," the Colonel said, "It would have taken us a week to find a decent trail and get that herd down into the canyon without you guiding us."

With a long mesquite limb, he stirred the coals of the fire, picked up the coffee pot and refilled their cups with the steaming brew. Rubbing the mat of whiskers that covered his face, he asked inquiringly, "How'd you come to be scouting for Mackenzie?"

Ned smiled, took a sip of coffee, then replied, "It's kind of a long story, Colonel."

"Well, looks like we got all night, start at the beginning," Goodnight chuckled.

Ned thought a bit as he looked into the fire, then began. "It was in Virginny, 1865, and we was getting the hell beat out of us by the Yankees. I was just a kid from Kentucky in Colonel Cole's regiment. The Colonel was shouting for us to retreat to the river and about that time, canon grape took off his right arm and he fell off his horse next to me. Seemed like the only thing for me to do was to try to stop the blood. I tied his sash around the stump, helped him back into the saddle, and ran to the rear, leading his horse. Well sir, shells and bullets were flying all around us but we made it out of the swamp and escaped the damned Yankees. Took us a week to get across the Blue Ridge and into Kentucky. Then we heard that General Lee had surrendered so we stopped at my pa's farm and rested up for a couple of weeks. Colonel's arm mended up and we set out for Texas."

Ned stopped, trying to determine how much of the story he needed to tell. He took a sip of coffee and looked at Goodnight and the Colonel nodded for him to continue. Enthralled, the other cowboys had gathered round and were listening intently.

"Colonel Cole told me that he was going to the Texas Panhandle and scout out a ranch which had been granted to him by the Republic of Texas. He had fought with General Houston during the revolution, nearly got caught in the Alamo with Jim Bowie and Davy Crockett. When the General was made President of the Republic of Texas, he convinced the legislature to make Colonel Cole the land grant. Much of Texas had already been divided into Spanish land grants, and at the time, no one thought this country up here was worth a damn, just buffalo and Indians. Well, sir, I didn't have nothing else to do so I tagged along with him.

"When we was coming across Oklahoma Territory, we rescued an Indian who was stuck in quicksand in the Canadian

River. You ain't going to believe this, Colonel, but that Indian was blue-eyed Quanah Parker, son of Comanche Chief Nokona. The old Chief was so thankful that he made us blood brothers to Quanah and promised us that the Comanches wouldn't bother us when we got our ranch started."

"The hell you say -- Quanah Parker himself!" Goodnight interrupted.

"Yes, sir -- me and him was about the same age and became good friends. If it hadn't been for that friendship, our hair would be hanging from some Indian's lodge pole by now, for certain," Ned replied.

"We kinda staked out where we thought the grant was located, found a good place for headquarters on the Red Deer Creek, then high-tailed it to Waco where we gathered five thousand head of maverick longhorns that were running wild along the Brazos and Colorado Rivers. It took us all winter and before we started our drive in the spring, Colonel Cole started courting a nice widow lady, Belle McCardle. Would you believe it, they got married and she and her two kids made the drive with us."

Stopping, as if not knowing how to continue, Ned looked around at all the faces gazing at him intently, wanting to hear more. He chuckled, then said, "Miss Belle had a daughter my age and we struck it off real good after we got up here in Indian country, and we got hitched. Colonel Cole, himself, tied the knot for us. That was in '66. We've got a son now who is ten years old."

Leigh laughed, "This is '76, Ned. Sounds like you didn't waste any time getting her in the family way!"

Ned blushed as all the cowboys laughed at his embarrassment. Continuing, he said, "We got along with the Indians, even furnished them beef when the buffalo got scarce. But when the buffalo hunters came in and started slaughtering the herds, the Comanches joined up with the Cheyennes and Kiowa, and started killing everything that had white skin. That's when Colonel Mackenzie asked me to take on scouting for his troops. Well, I didn't cotton to doing anything that would hurt Quanah and his tribe but I knew the sooner we could get the war over, the less Indians would be killed. We never did really whip the Indians, we finally caught them down here in the bottom of the Palo Duro, captured their horse herd and burned their village. Without horses or food, they finally all ended up at Ft. Sill and surrendered.

"I guess that's about it, Colonel. We figure we've got about twenty-five thousand head of cattle now and we've trailed several thousand to Dodge City and sold them to the eastern buyers."

Billy spoke up, "That ain't all, Colonel -- Ned didn't tell you about some of the battles he was in. There was one called Buffalo Wallow where he and five other soldier boys fought off over one hundred Cheyenne warriors for two days. They were all awarded the Congressional Medal of Honor for that little scrape!"

"Well, damnation, Ned. A Medal of Honor winner! How about that!" Goodnight said as he slapped Ned on the back.

Ned ducked his head in embarrassment and mumbled, "I was just doing my job, Colonel."

"I hope you stay a spell with us, Ned. I'd like to learn more about the country and it appears to me that you probably know more about it than any living white man."

"Glad we could help, Colonel, but I 'spect we'd best be heading back to our ranch at day break before the folks give us up for dead," Ned replied, smiling.

"Will you be going out the same way we came in?" Good-night asked.

"No, sir. Ceebara is northeast of here. I know a trail going out on the east rim which will save us nearly a days ride," Ned answered as he took a sip of the steaming hot coffee.

....

Storm clouds began to roll in the west as the two Mexicans arrived on the rim of the canyon. The sun had set behind the black, rolling cloud and huge rain drops began to fall as the wind shifted, lightning flashed and thunder echoed from the canyon walls.

"There, Senor," Pedro said as he pointed to a dim light on the canyon's floor, "is their camp."

Sostenes strained his eyes, looking through the swirling rain in the direction Pedro was pointing. "*Sí*! I see it! How do we get down?"

"The trail begins there," Pedro directed his finger towards the cut in the caprock.

Without waiting, Sostenes kicked the black into a trot and headed for the trail's opening. Pedro followed on his sorrel pony. The ride down was treacherous, and they were forced to stop several times in the protection of overhanging rocks until they could see through the rain.

Reaching the canyon's floor, they traversed the river for a mile before reaching the Casner's headquarters, which was five miles upstream from Goodnight's camp. "Hallo, the camp," Sostenes yelled before approaching the wagon.

A tarp had been strung from the side of the wagon to a nearby hackberry tree and a warm, dry fire was blazing beneath the shelter of the canvas lean-to. A lantern shone brightly, casting shadows on the white background of the wagon's cover. The two Casners and two Indian sheep herders were huddled around the fire, drinking hot coffee and discussing tomorrow's plans. Picking up his rifle which was leaning against the side of the wagon, Steve answered, "Come on in and identify yourself. Keep your hands away from your guns."

Sostenes and Pedro rode in, dismounted and shook the water from their hats as they sought shelter under the tarp.

"I am Manuel and this is my friend Pedro,' Sostenes lied. "We are looking for Colas Martinez's sheep camp. We were told in Atascosa that he was grazing in this canyon."

"No one but us in this canyon -- you must be mistaken, my friend," Steve replied, as he replaced the rifle against the wagon wheel.

"*Maldecir!* " Sostenes cursed., then in English, "Damn! We must have received bad information. We need to find Martinez, his wife is *mucho malo*...sick, and needs him."

"Well," James said, "He is not here -- this is the Casner camp. You may as well pull off them slickers and spend the night. Looks like this storm ain't going to quit any time soon. Grab a cup of coffee, it'll warm you up."

Sostenes removed his slicker, dropped it next to the fire, then, without warning, quickly pulled his pistol and began firing. Steve, reaching for the rifle, was hit first in the head, and fell against the wagon wheel. James, unarmed, looked on with surprise as Sostenes turned the pistol and fired, hitting him in the chest. Blood spurted from the wound as he fell dead next to his brother. The Indians attempted to run and were shot in the back before they had taken three steps toward the darkness.

The two dogs growled and were shot as they made a lunge for Sostene's leg. One of them fell mortally wounded, the other, howling with pain, disappeared into the darkness surrounding the camp.

Sostenes replaced the pistol in his belt, removed his knife, and quickly slashed the throats of the three men. Pedro looked on with fear and astonishment.

Turning to Pedro, Sostenes waved the bloody knife in the air, "Where did you see the gold?" he demanded.

Without speaking, Pedro pointed nervously toward the rear of the wagon.

Sostenes picked up the lantern and disappeared inside the wagon. Pedro, frightened, realized that his uncle could not allow him to live after witnessing this atrocity. Grabbing his slicker, he quickly mounted his pony and disappeared into the darkness. Kicking the pony into a run, he rushed through the storm, found the trail as lightning flashed, and rode to the plains above. As he came out on top, he glanced backward, and as lightning lit up the canyon's walls, he could see that Sostenes was nowhere to be seen. Turning his pony toward Tascosa, he kicked him into a ground eating trot. Maybe he could reach Borregos Plaza and the protection of his father before Sostenes caught up with him.

He needn't have worried. Sostenes had located the trunk inside the sheep wagon, but only a few gold coins were found, payment for a shearing of wool before leaving New Mexico. Cursing, he began to destroy everything inside the wagon, searching unsuccessfully for the gold. When none could be found, he returned outside and surveyed the grisly scene which he had perpetrated. In anger, he once more drew his pistol, reloaded and emptied it once more into the dead bodies of James and Steve Casner, then dragged the four bodies and the dead dog into the darkness surrounding the camp.

It was then he became aware that his nephew had disappeared. He shouted for Pedro, but received no answer. Realizing it would be impossible to find him in the darkness of the storm, he unsaddled his stallion, tied him to a tree, and returned to the protection of the wagon. Tomorrow he would find the gold, then find Pedro and take care of him.

Throwing out much of the contents of the wagon, he rolled out his bed roll, and without remorse, crawled under the covers and was soon asleep.

....

In the Goodnight camp, they were startled when a loud noise echoed off the canyon walls. "Sounds like a gunshot," Ned said as he peered into the darkness.

As a bolt of lightning struck a tree nearby, Goodnight shook his head, "I don't think so, Ned. Probably just thunder."

Goodnight's camp was five miles down the canyon from the grisly scene at the sheep camp. They, too, were huddled under a canvas lean-to where a large fire was blazing.

"Yeah, I guess you're right, Colonel," Ned replied as he stepped to the fire, picked up the coffee pot and poured himself another cup. "Couldn't be a gun shot, ain't no one else between here and Tascosa."

....

The pony was nearly dead from exhaustion when Pedro finally reached the protection of Borregos Plaza the following night. He fell from the saddle as his father rushed from inside the hacienda, picked him up and carried him into the lighted room.

"Pedro! What has happened? Where is Sostenes?" Colas asked.

In a whisper, Pedro replied, "He killed them, Papa! He killed them all!"

"Who killed who?" Colas demanded.

"Uncle Sostenes -- he killed the Casner's, their herders and their dogs. He killed them all!"

"Why, Pedro? Why would he kill them?"

"He wanted their gold, Papa. I ran so he wouldn't kill me. He's coming, I know he's coming to kill me."

"No, Pedro. He will not kill you, I will see to that. Even though he is my wife's brother, I will see that he kills no one else."

"But he is crazy, Papa. He will kill you, too."

"No, I will get help from the other men of the Plaza. He is like a mad wolf, and we will set a trap for him," Colas replied.

....

The next morning Colas called a meeting of the men of Borregos Plaza and told them what had happened.

"We cannot allow such as this to happen. Senor Goodnight has warned if there is any trouble in his canyon, he will return with his cowboys and run us all out of Texas. I promised him that if Sostenes caused trouble, we would take care of him ourselves," he said.

"What can we do, Colas?" Florentine asked. "He is too fast with the gun!"

"Sostenes can't resist a good poker game. When he returns we will pretend we know nothing about the murders and invite him to join us in a game of cards. As he enters the cantina, we will follow him, draw our guns and all shoot at once. We cannot give him a chance to draw his guns, because he would certainly kill some of us."

The next day, Sostenes rode into Borregos Plaza as if nothing had happened. Colas wife fed him a good dinner, then Colas suggested he join him and some of the other men at the cantina for a game of poker.

"Good," Sostenes replied, smiling, "I would like to win some of your gold -- my purse is getting empty."

They walked from the Martinez hacienda and were joined by four more of the Plaza's men. Sostenes, suspecting nothing, led the way into the cantina. As the others stepped in behind him, they all drew their pistols and fired at once. Sostenes fell to the floor, cursing. The men fell upon him with their knives and struck him several blows. He still refused to die.

Florentine, superstitious, believed that it was the devil in him that kept him alive, and grabbed a gold crucifix which hung from around Sostenes neck. As the crucifix fell away, the outlaw Sostenes breathed his last breath and died.

They dragged his body to the banks of the Canadian River and buried him in an unmarked grave. Colas Martinez then searched the belongings of the outlaw, looking for the gold, but none could be found.[3]

3Panhandle Pilgrimage - Robertson - Panhandle Plains Museum

4

Daybreak found Ned and Billy mounted, their saddle bags full of food from the cook's chuck wagon -- sour dough biscuits, cold cuts from the buffalo roasts, salt pork and fresh ground coffee for their two day journey. Colonel Goodnight waved farewell as they disappeared around a rock-fall in the bend of the river.

The rising sun painted the cliff sides with bright multicolored layers as the reds, blues, grays, yellows, greens and whites came alive with the light of morning replacing the dark of night. In the distance, the cottonwood trees along the river were draped in patches of rising fog, and a herd of white-tailed deer, drinking along the streams banks, bounded out of sight into a nearby plum thicket. Ned and Billy rode in silence, taking in and enjoying the grandeur of the scene.

After riding less than five miles upstream, Ned motioned for Billy to stop and held his hand to his ear listening. A strange sound emerged from across the river -- the sound of sheep bleating!

"Danged if that don't sound like sheep, Billy," he said as he urged the buckskin across the shallow stream.

They were aghast at the sight which lay before them. Thousands of sheep were being herded by a huge sheep dog which was dragging a bloody broken hind leg. Next to the flock was a canvas covered wagon and the ground around it was littered with its contents. Several buzzards took flight as they approached and they saw the remains of the two Casner brothers, the Indian sheep herders and a dead sheep dog, piled twenty yards to the rear of the wagon.

Dismounting, Ned moved closer to the carnage and was able to see that the men had all been shot several times and their throats had been slashed. Billy joined him and asked, as he held his hand over his nose, "Indians, Ned?"

"No -- maybe Comancheros but not Indians. Indians would have scalped them, not cut their throats."

Looking around, he could see the hoof prints of Sostene's horse. "Probably whites, whoever did it was riding shoed horses. I'd best ride back and tell the Colonel. You see if you can help that crippled dog and keep the buzzards away from the bodies until I return. Keep a sharp eye out, the murderers that did this may still be around."

Ned lit a shuck back down the canyon and didn't let the buckskin rest until he slid to a stop next to the Goodnight camp. The Colonel rushed out as he dismounted and shouted, "What's happened, Ned? Is Billy hurt?"

"No, sir, " Ned replied, "You've got to come quick, Colonel -- you ain't going to believe it!"

"Believe what? Calm down Ned -- believe what?" Goodnight asked.

"Four or five miles up the canyon .... a flock of sheep .... four dead men -- and a dead sheep dog!" Ned answered, breathlessly.

"Bring my horse, Leigh -- and hurry!" Goodnight shouted to his brother-in-law, Leigh Dyer.

Several of the cowboys joined them as they mounted and

headed back up stream.

Billy, binding the broken leg of the white sheep dog, was waiting for them. He pointed to the piled bodies as buzzards circled overhead.

"Damnation!" the Colonel said as he looked the carnage over, kicking an upturned coffee pot in anger.

"Do you know them, Ned?" he asked.

"No, sir. Never seen them before. They ain't Mexicans, for sure. I thought there were only Mexican sheep men in the area," Ned responded.

"The Casners! Romero told me about two Anglo brothers who had headed towards the Palo Duro with their sheep. This must be them," Goodnight said.

"But why would someone kill them like this?" Ned asked. "Looks like whoever done it was mad as hell at them -- shot several times and their throats cut."

"Romero told me that the Mexican outlaw, Sostenes has been staying with his brother-in-law at Borregos Plaza. I heard about him the last time I trailed a herd up the Pecos river -- he is probably vicious enough to do something like this. They say he hates gringos," the Colonel replied.

"Yeah, I heard that he killed a buffalo hunter in the cantina at Atascosa," Billy said. "Stuck a knife in his chest before the buffalo hunter knew what was happening."

"Well, I can't allow something like this to happen in my canyon -- I'll be riding to Borregos Plaza to find this Sostenes feller. If he did it, I'll hang him from the nearest cottonwood tree."

"I'll go with you, Colonel," Leigh Dyer, his brother-in-law, said, "You might need some help."

Goodnight shook his head, "Alright, Leigh, I wish the rest of you men would stay here and get the cattle settled and look after these damned sheep until we can find out who they belong to -- I'll be alright."

"Colonel," Ned interrupted, "if you don't mind, me and Billy would be proud to go along with you, too. I know Colonel Cole would feel the same way as you -- we can't be allowing someone as vicious as this to be running loose in our area. Besides, I know another trail close by which we can take which will save you some time."

"Thanks, Ned. I'd appreciate it, you lead out," Goodnight replied.

....

Although too far away for Ned to see as they rode up the narrow trail which the Casners had used to bring in their sheep, a crow was perched on the limb of a large juniper tree which was growing just below the caprock. The early morning sun reflected off a bright gold coin which it held in its beak.

....

It was nearing midnight when Goodnight, Ned and Billy reached Atascosa. Their plans were to first visit Casimiro Romero, tell him the story of the murders, and enlist his aid in searching out Sostenes. Riding up to the Romero hacienda, they could see a light shining from the kitchen area.

"Hallo, the house," Goodnight yelled. Movement could be seen through the window, and the old *Don* stepped from the doorway onto the porch.

"Who is it?" he asked, shielding his eyes from the light of the lamp which he held in his hand.

"Charles Goodnight," the Colonel responded.

"Come in, Colonel -- come in," Romero invited.

They dismounted, tied their horses and walked up onto the porch. Romero led them into the lighted kitchen where they were greeted with the smell of coffee boiling on the stove.

"I was waiting for one of my herders who should have been here two hours ago. I guess you men can help drink this pot of coffee," he said as he pulled three cups from the cupboard.

"Smells good, Casimiro. We've been riding hard all day and didn't take time to stop," the Colonel said as he took the offered cup, blew on it and took a sip.

"You look worried, Senor," Casimiro said, " what has happened?"

Goodnight proceeded to tell the story of the vicious attack in the canyon as they all sat down around the huge table. "I suspect it was that Sostenes feller you was telling me about. I've come to hang him. I won't be allowing anything like that taking place in my canyon. Next thing you know, they might decide to rob me or kill some of my cowboys."

"I don't blame you, Senor Goodnight, but I'm afraid you can't hang him," Casimiro replied.

Angrily the Colonel said, "Damn right, I can hang him -- and I intend to at first light. And I'll hang anybody else that sets foot in the Palo Duro without my permission."

"No, Senor, he is already dead," the Mexican said. "My friend, Colas Martinez, Sostenes brother-in-law, learned of the atrocity from his son who had guided Sostenes to the canyon, and he and some of his men shot and killed the outlaw only this morning."

"How do I know that is true?" Goodnight asked.

"We will go to Borregos Plaza in the morning and you can

talk to Colas. I suppose if you don't believe him, you can dig up the grave and see for yourself. In the meantime, you must sleep. I have beds," Casimiro answered, adding, "I'll see to your horses."

....

After a sleepless night, Goodnight arose at daybreak. Casimiro was already up and was directing his cook to prepare breakfast for himself, Goodnight, Leigh, Ned and Billy.

Drinking coffee, Ned asked. "Senor Romero, why would this Sostenes feller kill the Casners?"

Romero replied, "Because there are rumors that the Casners were carrying twenty-five thousand dollars in gold coins. Sostenes has been known to murder a man for a lot less."

"Well, I promise you one damned thing, if he ain't lying dead in that grave, I'll hunt him down and see that he finds a grave that will fit him," the Colonel said.

They finished their breakfast as the sun rose in a cloudless sky, walked to the stable, saddled their mounts and rode down river toward Borregos Plaza.

....

"*Buenas dias*," Colas Martinez greeted as they rode up to his *casa*. Pedro stood at his side and held Casimiro's horse as he dismounted. "Welcome, my friends. What is your business so early in the morning?"

"It is business concerning your brother-in-law, Colas," Casimiro said. "Senor Goodnight says someone murdered the Casner brothers in Palo Duro Canyon. He has come to hang Sostenes for the deed."

Colas looked frightened as he replied. "*Si*, it is true, Senor Goodnight. Colas did it. My son, Pedro here, was with him and witnessed the murders. He too would have fallen to Sostenes knife, except he was able to slip away during the storm."

"Damn his soul to hell," Goodnight said, angrily. " Where will I find him? I intend to hang him from a cottonwood tree on Main street in Atascosa so that all can see that I do not intend to allow such lawlessness to invade our area."

"Sostenes is already dead, Senor," Colas said. "I promised you that if he caused trouble, I would kill him myself. He is buried yonder, next to the river."[1]

"I must see with my own eyes, Colas," Goodnight said. "Only then will I be satisfied that he has been punished."

"Pedro, fetch two shovels. We will dig up the body," Colas instructed.

Ned and Billy helped Pedro dig in the soft earth of the newly covered grave. Brushing the sand from the body, Sostenes was easily identified by his fancy clothes. There were several bullet holes in his back as well as many knife wounds.

"Thank you, Colas. You are a man of your word. Throw the dirt back on the body, boys," the old cattleman ordered.

Ned and Billy completed the grizzly task, then accompanied the Colonel and Casimiro back to Atascosa. They reined up at the cantina, dismounted and tied their horses to the hitching rail. Several buffalo hunters, teamsters and sheep herders were already crowding the bar.

Colonel Goodnight entered, with his Winchester held loosely in his right hand. All eyes turned to him as he thundered, "You men listen up! My name is Charles Goodnight, and I have a ranch in Palo Duro Canyon. The Mexican outlaw, Sostenes paid a visit to the canyon, murdered and robbed two sheep men and

_____

1 Amarillo Sunday News-Globe, Sept. 25, 1966

their herders, thinking he was going to steal twenty-five thousand dollars. I followed him here with the intention of hanging him from a cottonwood limb. Senor Martinez and his men beat me to it. He is lying dead in a grave five miles down river. I am here to tell all of you that I will not tolerate this kind of behavior from any one. My cowboys have orders to hang anyone caught shooting buffalo on my range, rustling my cattle or stealing my plunder. I advise you to keep your distance from Palo Duro Canyon."

He turned and stalked out of the cantina, followed by Ned, Billy and Casimiro.

....

The men in the cantina were dumbfounded, and not until Goodnight had turned and stalked from the cantina did any of them say a word. "Who the hell does that old cowboy think he is?" Bill, a grizzled and stinking buffalo hunter growled. "This here country don't belong to him or nobody. We got a right to hunt buffaler anywhere we please!"

"That's right," Buck, a short, buck-toothed hunter, shouted. "If'n there's buffaler in that there Palo Duro Canyon, they belongs to the first man that shoots 'em!"

"Who wants buffalo when there's twenty-five thousand in gold coins hid in that canyon somewhere?" a teamster asked.

"Twenty-five thousand? Who says?" hunter Bill questioned.

"You heard what that old bastard said, them sheep herders had twenty-five thousand dollars in gold coin when they left Atascosa and went into the canyon. That Mex didn't find it so it must still be hidden somewhere," the teamster responded.

Bill scratched his dirty whiskers and said, "I seed that canyon from the rim one time, and there's ten zillion places where a man could hide his poke and no one would ever find it."

"I don't know about that, Billy," Buck responded, pausing as he took a drink from his glass. "If'n we knew where that sheep camp was set up, the gold would have to be somewhere nearby."

Bill turned up his glass and drained the cheap whiskey into his mouth. After wiping his mouth he said, "By grabs, I think you're right, Buck. Maybe we best take a look at that canyon. Might be more profit in gold prospecting than in hide hunting."

....

Ned's ten year old son, Cole, and Chief, Quanah's son, were cleaning out the stables when he and Billy rode in from Atascosa. The two boys dropped their shovels and ran to greet them. "Howdy, boys," Ned said. "I'm glad to see you've kept busy while we were gone."

Cole smiled, and replied, "Howdy, pa. We 'bout give you up for dead. I surely am glad to see you home."

They dismounted and gave the reins to the boys who led them into the barn and began removing the saddles.

"Better rub them down good, son, they've been rode hard all day," Ned ordered.

Colonel Jim Cole, seeing them arrive, walked from the ranch house and joined them at the barn. "Guess you boys must have found a lot of strays, seeing as how you've been gone nearly two weeks," he said as he shook their hands.

"We run into all kinds of problems, Colonel," Ned replied as the two boys began removing the saddles and listened spellbound. "We choused a bunch of strays out of the breaks east of Atascosa and just as we was fixing to head home, we run across a feller by name of Goodnight, trailing a herd of longhorns towards the Big Canyon -- he called it the Palo Duro. Said he was setting up a ranch down in the bottom."

"Goodnight? Charlie Goodnight? I knew him before the war," Jim said. "Down by Waxahatchie. It will be nice to have him for a neighbor. Probably no more than sixty or seventy miles from here to the big canyon."

"Yes, sir, it shore will be good to have neighbors. Colonel Goodnight seems like a right nice feller. Me and Billy went a ways with him and showed him a trail into the canyon then helped him get his eighteen hundred head and plunder down to the bottom. He asked us to spend the night. Next morning me and Kid struck out for home when we come onto a sheep camp that had been raided by a Mexican bandit -- killed two brothers and their Mexican herders not more than five miles from Goodnight's headquarters down in the canyon. I'm telling you, Colonel, I never seen the likes of such a slaughter. Looked like he shot each one of them a dozen times after they were dead, then cut their throats. He even shot the herders sheep dogs.

"Anyway, when we told Colonel Goodnight what we had found in his canyon, he swore he'd find the bandit and hang him to a cottonwood tree. We rode with him back to Atascosa and discovered other sheep men had already killed the bandit. We dug him up to be certain they were not lying to us. It was him, alright. They called him Sostenes."

"You did well, Ned," Jim said, "we can't be having that kind of lawlessness taking place. First thing you know, we'll have all kinds of outlaws killing our cowboys and stealing our cows if they aren't punished."

"Why'd the bandit kill them, pa," Cole asked?

"Seems the sheep men were supposed to be carrying twenty-five thousand dollars in fresh minted gold coins. If they had it, he didn't find it. Reckon they hid it somewhere in the canyon."

"Since the bandit is dead, I guess it would belong to anyone that finds it now, huh Pa?" Cole asked. "Maybe me and Chief could find it."

Ned laughed, "You boys are a little short in the britches to be thinking about treasure hunting."

"We'll be big enough some day, Pa" Cole replied.

"They certainly will, Ned. These boys are growing like weeds. Won't be no time 'till they'll be running this ranch," the Colonel said, smiling.

Cole smiled -- he liked to hear his grandad brag on him.

....

Colonel Goodnight's first order of business was to have his cowboys dig a half-dugout for a ranch headquarters, covering the top with a sod roof. It would be sufficient to keep warm and dry until a ranch house could be constructed. A brush arbor was thrown up to act as a temporary bunk house for the cowboys, and corrals were built to hold the horse herd.

Leigh accompanied him as he paced off a spot where he wanted the ranch house to be built. "You boys get started hauling rocks for the foundation and cutting logs for the walls, I'm going to head back to Pueblo to pick up Mary Ann and more supplies. I'll bring back a load of lumber. I may be gone two or three weeks."

"Alright, Colonel -- we'll keep busy," Leigh replied.

5

The first thing Colonel Goodnight did when he reached Pueblo, was stop by the newspaper office. *"Buenos Dias*, Senor Goodnight," Juan Lopez, the editor said as Goodnight entered. He stepped forward and shook the hand of his old friend. "I did not know that you had returned from Texas."

"Just got in on the train, Juan. Don't plan on staying long. Need to tend to some business, pick up a couple of wagons, load Miss Molly and her trappings and head back to Texas."

"That Texas country as good as you thought it would be?" Juan asked.

Smiling, the Colonel replied, "Better, Juan -- grass up to a steers belly, spring water clear as a mountain stream, canyons as beautiful as a senorita's smile, and nobody for a hundred miles to crowd me out."

"Sounds great -- what can I do for you?" Juan asked.

"Need to run an add and then I need a favor."

"Alright, what should the add say?"

"Two sheep men murdered in the Texas Panhandle. Five thousand sheep being held by cattleman Charles Goodnight. Looking for relatives. Present proof and pick up your sheep. Inquire with Casimiro Romero, Atascosa, Texas."

Juan looked up from his writing, "Sounds like a good story for the paper -- got time to tell it to me?"

"I'll tell it, but promise you won't mention any names other than mine and Romero's. Don't want every sheep man in the country trying to claim those sheep."

"I understand, Colonel," Juan said as they sat down next to his desk and he took pen and paper and began to write.

Goodnight told the entire story, even to his warning that he would hang anyone who rustled his cattle or killed buffalo in the Palo Duro. When he had finished, Juan asked, "The favor, Colonel -- what can I do for you."

"I need to borrow a horse and saddle to ride out to my ranch east of town. I haven't seen that pretty wife of mine in several weeks."

"Marty!" the editor shouted, "Go out back and bring my horse up front for Mr. Goodnight."

A young boy, with an ink stained apron around his middle, said "Yes, sir, Mr. Lopez," and headed for the back door.

....

Colonel Goodnight had been a wealthy cattleman and invested heavily in the banking business in the Pueblo area for several years before the financial collapse of 1873. When his bank failed, he lost everything except the small ranch and home a few miles east of Pueblo on the Arkansas River. He was well known and respected in the area, and when a wealthy banker in Denver, John Adair, heard that Goodnight was looking for a partner in his Palo Duro venture, he came to Pueblo and met with him.

Goodnight convinced him to travel back to Texas with him and Mrs. Goodnight and look over the proposed ranch. Adair returned to Denver, fetched his wife, Cornelia, then rejoined the Goodnights for the trip.

Driving a herd of one hundred head of registered Short Horn bulls, they set out with four wagons loaded with Miss Molly's household goods. She drove one of the wagons and the Adairs rode horses.[1]

Adair was so impressed with the Palo Duro Canyon and Goodnight's plans, that he signed a five year contract to furnish the finances to purchase land, cattle and operating expenses with the idea that the holdings would eventually encompass one million acres with over one hundred thousand head of cattle.

After two weeks the Adairs returned to Colorado, leaving the Goodnights and their cowboys to begin the JA ranch dynasty.

....

The ranch grew quickly under the Colonel's supervision, and soon a comfortable ranch house was constructed along the river in the floor of the canyon. Working corrals were constructed and more cattle were purchased .

Goodnight was forced to leave the ranch once again to conduct business with Mr. Adair in Colorado, leaving Miss Molly and her brother, Leigh Dyer to watch after the spread.
Returning after nearly three weeks absence, Leigh welcomed him with a frown on his face.

"What's the matter, Leigh," Goodnight said, "You look like you just lost your last friend in the world."

"Almost as bad, Colonel," Leigh replied, "Come on in the house and have a cup of coffee while I tell you about it."

Over steaming coffee, Leigh said, "We been having all kinds

[1]Charles Goodnight - J.E. Haley

of trouble since you left. I've had to chase several riders out of
the canyon who claimed they were looking for those dead
sheep herders gold. On top of that, some buffalo hunters have
been killing shaggies down toward the lower end of the canyon
and stampeding our cattle all over hell and half of Texas. I
found where they killed and butchered one of our steers. I ain't
for sure, but I think we might be missing some cattle to
rustlers."

Goodnight pounded the table with his huge hand and
cursed, "I left word in Tascosa that I wouldn't tolerate none of
that. First thing tomorrow I want you to show me where they
killed that steer. Maybe we can follow their trail."

....

There was little remaining of the dead steer. Whoever had
killed it had taken the best cuts of meat off of it and coyotes
had disposed of everything except the hide and bones. Nearby,
next to the bank of the river, they found where a camp had
been made. "Probably a week or more since they broke camp,"
Leigh said, "but we haven't had any rain, so their tracks are still
plain."

The four of them -- Goodnight, Leigh, Joe and Sam -- followed the tracks downstream for nearly a mile before the horse
tracks were mingled with the tracks of several cattle. "Looks
like they picked up a few head and started herding them toward
the west wall of the canyon," Goodnight said, "how many you
make out?"

Leigh dismounted and kneeled next to the tracks, looking
closely. "Ain't but three riders, Colonel. They ain't buffalo
hunters -- hunters would have wagons. These are rustlers and
looks like they might be pushing twenty or thirty head in front

of them."

The tracks led to the canyon wall then followed it to an Indian trail which wound around rocks and boulders toward the top. The trail was wide enough for two horses to walk, side by side, along the talus slope. It cut through a thick stand of junipers and came out just below the caprock. They followed it along the base of the caprock until it reached a point where water had cut through the rock and falling boulders had made a natural bridge, sloping to the top.

"I sure as hell didn't know about this trail, Colonel," Leigh said, as they came out on top.

"We'll probably find a lot more, once we've had time to scout out the canyon," the big cattleman replied.

Following the well preserved prints of the cow herd, they rode across the prairie in grass that was half knee high on their horses. Topping a slight rise, no more than a mile from the canyon's rim, they surprised a small herd of buffalo which were standing knee deep in a shallow playa lake. The buffalo snorted and bounded out of the water and stampeded to the west. Next to the lake was the remains of another camp fire.

"They must have spent the night here, Colonel," Leigh said, as he dismounted and kicked the cold ashes of the fire."

Goodnight, with his hand shading his eyes, looked north and said, "They are headed toward Atascosa. I guess they figure they can sell them to some of the merchants and pick up a few whiskey dollars. Joe, you ride back and tell Miss Molly and the other boys that me and Leigh and Sam are going to stay on the trail until we catch these thieving sidewinders. We got to send a message to anyone else that thinks they can steal our cattle and get away with it! May be two or three days before we get back."

....

The trail led to two more campsites before they reached the Canadian River breaks. In the distance they could see the river winding its way to the east. Smoke on the horizon indicated the frontier settlement of Atascosa.

"I was hoping we would catch up to them before they reached the river," Goodnight said.

Leigh pulled a sack of Bull Durham smoking tobacco from his shirt pocket and proceeded to roll a cigarette as he stared in the direction of the town. "I 'spect we may run into a peck of trouble, Colonel, if those thieves have friends in Atascosa," Leigh said, as he struck a match on his saddle horn and lit his cigarette.

Goodnight, waiting for Leigh to complete his smoke, pulled a plug of Star chewing tobacco from his vest pocket, bit off a corner and allowed it to soak a little before beginning to chew, all the time lost in thought. "I reckon as how you're right, Leigh, but we've got to make an example out of these rustlers and let everybody know that I won't tolerate thieves on my range."

"What you aim to do to them, Colonel," Sam asked, "there ain't no law in Atascosa?"

"I aim to stick to my word. I said I'd hang anyone caught messing with my cattle, and it looks like we're about to catch us three law-breakers." Goodnight spit a brown stream of tobacco juice which splattered on a flat rock, wiped his beard and kicked the blue roan into a ground-eating trot down the well worn trail.

....

The trail of the cattle and rustlers led to the river, then

across the river and into the rustic frontier town. A pole corral at the rear of the Equity Saloon was filled with the twenty-seven head of Goodnight steers. The colonel, Leigh and Sam dismounted and tied their horses to the middle rail of the pen. Leigh climbed up on the top rail and slowly cast his gaze around the herd. "They're ours, alright, Colonel, every damned one of them. The JA brand is as plain as the nose on my face."

"Alright, Leigh, here's what we're going to do. Me and Sam will go in the front door, you slip around to the rear and come in from the back. You just stay out of sight until I figure who the thieves are. When I pull down on them, you come out with your Colt in your hand. If they try to resist, shoot the thieving bastards."

There were six horses tied to the hitching rail in front of the saloon. Goodnight circled around each of them, feeling of their shoulders. Three of them were still damp with sweat. He motioned for Sam to follow him and they entered the cool interior of the adobe building.

Three men, who looked like buffalo hunters, were bellied up to the bar with their backs to the door. The bartender was pouring drinks. The other three were seated around a table, playing poker.

Goodnight, with his Winchester held loosely in his right hand, spoke. "I'm looking for the men who own those steers in the back?"

The card players never looked up from their game. The three hunters at the bar, turned as one, and a huge, dirty, buckskin clad hunter said, "They be mine. You looking to buy?"

"Afraid not, I'm just looking for the men who stole them

from my pasture and drove them for three days to this pen in the back."

The big hunter smiled as he slowly slid his hand toward his hip. "I wouldn't do that if I was you, Leigh said from the rear. It might be the last move you ever made."

Fear showed in each of their faces as they glanced back and saw Leigh standing in the shadows with his gun pointed toward them.

"Well, lookie hear, Leigh," the colonel said, "These are the same buffalo hunters that were here when I gave a warning last month to stay away from the Palo Duro."

"Damned if I don't think you're right, Colonel. Well as I remember, you said you would hang anyone caught looking for gold, killing buffalo or stealing your cattle. Looks to me like these three pilgrims might be guilty of all three crimes," Leigh said with a smile on his face.

"Sam, get their guns and their knives," Goodnight instructed as he brought the barrel of the rifle up with his finger on the trigger, pointed at their guts.

"Now wait a minute mister!" the big hunter shouted, "We found them steers just the other side of the Canadian, wandering around like they was lost. We just thought we'd do you a favor by penning them for you."

The bartender was wiping glasses, nervously. Goodnight turned to him and asked. "These fellers been trying to sell those steers to you?"

"Look, mister, I don't want to get mixed up in this," he said, placing a glass back on the shelf.

"You're already mixed up in it -- yes or no, they been trying to peddle my cows?"

Ducking his head and looking at his hands, the bartender answered weakly. "Not to me but to my boss, Jack Ryan."

Goodnight nodded as he motioned for the three rustlers to take a seat at one of the empty tables. Turning to the three card players, he said, "Court is in session and I appoint you as jurors -- I'm the judge. Sam, I'm appointing you as counsel for these criminals."

'Aw, hell, Colonel, I don't know anything about counseling. I ain't never been in a court house but once when I got arrested for drunk and disorderly in Dodge City when we brung up a herd of 'horns from South Texas."

"Ain't nothing to it, Sam. Just try to figure out why these rustlers don't deserve to hang for stealing my cows," Goodnight replied. "Now, Leigh, I appoint you as prosecutor. You're first up. Let's hear why you think these men are guilty and deserve to hang."

"Damn, Colonel, you know well as I do that they are guilty as hell. We found two dead buffalo and a dead steer where these men were camped on our range. Then we followed their trail where they picked up twenty-seven steers and choused them out of the canyon. Then we followed their trail from the Palo Duro to this here saloon, and the steers are penned up out back." Leigh paused, realizing he was making a pretty good presentation for the State.

"What about witnesses? You got any witnesses, Mr. Prosecutor?"

"Well, there's you and Sam and me -- and I guess this here bartender. He says he heard them trying to sell the steers to his boss."

"O.K. Leigh, I guess you'd best call the bartender as a witness, seeing as how me and Sam are disqualified."

Leigh asked the bartender to come around. Looking at Goodnight, he asked, "What do I do now?" Colonel.

"Swear him in."

"Do you swear that what you're fixing to say is the truth?" Leigh asked.

The bartender, nervous as a whore in church, said meekly, "I do."

"Tell the court what you know about this whole affair," Leigh said.

"Well, I don't know much," the bartender said, "only that I heard these gents trying to sell those steers out back in the corral to Mr. Ryan."

"I 'spect its your turn, Counselor. Got any witnesses that says these men are not guilty of stealing my steers?"

"Just the rustlers, themselves, Colonel. They say they're not guilty."

"Call your first witness," Goodnight ordered.

The big buffalo hunter started to get up from his chair and Leigh shoved him back down with the barrel of his pistol. "Just tell your story, mister, we can hear you setting down."

Nervously, the hunter said, "I guess maybe we did steal them steers, but we had good reason. We'd been looking for them sheep herders' gold for about two weeks afore we ate up all our grub. We saw all them horns grazing and decided we'd kill one for some meat. Then we figured you wouldn't miss a few head if we choused them out of the canyon and drove them to Atascosa. All we was wanting to do was get a little grubstake so's we could get back to Dodge City."

"Alright, that's enough," Goodnight said. Looking to the

three jurors he asked, "How does the jury find these men, innocent or guilty?"

The older of the three spoke, "Well, hell, mister, seems they ain't no question about it, they's guilty!"

Removing his pistol from its holster, Goodnight pounded the table with the butt end. "You men know what the penalty is for molesting women and stealing horses or cows. I sentence you to be hung to the nearest cottonwood until you are dead. May God rest your soul. Sam, you go get our lariats from our saddles."

They led the rustlers out of the saloon and to a large cottonwood tree which was growing on the banks of the Tascosa creek. Sam brought up their horses and after placing a rope around each of their necks, forced them to mount up as he threw the ropes over a low, overhanging branch. All the while, the three rustlers were begging for leniency.

Several onlookers had followed the procession to the tree and were looking on with interest. The Colonel turned to them and said, "My name is Charles Goodnight. We just held trial for these three men and they were found guilty of rustling cattle, killing cattle, hunting buffalo and searching for gold on my ranch in the Palo Duro Canyon. Now you all know, I put out the word that since there ain't any law in this country, I'll hang anybody who I catch stealing or trespassing on my land. I hope you will all spread the word that until we get duly elected law enforcement officials, I am the law in Palo Duro Canyon and anyone breaking my law will suffer the same consequences as these men."

He slapped the horses on the rear, all three bolted forward and the three rustlers were left swinging at the end of the ropes.

As he watched them swing slowly back and forth, he asked, "Is there an undertaker here?"

A tall, slender, bald-headed gentlemen dressed in a black and white stripped shirt, black trousers, and with a white apron around his middle, stepped forward. "Yes sir. I am the local barber but I also act as undertaker," he said.

Colonel Goodnight pulled a ten dollar gold coin from his pocket and flipped it to the undertaker. "Cut these men down and bury them," he said as he, Leigh and Sam turned and walked back to their horses, opened the gate to the corral, mounted and drove the cattle back across the river and toward the Palo Duro.

6

The Colonel's add in the Pueblo newspaper soon had results. John Casner and his eldest son were prospecting in Silver City, New Mexico when they saw the add and realized that the two murdered sheep men were probably his two younger sons. Riding up to the Goodnight headquarters, they identified themselves to the Colonel and offered proof that they were Casners, father and brother of the two murdered sheep men.

"Sorry about your loss, Mr. Casner," Colonel Goodnight said, " but the sooner you can get them damned sheep out of my canyon, the better I'll like it."

"I thank you Colonel, for seeing that my boys were buried proper," John Casner replied. "I intend to find and hang the people who did this -- can you give me any information as to who is responsible."

"You're too late, Casner," Goodnight replied, "It was Sostenes L'Archevegue and he lies dead and buried in a grave at Borregos Plaza -- killed by his brother-in-law, Colas Martinez."

"Thank you, sir," Casner said, "I'll be taking my sheep and heading for Borregos Plaza. I intend to kill a few Mexicans and recover my gold."

"I don't expect you'll be finding any gold, seems everybody believes your boys buried it somewhere."

....

Gathering a group of outlaw types in Tascosa, the Casner's arrived in Borregos Plaza, inquiring the whereabouts of Colas Martinez. Finding him, they pretended to be interested in hiring him as a guide on a hunting trip to Palo Duro Canyon. Colas agreed to accompany them, but after traveling only a short distance away from the Plaza, the Casner's turned on Colas and accused him of being in on the murders of the two boys and stealing the gold.

Colas denied, to no avail, and the Casners shot and killed him, then returned to Borregos Plaza and began killing everyone they could find. Most of the people escaped, but they captured two of the men, tortured them seeking information, then hung them with a chain. Riding to the Martinez home, they searched the premises and questioned Colas' widow who was unable to give them information on the gold.[1]

"Lew," John Casner told his son, "that gold has got to be somewhere, but seems these pepper bellies don't have it. Maybe we've been looking in the wrong place."

"What about that Goodnight feller," Lew replied. "He could have found the gold and is keeping quiet about it."

"Don't think so, son," John said. "He don't strike me as that kind of person. If he had found it, he'd tell us."

One of the men who had helped them with the Mexican murders, suggested that an outlaw named Goodanuff, an army deserter from Fort Elliot, was holed up in nearby Robber's Roost. He had been seen associating with Colas Martinez and

1 Amarillo Sunday News-Globe, Sept. 25, 1966

Sostenes and suggested he may have been in on the murders of the Casner boys.

"I think we need to locate this Goodanuff feller, pa. Sounds like he could have been involved," Lew said.

They set out to find Goodanuff, but hearing about the viciousness of the Casner gang and that they were looking for him, he was able to elude them and escaped to Hidetown. Hearing that they were on his trail and fearing for his life, he surrendered to the military authorities at nearby Fort Elliot.

The nearest jail was two hundred miles to the south at Henrietta, and the post commander decided to transport Goodanuff to Henrietta where he would stand trial for crimes committed in the Texas Panhandle. The first night on the trail, the Casner gang was able to steal Goodanuff from the guards and hung him in a nearby cottonwood tree.[2]

Unable to learn anything from Goodanuf, the Casner's decided it was useless to continue the search.

"I guess we best head for California, Lew," John said, "and see if we can find another gold strike."

....

All of the cowboys called her *Miss Molly*. Some of them looked on her as the only mother they had ever known. They knew she was *Mrs. Mary Goodnight*, but the name, *Miss Molly*, carried a tone of affection. They all tried to make her life a little easier and a little happier in this wild and rough, man's country.

Miss Molly tried to keep busy but she worried all the same. Her husband, brother and one of the ranch hands were off chasing rustlers and could be in all kinds of trouble. The re-

2Amarillo Sunday News-Globe, Sept. 25,1966

mainder of the ranch crew were riding out the lower pasture, fifteen or twenty miles to the south, hunting any other trespassers that might be trying to run off some of Goodnight's stock.

Sour Dough, the ranch cook, had been working for Charles Goodnight for nearly twenty years. The boss had told him to always stay close to Miss Molly and protect her when he was gone. With the nearest town being sixty miles away, with no neighbors in between, there was always the danger of outlaws or renegade Indians making a raid on headquarters.

Sour Dough was working on the corral fence about a quarter of a mile to the south of the headquarters buildings. Once in a while, he would look up to make certain she was alright. In a little while, he would have to start supper so it would be ready when the crew arrived back at headquarters about sundown.

Headquarters was not much protection -- a few pole corrals, the rough beginnings of a ranch house for the boss and Miss Molly, and a lean-to for a bunk house. The ranch house was livable and was still being worked on by the ranch crew, but they only worked on it when there was no other chores to take precedent. Sour Dough, with Miss Molly's help, did the cooking for all of the ranch family outside under the brush arbor.

She enjoyed working outside, cleaning brush away from what she considered to be her front yard. Jesse, one of the ranch hands, had purchased a dozen laying hens for her, after spending a weekend in Mobeetie, and had carried them in a burlap sack tied to his saddle, all the way to the Palo Duro. They became her favorite friends when no one else was around. She would talk to them and they would cluck to her, sometimes even jumping up on her chair and eating crumbs from her hands. They kept her mind from dwelling on the isolation and loneliness of frontier life.[3]

Today was a beautiful day -- bright sunshine with a few fluffy white clouds drifting overhead. There was very little wind and she could see the multicolored bluffs on both sides of the canyon. Moving her rocking chair from inside the house to the outside, she set it in the shade of a large cottonwood tree. Bringing her sewing to keep her fingers and mind busy, she began to sew a rip in a faded shirt. Kevin, one of the younger cowboys (fourteen years old) had ripped his shirt while chasing a steer through a plum thicket.

"You take that shirt off and I'll sew it for you today," she ordered at breakfast.

"Gosh, Miss Molly, I only have one more shirt and its my Sunday-go-to-meeting shirt. I hate to work in it," Rusty objected.

"Makes no never mind," she replied, "You can wear your good shirt and be careful for a change. I'll have the torn shirt ready for you tonight."

Miss Molly considered all the cowboys her children, and treated them as such. Most of them were not much older than Kevin. He didn't argue with her, said "Yes Ma'am", turned his back and walked toward the lean-to. He returned shortly, dressed in his good shirt and carrying the torn one.

She had been sitting in the rocking chair under the cottonwood tree sewing the shirt when about a dozen crows flew in, and landed in its branches. They too, were old friends, coming to visit now and then and begging a few crumbs from her table. One of them had become so bold as to fly down and land on her chair and she had named him *Coaley* because he was so black. Of course she could not tell one from the other as long

_____
3Charles Goodnight, J.E. Haley

as they remained in the tree or were flying about. But Coaley was missing one toe on his right foot, and when he would get close, Miss Molly would recognize him and strike up a conversation.

"You old thief," she said, "always begging for something. You just stay here and I'll bring you a cold biscuit."

Miss Molly lay the shirt, her thimble, needle and thread in the seat of her chair and walked inside the house. She was gone no more than ten minutes, but when she returned the crows were gone. She reached for the shirt and her sewing tools. Startled, she pulled her hand back. Where she had left her thimble was a shiny, bright twenty dollar gold coin! The thimble was gone.

"I declare!" she said to herself, as she picked up the coin and placed it in the palm of her hand. Looking around she searched for the cowboy who had left the coin and had taken her thimble. There was only Sour Dough and he was still working diligently on the corral fence, nearly a quarter of a mile away. "I declare," she said again as she looked at the coin, puzzled.

7

News of the hangings spread across the plains and gold prospecting in Palo Duro Canyon came to a halt. However, cattle rustling became progressively worse as more and more cattle were trailed into the area and new ranches were established. With no fences and no survey, neither the cowboys nor the cattle recognized property lines. The cattle strayed and mixed until it was virtually impossible to know whose cattle were where, and how many were being stolen by thieves. Many of the cowboys learned that they could make more money stealing cattle than they could herding cattle. And it was suspected that some of the ranchers began replacing their missing cattle with neighbors livestock, changing brands with running irons.

Tempers were running high, and accusations and rumors were rampant. A range war loomed on the horizon.

After a terrible blizzard during the winter of 1878 resulted in cattle drifting south, and thousands of cattle had sought protection in the deep canyons of the Palo Duro, Colonel Goodnight sent messengers to each cow camp, announcing a meeting to be held in Hidetown for the purpose of making plans for a cooperative roundup, where the cattle could be identified by brands, separated and driven back to home pastures.

"Men," he said, when all had gathered at the Lady Gay Saloon in Hidetown, and had their drinks poured, "We need to do something about this problem. We have no idea in hell how many cattle are missing or who is responsible. I have seen thousands of head of your brands mixed with mine. I will be rounding up my cattle beginning the first day of April. What I am suggesting is that you all send a few cowboys to help with my roundup and they can cut out each brand and drive them back to your home range."

Deacon Bates, owner of the LX, placing his drink on the table, said, "Sounds like a good idea, to me Colonel, but I suggest we do the same on each of our ranches. I know there are a lot of strays mixed with the LX brand. We could work together putting all of our cowboys on a drive in the Palo Duro, then make a drive on the Ceebara range, the Quarter Circle T, the LIT, the LX, the LE and the LS along the Canadian River. That way, we could make a count of all of our brands and determine how many head have been driven off by rustlers."

There was a nodding of heads as each of the ranchers agreed.

"Just finding out how many are missing ain't going to solve the problem," Ned said. "Seems to me we need some law established."

"What are you suggesting, Ned," Tom Bugbee asked, "You know the state's broke and can't afford to send any rangers up."

Ned, rolling a cigarette, licked the paper before replying. Lighting the smoke he said, "I've given it a lot of thought, Tom, and seems to me we need to form an organization and hire some rangers of our own. The only thing that's going to stop this rustling is to catch a few and hang them the way Colonel

Goodnight did at Atascosa."

They all nodded in agreement and Ned said, "After the roundup and we get a tally of our losses, I suggest we meet back here and put together a plan."

"Sounds good, Ned," Goodnight said, "Bring your chuck wagons and crews and gather at the south line camp of the JA, the last week in March and we will spread out and drive the cattle to holding pens at ranch headquarters. I'll try to have everything ready."

....

Ceebara cattle had been trail driven to market at Dodge city for the past seven years and Cole had been allowed to make the last drive in 1878, when his grandfather, Colonel Jim Cole was gunned down by outlaws on the streets of Dodge City.

Cole could remember that drive as if it happened yesterday. He had learned a lot, riding with his pa and grandpa, heading three thousand head of mangy longhorns up the trail to Dodge City.

The drive took twelve days and they had little trouble before reaching Dodge City, but once there, all hell broke loose.

Cole had been sitting on the top rail of the stock yard fence, watching their cattle when another herd arrived. As the cattle moved down the alley in front of him, he noticed that some of them had brands that appeared to be C Bar A with another fresh brand burned over it.

Running to get Ned, he said, "Pa, there's a herd of cattle just arrived with our brand on it."

"Are you sure, son," Ned asked.

"Yes, sir -- the brand has been doctored but it's plain they are our cattle."

Ned accompanied him to the pen holding the newly arrived herd, and without arousing any suspicion, looked closely at the herd and decided that Cole was correct.

Returning to the Colonel, Ned reported what they had discovered. Colonel Cole decided that the best thing to do was notify Vince of the situation and have him purchase the cattle. Once payment was made, then Sheriff Masterson could arrest them for selling stolen cattle.

As the rustlers stepped out of Vince's office, shoving money from the sale into their saddle bags. Bat and Ned stepped forward, pistols drawn, and shouted, "Alright, drop those bags and unbuckle your gun belts. You're under arrest for rustling and selling stolen cattle."

The leader of the outlaws, Dutch Henry, dropped to one knee and quickly drew his revolver and fired, hitting Bat's hat and knocking it from his head. Ned's shot caught Dutch in the shoulder and knocked him to the ground.

When Colonel Cole, standing on the boardwalk, saw what was happening, he quickly drew his Colt and fired, hitting the nearest outlaw in the head. However, Dutch, lying prostrate on the street with blood flowing from a wound in the shoulder, turned his gun toward Jim, fired and hit him in the chest. He was knocked backward and fell in the street.

Cole, standing next to his grandad, watched as blood flowed from the wound. Crying, he knelt and placed his hand over the wound, trying to stop the blood.

The other six outlaws ducked behind the horses and began firing. Ned and Bat returned the fire, taking their eyes from Dutch.

Dutch, rising, staggered toward Jim and Cole, cursing, with

his gun pointed toward Jim. Cole picked up his grandad's pistol, holding it with both hands he pointed it toward the outlaw and pulled the trigger. The shot caught Dutch square in the chest and knocked him backward. Dropping his revolver, he fell dead at Cole's feet.

General Dodge, commanding officer at Fort Dodge, sent an army ambulance pulled by a span of mules, and they carried the Colonel back to Ceebara headquarters for burial.

Cole remembered that people from all over the Panhandle had attended the funeral, even Chief Quanah and General Mackenzie from Fort Sill in Oklahoma.[1]

Chief had remained with him on the ranch after the funeral and had been living with him ever since.

He and Bold Eagle were now thirteen years old, and when Kate wasn't teaching them their book lessons, they were working along side of the other cowboys, roping, branding and riding the range. They thought they were full grown.

"I guess you boys better get your bed rolls ready," Ned ordered one night in late March, "We'll be heading for the Palo Duro to help Colonel Goodnight with his roundup tomorrow morning."

Cole caught his breath, he wanted to shout for joy. He had never seen the Palo Duro Canyon but had heard other cowboys talk about its beauty, grandeur and wildness. Instead of shouting he said, "Yes, sir!" with all the emphasis he could muster.

"Come on, Chief," he said, "We got work to do."

His name was Jim Bold Eagle, but Cole had named him *Chief* when they were only six years old. Chief Quanah would come by the ranch to visit before the Red River Wars, and Cole and Chief would play together on Red Deer Creek. The name

[1]Dry Bones - Gerald McCathern

stuck and everyone around the ranch called him Chief. He had been living with the Armstrongs for three years.

They rushed to their room and began putting together extra clothing, slickers and blankets in their bed roll. Once complete, they rolled everything in a small tarp to protect it from the weather.

"Chief," Cole said as they were completing the task, "the Palo Duro used to be your home, didn't it?"

"Yes," the young Comanche said, "I remember it was our winter home. And I remember the day when the blue coats came, stole our horses and burned our lodges. They captured my mother and father and me, but your pa helped us escape. That's when your pa led our people here to the big ranch house and fed and protected us until spring. My father, Chief Quanah, then led our people to the reservation because he knew that we were few in number and had no chance of fighting the horse soldiers."[2]

"I'm glad he allowed you to remain with us, Chief. You are my best friend."

"And you are mine," Chief replied.

Cole tied his bed roll together, sat back and said, "I been thinking, Chief. They say that there is a lot of gold hidden somewhere in the canyon. Maybe you and I will have a chance to search for it."

Chief smiled, "I know the canyon and maybe we will find it."

Stars were still sparkling in the clear North Texas sky when the Ceebara crew mounted up and headed southwest for the two day journey to the Palo Duro. Ned, Cole, Chief, Smokey,

Sonny and ten cowboys were horseback. Biscuit and Manuel were bringing the chuck wagon which was being pulled by a team of bay mules. They crossed Red Deer Creek then took the trail up the talus slope to the cut in the caprock. As they came out on top of the plains, the sun made its first appearance in the east, its rays painted the white caprock a deep golden color -- a good omen for Cole and Chief, thinking about buried treasure as the crew headed southwest.

The air still had a touch of winter in it, and they shivered as it penetrated their heavy coats. Within two hours, however, they removed their coats and tied them behind their saddles as the temperature rose to a comfortable level.

Ned, riding along side of Cole and Chief, said, "That's the trouble with the weather this time of year. You never know how to dress, you can have winter, spring and summer all in the same day."

"That's for dang sure, pa," Cole replied as he removed his coat. "I'll bet we don't ever need these coats again."

Chief smiled, "Probably not until the sun sets this evening."

They rode in silence most of the day, listening to the squeaking and banging of the chuck wagon. They passed several small playa lakes which were brim full from recent rains. Small herds of buffalo and antelope watched with wary eyes from the edge of the lakes as the small caravan passed. Several large herds of longhorns, wearing a variety of brands, were grazing contentedly around the lakes. By sundown, they had crossed the North Fork of the Red River and camped for the night in the valley of the Salt Fork

"Whose ranch are we on now, pa," Cole asked

"I suppose this must be the Quarter Circle Heart, son -- Mr.

Carheart's spread," Ned said. "We'll probably gather the cattle here when we finish with the JA" .

While the boys tended to the horses and mules, Manuel gathered fire wood and started a fire. Biscuit soon had coffee boiling and steaks broiling. Cold beans were being warmed in a large pot and sour dough biscuits were being cooked in a cast-iron Dutch oven. Cole and Chief, their chores complete, sat next to the fire, mouths watering as they smelled the aroma of Biscuit's highly seasoned food.

With supper complete, they sat around the campfire for awhile and listened to two of the cowboys play a guitar and harmonica. Cole couldn't remember when he had ever enjoyed a day as much.

Curled in his bed roll he said, "Pa, I surely do thank you for bringing me along."

Ned smiled in the dark, "You're surely welcome, son."

....

They rode into the south cow camp of the JA two hours before sundown and discovered they were the last of the roundup crews to arrive. Chuck wagons were scattered among the cottonwood trees along the bank of the South Fork and hundreds of cowboys were busy with horses and tack. Biscuit chose a site next to a clear pool for his chuck wagon and started issuing orders to Manuel, Cole and Chief. The mules were soon unharnessed, hobbled and released on the prime grass next to the river. Cole and Chief gathered wood for the evening meal and the morning breakfast.

Colonel Goodnight rode up on his huge blue roan gelding and dismounted, shaking hands with all the men. He smiled at Cole and Chief as he took their hands, "Well," he said, shaking

Cole's hand, "seems to me Ned brought the best cowboys on his ranch to help out. I reckon we won't have any trouble finding all the strays with you two cowboys riding with us."

Cole and Chief beamed. Colonel Goodnight, himself, bragging on them!

"Biscuit," the Colonel shouted, "No need to prepare any supper, we've got a steer turning on the spit, and beans boiling in the pot. There's enough for everyone."

Biscuit had the coffee boiling and Ned poured two cups and offered one to the Colonel. "Where do you want us to begin, Colonel," he asked.

"I wish you would take your crew to the upper end of the canyon in the morning and start chousing the cattle out of those branch canyons back down to the corrals at the headquarters. I figure it's nigh onto thirty miles up river to where you will need to start. You should be ready to start your drive back down the river by the time we get the rest of these boys fanned out and pushing the cattle up river."

"That would be another three or four miles above the spot where them sheep herders were murdered, I reckon, Colonel," Ned replied.

"That's right, Ned. Maybe a little farther. You'll be able to tell where the canyon narrows. It will take you the better part of tomorrow to get in place, and a good day to ride out those subcanyons. I figure you should have your herd to the corrals about the same time we get there with ours."

"How many you reckon we'll find, all together?" Ned asked.

"JA should have about twenty-five thousand head -- I don't know how many strays we will find, a good many I suspect," Goodnight replied as he removed a plug of chewing tobacco from his chaps and a knife from his pocket. Cutting a large plug he gave the knife and tobacco to Ned, who cut a plug and handed it to Billy. They all chewed and spit and listened to the Colonel tell his plans.

Turning to Cole and Chief, the Colonel smiled and said, "When you boys pass my ranch house, stop in and meet Miss Molly. I bet she'll have some cookies she baked up, just for a couple of hungry cowboys like you."

Cole smiled and replied, "Yes sir, we'll surely do that!"

....

The next morning, Cole and Chief wolfed down their breakfast and caught up their horses. "Pa, we're going to ride on ahead," Cole said, "we'll wait for you at the ranch house."

"Alright, Cole, but don't you go to pestering Miss Molly. See if you can haul her some water from the creek and bust up some kindling for her stove."

"Okay, pa," Cole yelled as they kicked their horses into a lope and disappeared in a cloud of dust.

....

Chief pointed out landmarks which he recognized as they rode northwest. "There, Cole," he would point. "That bluff that looks like a buffalo's head is where my father killed a bear. I remember the bear skin in our tipi. But we lost it when the buffalo soldiers burned our lodges during the war."

"That's a dang shame, Chief," Cole said. "Ain't very many bears left in this country. In fact, I haven't seen a one on Ceebara range."

Chief nodded, "I know, but there's still plenty of bob cats and cougars. Maybe we will see some of them when we start our drive."

"I hope so, Chief," Cole replied. They had been hunting together since they were seven years old.

They soon outdistanced the slow moving chuck wagon and had the grandeur of the canyon to themselves. Now and again they would pass small herds of buffalo mixed in with herds of longhorns, and both breeds would bolt into the rocks and trees as they rode by.

They saw several flocks of turkeys, and Cole nearly lost his seat when a covey of Bob White quail took flight below Comanche's feet, sounding like a den of rattle snakes. The horse jumped about six feet, and Cole had to grab leather in order to remain aboard.

Soon their conversation turned to the sheepherders gold which was supposedly hidden somewhere in the canyon. "I didn't realize this canyon was so large," Cole said. "We could search for years and never find it."

"Maybe we find it," Chief replied. "I remember some caves where my friends and I used to play. They are hidden in the rocks, and hard to find. Maybe one of those caves is where the gold is hidden."

They rounded a bend in the river and could see a small column of smoke rising in the distance. Cole kicked his chestnut gelding into a lope as he pointed, "I can smell cookies cooking," he shouted.

When they pulled up in front of the ranch house, Miss Molly was standing in the doorway, wondering what all the shouting was about. "My land!" she said as the two boys dismounted. "Who might you be?"

"I'm Cole Armstrong, Miss Molly, and this is my friend, Chief. We're from the Ceebara ranch. Mr. Goodnight said we should stop by and give you a message."

"A message? What did he say?"

"He said to tell you that we would appreciate some of those fresh cookies that you baked," Cole replied with a grin.

Miss Molly smiled and said, "I think I might have one or two left. My boys just about ate them all before they left for the cattle drive. Come on in and we'll have a look."

Most of the cowboys on the JA were not much older than Cole and Chief and Miss Molly called them all *her boys*. She and Mr. Goodnight did not have any children of their own, so she pampered them all as if they were her own.

She led the two boys into her kitchen, and pointed to a large platter filled with cookies. "I'll swan," she said, "Looks like they left a few for you. Now you boys step out on the back porch where you will find soap and water. Wash some of that dust off your faces while I pour a couple of glasses of buttermilk to go with the cookies."

When they returned, the dust washed from their faces and hands, there were two glasses of buttermilk and a large platter of cookies setting on the table. She sat beside them as they began to eat. "Cole," she said, "I can see that you two are not brothers. I suspect that you must be Ned's son, but who does Chief belong to?"

Between bites, Cole explained, "Chief is Quanah Parker's son, Miss Molly. When Quanah took his tribe to Ft. Sill, he left Chief to live with us so he could learn the cattle business.

"Quanah Parker! My land," she said, "This canyon was one time his home. It's such a sad story, how the soldiers burned their lodges and killed their horses."

"Yes, ma'am," Chief said, "I remember our camp was just

about where your corrals are located. When the soldiers attacked, we hid in the rocks and trees. Only four or five of our warriors were killed, but we lost our food, clothing and tipis. The soldiers drove off our horses and then shot them. If Mr. Ned hadn't led us to Ceebara headquarters and took care of us during the winter, we would have all died."

"So, now your tribe is on the reservation at Ft. Sill?" Miss Molly asked.

"Yes, ma'am," Chief replied, "but not happy. I suspect my father will soon bring our tribe back to this canyon."

Cole interrupted, "Chief thinks he can find the sheepherder's gold, Miss Molly. He knows a lot of good places where it could be hid."

"Well, good luck, boys," she said, "but my cowboys have spent a lot of time looking for it. They haven't found hide nor hair of it and I suspect you won't have any better luck. I think Mr. Goodnight would like for someone to find it, so people would stop looking. They slip in and kill our cattle and start grass fires. I tell you, it's a real problem."

"We don't intend to do that. We just thought we could look a little as we chouse the cattle out of the canyons," Cole said as he took a sip of buttermilk.

"Well, I'll tell you this much. I have never told anyone, but one day while I was sewing out under that cottonwood tree next to the porch, my thimble disappeared. But when I started searching for it," she paused and placed her hand in the pocket of her apron and pulled out a coin, "I found this gold coin laying on the shirt. We've got a pesky crow that comes in and steals every thing that is bright and not nailed down. I didn't see him do it, but I suspect he left the coin and took my thimble,"

Miss Molly said.

"Well, I be da---" Cole caught himself. Ned had told him to always watch his language around ladies. Embarrassed, he said, "I mean, gosh, do you think it is a part of the sheepherder's gold."

Miss Molly laughed, no one in Texas did more cussing than Mr. Goodnight but she appreciated Cole's reserve. "I don't know. I guess it could be, or it could have been lost by some of the soldier boys during that battle with the Comanches. But if I was going out looking for gold, I would look for a crow that might be carrying a thimble in his beak. Maybe he would lead you to his treasure,"

As they talked, unknown to them, back in the sub-canyon where the tall lighthouse formation was located, a crow circled on the updrafts of the breeze, and the sun's rays reflected off a bright gold coin he clutched in his beak."

....

When the chuck wagon arrived, Cole and Chief joined the other Ceebara cowboys and rode another five miles until Ned called a halt. "Make your camp next to the river," he instructed Biscuit. "You boys hobble your horses and put them to graze behind the chuck wagon. Cole, you and Chief help Manuel gather enough fire wood to last a couple of days. Tomorrow some of you will ride on upstream a couple of miles and pick up any cattle on the way back. A couple of you will ride out this smaller canyon on the west side of the river."

Cole spoke up, "Pa, me and Chief will take this canyon."

"Alright, son, but don't miss any cattle -- and be careful."

....

Cole took the lead, following the small meandering stream

which wound along the valley floor. As they rode farther, the canyon walls became closer together, indicating that the end was getting closer. Still they passed several cows and calves, because the grass was thick and plentiful.

"Look, Cole," Chief said as he pointed ahead. "There is the tall rock I was telling you about, straight ahead."

Cole pulled his pony to a stop and looked with awe. There ahead was a tall formation, resembling some of the pictures of coastal light houses he had seen in one of the books he had been studying. "Must be three or four hundred feet high," he said, "and not much larger at the bottom than it is on the top. Wonder what keeps it from falling?"

Chief had no answer to that question but related how he and his Indian friends would ride their ponies up to it, then dismount and try to climb it, but the walls were too steep and they could only go a short distance.

Cole gazed in silence as he thought. "You know what I am thinking, Chief. If I wanted to hide gold in this canyon, I would pick a good spot close to this formation so that I could use it as a landmark when I returned. I'll bet the gold is nearby."

"Yes, I think you may be right," Chief replied as his eyes moved along the rim of the canyon, searching for signs of a cave.

A cow bawling for her calf broke their reverie and Cole said, "Let's ride on ahead and start the cattle back down toward the main canyon. We don't want pa to be worrying about us and send some of the hands looking for us."

Remounting, they continued toward the upper ends of the canyon. The trail was now more dim, with huge boulders blocking their way. They could hear the sound of the cow, closer now, bawling for her calf.

"I wonder what's wrong with that cow," Chief asked, "she doesn't sound right."

Cole negotiated his horse around a huge boulder, looking down to make certain he kept to the trail. Looking up, suddenly he saw a large cougar in the middle of the trail, feeding on a young calf. The huge cat, surprised, leaped at Cole and his horse. The horse screamed, reared and fell backwards. Sharp claws grabbed at Cole's leg as he rolled from the horse's back. The frightened horse kicked and scrambled to get up as the cougar landed on top of Cole.

Realizing what was happening, he screamed, "Cougar! Cougar, Chief!"

Quickly pulling his Winchester from the saddle boot, Chief worked the lever, pushing a shell into the chamber. In one motion he threw the rifle to his shoulder and fired as the cougar clawed at Cole's back. The bullet pierced the cougar's neck, breaking it and piercing the spinal cord. It fell limp on top of Cole.

Chief dismounted in a flash, dropped the rifle, pulled his Bowie knife from his belt, and landed on top of the huge cat. His momentum knocked the cougar from Cole's back and they rolled down the small incline, stopping in the stream bed. With his legs wrapped around the cat's torso, he looped his arm under its jaw and brought the sharp blade of the knife across the tight skin of the neck, slicing through the jugular vein. The cat jerked its legs a couple of times and died.

Rushing back up the hill, Chief turned the blood covered body of Cole over and was relieved to see his friend smiling at him, even though he had a mouth full of dirt and grass. Cole struggled to his feet, clawing at the dirt in his mouth. When he could finally speak, he said, "Good shot, Chief, that big sonofagun nearly had me."

"What you mean, nearly? Seems to me he got you! Look at all the blood."

Cole felt around his torn shirt and his chaps. A large chunk was torn from his chaps, and deep scratches were in his leather vest, but the claws had not penetrated his skin. "Must be the cougars blood, I don't think any of it is mine," he said nervously.

"What we going to do now, Cole?" Chief asked.

"First thing we're going to do is skin that cat. I want some proof when we start telling our story, otherwise, no one will believe us."

After skinning the cougar, they rolled the hide and tied it behind Chief's saddle then rode on to the head of the canyon. Only the one cow which had lost her calf to the cougar was found before they turned around and started their drive back down the canyon. Reaching the Lighthouse formation, Chief looked up and saw a lone crow, perched on a Juniper limb, which was growing just below the caprock.

Pointing, he shouted for Cole to look. They both swore there was something bright in his beak. Cole dismounted, reached into his pocket and pulled out a shiny, silver dollar. Positioning it on a flat rock so the sun's rays would reflect toward the crow, he remounted and motioned for Chief to follow him. They rode down the trail about fifty yards, stopped, waited and watched.

The inquisitive crow took flight, circled and landed on the flat rock, dropped what was in his beak, picked up the silver dollar, and once again took flight back to his Juniper perch.

The two boys rode back to the rock and Cole reached down and picked up the twenty dollar gold piece. Laughing he held it up for Chief to see, "I'd say that crow made a bad deal, trading twenty dollars for one dollar."

Chief took the coin, examined it and replied, "Must be an Indian crow -- he trades with white man the same as the Indians do."

Cole looked at his friend, astonished, then laughed at his sense of humor.

Chief returned the coin to Cole, and he put it in his pocket, saying, "Let's keep this a secret. We need to finish our drive and the first chance we get, we'll come back and have a look up there in that crow's nest. I'll bet my hat there's more where that came from."

8

The two boys swept the canyon floor, riding back and forth, shouting and whistling, pushing the cattle downstream. By the time they reached the river, dust could be seen rising from the canyon, approximately one mile to the north. "Looks like we made it just in time, Chief," Cole said. "Pa and the other cowboys will be here shortly with their herd."

"And it looks like they found many, by all the dust that is being kicked up," the young Indian replied.

Holding their herd, they waited in the mouth of the Lighthouse canyon, and watched as over four thousand head rushed by. Now they could hear the shouting and whistling of the Ceebara cowboys as they pushed the herd downstream. Cole and Chief blocked their canyon, preventing any of the big herd from entering.

Ned rode up, smiling. "Looks like you boys did a good job. How many do you figure you brought out?"

"Probably close to eight hundred head," Cole replied.

Noticing the blood on Cole's clothing, Ned's smile disappeared. "What the hell happened to you, son? Are you hurt bad?"

"No, sir. Ain't hurt none at all," Cole replied, smiling. "We had a little disagreement with a cougar."

"Looks like the cougar might have won the argument," Ned replied.

Chief turned in his saddle and lifted up the cougar's head. "No, sir, Mr. Ned. The cougar lost. That's cougar blood on Cole," he said.

Cole smiled proudly, "You should have seen the fight, Pa. That cat made a jump at me and my horse. The horse fell backwards trying to get out of his way. There I was, laying flat on the ground with my leg caught under old Comanche, and Chief pulls his rifle and shoots the cat in the neck. I was pinned under the cougar and Chief bailed off his horse, landed smack on the cougar's back with his knife in his hand. He cut that cougars throat and it bled all over me."

Ned smiled and said, "You did good, Chief, I'm proud of you."

Turning to Cole, he asked, "You sure you ain't hurt?"

"No, sir. He kinda made a pin cushion out of my chaps and vest, though," Cole replied, holding his leg out so Ned could see the tear in the chaps. "We skinned him out so we could prove to you what happened."

Ned laughed, "It would be hard to believe if you didn't have the proof."

....

Ned's crew had nearly five thousand head in front of them and they picked up another thousand as they continued the drive to the corrals and headquarters. The first of the big herd was just arriving and Ned and the Ceebara cowboys blocked the valley floor, preventing the herd from continuing on upstream.

The floor of the canyon, from one side to the other, was filled with bawling cattle.

Colonel Goodnight appeared out of the dust, riding his big blue roan. "Corrals are not large enough to hold them all," he shouted. "We'll push them into that small box canyon behind the ranch house. They can't get out of there and there's plenty of water and grass to hold them until we can get them worked."

Ned nodded in agreement and motioned for his crew to allow the cattle to enter the box canyon. Dust from the thirty thousand cattle filled the canyon and obscured the canyon walls as the two hundred cowboys formed a half circle around the herd, allowing them to flow into the natural corral.

....

Goodnight's cook, Sour Dough, and Miss Molly, had been working all day, preparing the evening meal. Another steer was turning on the spit over a huge bed of coals next to the ranch house. A large cast iron pot of beans was boiling, and a tub of biscuits were warming next to the fire.

The cowboys ate in shifts -- while one group kept the cattle inside the small canyon, another group rode in and ate. Soon, they all had eaten and were talking about the days activities. The story of the two boys' battle with the mountain lion had made the rounds, and several cowboys made a point to come by and see the huge hide and congratulate the two young cowboys on the success of their adventure.

Cole didn't know if he should mention the crow incident, but when Miss Molly invited him and Chief to share another cookie and buttermilk in her kitchen, he decided to confide in her.

"Miss Molly, we met your crow today," he said as he took a

swig of the buttermilk. "

"That's nice, Cole, but how did you know it was old Coaley?"

Pulling the coin from his pocket, he gave it to her and said, "We traded him a silver dollar for this twenty dollar gold piece."

"Well, my land," she exclaimed. "Just like when he took my thimble and left me an identical coin."

She gave the coin back to Cole and asked, "Do you know where he got it?"

"Not exactly, but we think we might be able to find it. Do you reckon Mr. Goodnight would mind if we came back someday and prowled around a little?"

"I'm sure he wouldn't mind, Cole. But I've got a little influence around here, too. You come anytime you want to as long as you promise to come by and have a cookie and buttermilk with me," she said, smiling kindly.

"I know the story is that the gold belonged to some sheep men named Casner. If we found it, would it still belong to them?" Cole asked.

Miss Molly thought about the question before answering, "Yes, I suppose so, if we knew their whereabouts, but Mr. Goodnight tried to locate them last year and couldn't find them. I suppose we could advertise and if they didn't respond, it would be yours."

"But if it's on your property, wouldn't it belong to you?"

"Not necessarily. I've heard Mr. Goodnight say he wished someone would find it and get it off his ranch. He says our cowboys have dug up half of our grass looking for it. Besides they are spending more time prospecting for gold than they are tending to cows. You find that gold and I'm sure it will be yours to keep."

"We don't have time to look this time, but if Pa will let us, we will come back before fall," Cole responded.

"You do that, Cole. It gets mighty lonesome for me here in the canyon. Mostly, all the cowboys are gone two or three days at a time, and some times, Mr. Goodnight is gone for weeks. All I've got to keep me company is my chickens, and an occasional visit by old Coaley. I would surely welcome your visit."

....

Breakfast was complete before sunrise the next day and separation and identification of the cattle began. The corrals would only hold two thousand head, so the cowboys would cut out that many and drive them into the pens. They would be driven down a narrow chute and all the JA brands were cut into one pen, the mixed brands into another. Then the JAs were released and driven up the main canyon a short distance.

It was decided to cut the LS, LE, LIT, and LX brands into one pen, and then drive them out of the canyon on the west side, since those ranches were northwest of the canyon. The Quarter Circle Heart, C bar A, RO, Quarter Circle T and Turkey Track were cut into another pen, then driven out of the canyon on the east side, since those ranches were northeast of the canyon.

The west side cattle would then be driven together to the LX pens on the Canadian River where they would once again be cut according to brands and driven to individual ranch pastures. The east side cattle would be driven to C bar A corrals and re-cut into individual brands and driven to individual ranch pastures.

It was grueling work -- dusty and hot. For four days the

cowboys worked from daylight 'till dark, herding, pushing and shoving the cattle down the chute, examining brands. Some of the brands were grown over with hair and hard to identify. Several times, arguments erupted between crews as to who the rightful owner of a cow would be.

The tiger-stripped cow was large and unruly, fighting and refusing to enter the chute. Cole and Chief, sitting their horses near the chute, laughed as a horn of the cow caught an LX cowboy in the seat of his pants and threw him about ten feet where he landed in a fresh pile of cow manure.

When the cow turned to make another run at the floundering cowboy, Cole and Chief spurred their mounts forward as they unfurled their ropes. Cole rushed by the cow, let fly his lariat, and jerked it tight as it sailed neatly over the cows huge horns.

Chief, one jump behind the cow, released his rope and it slipped easily under the cow's belly. As her two hind feet stepped into the loop, he jerked out the slack, dallied his rope around the saddle horn, and pulled the cow to the ground. She fell three feet from the hapless, manure covered cowboy who was struggling to get up.

The other cowboys stopped their work and watched the action of Cole and Chief as they held the cow until the cowboy crawled safely out of the way. Cole dismounted, speaking to Comanche to back and hold the rope tight, then stepped to the cow, examined the brand and shouted, "LE!"

Speaking to Comanche who was watching him closely, he said, "Slack, Comanche." The horse took a step forward, the rope slackened and Cole pulled it from the cows horns. Chief continued to keep his rope secure while Cole remounted. Cole nodded to him, he released the dallie around his saddle horn, the cow kicked the rope loose, and stood, looking for someone where she could direct her anger. Everyone afoot, climbed to the top rail of the fence, and cheered as Cole and Chief drove her into the LX pen.

The next day, tempers were running high when an argument erupted between two LS and two LX cowboys about the brand of a spotted cow. A punch was thrown in anger, and the argument turned into a fight. When other cowboys from the two crews became involved, the fight became a brawl and the corral became filled with cowboys throwing punches, wrestling in the manure covered pen, shouting and cursing.

Soon, the top rail of the fence was covered with cowboys from the other ranches, yelling support for their favorites. Fearing gunplay could erupt, Ned, Tom Bugbee, and Colonel Goodnight rushed into the melee, pulling struggling cowboys apart and shouting for them to stop the fight.

An LX cowboy, swung a roundhouse right toward the chin of an LS cowboy -- the cowboy ducked and the fist of the LX cowboy landed solidly on the chin of Colonel Goodnight. The Colonel hit the ground as if he had been hit by an axe handle.

Sitting on the ground, cow manure on his face, Colonel Goodnight pulled his Colt and fired three quick shots into the air. The sound of the shots echoed back from the canyon walls and the fighting cowboys quickly fell prostrate on the ground, believing that someone was shooting at them.

The shouting ceased and Goodnight's voice boomed, "The next shot is going to be at the first one who throws another punch. Now get up, shake hands and let's get on with the inspections."

Grudgingly, the cowboys shook, then smiled and returned to their stations, content that they had been able to release some of their pent up anger. The only wounds were a few bloody noses and black eyes.

The cowboys lining the fence laughed as Colonel Goodnight pulled himself off the ground, wiping cow shit from his face. Tiny, a large cowboy from the Turkey Track, yelled, "Better leave the fighting to us younger fellers, Colonel!"

Goodnight glared at him and replied, "It wasn't my age, Tiny, it was that cowboy's aim."

Once the roundup and cutting was complete, a tally showed twenty-four thousand three hundred head of JA brands; three hundred LS, one hundred fifty LE; five hundred twenty LIT; six hundred LX; one hundred twenty Quarter Circle Heart; four hundred C bar A; eighty Quarter Circle T; fifty RO. and thirty-five Turkey Track.

Colonel Goodnight estimated he had probably lost seven hundred head to rustlers. The other ranches would not know their losses until the final roundups were made on each ranch.

After three days of brand inspections, the stray cattle were driven up narrow trails to the top of the canyon and headed north to home ranches.

After more than a month, the roundups were finally completed and the tally showed over two hundred thousand cattle had been checked for brands. Near eleven thousand head were declared missing, mostly a result of rustlers taking their cut.

"Eleven thousand head! That's a right many to just disappear, ain't it Pa," Cole asked.

"It certainly is, Son," Ned answered, "but without any law,

no fences and no more cowboys to ride the range, rustlers could take fifty thousand and we would never know until we had a roundup. Looks like we ranchers are going to need to form our own ranger committee and hang a few cow thieves if we are ever going to put a stop to it."

....

Chief and Cole continued to talk about the crow and were positive they could locate the gold but there was too much work to be done on Ceebara range for them to go treasure hunting. New calves had to be branded, cows pulled from quicksand in the Canadian River, corrals repaired, and lessons to be studied in Miss Kate's home school. The two boys loved the hard work with the cattle but hated school, and Ned's harsh words were required to keep them at their books.

Summer was soon gone and the fall cattle drive to market in Dodge City was fast approaching. The boys forgot about the gold and their lessons, and were anxious to make the trail drive to Dodge City. Even though they had made the trail drive two years before when Colonel Jim Cole was gunned down by outlaws on the main street of Dodge City, the excitement of another drive far surpassed their fears of another gun battle.

Three thousand head of three year old steers had been cut out and left in the Red Deer Creek pasture after the round up and were ready for the two week trail drive. Big Red, the old two thousand pound lead steer knew that he would soon be on the trail again and was restless, continually roaming the valley floor, bellering to let the other steers know that he was the boss. Once a day he would show up at Miss Belle's kitchen door and beg for sweets. He loved molasses and would not leave until

Belle had fed him a couple of spoonful of the sweet syrup.[1]

"Pa," Cole asked, " me and Chief surely do want to make the drive this year. We can do anything the other cowboys can do, and maybe even better."

"Well, I agree that you are two of the best hands on the ranch, but you know your mother, especially after your grandpa was killed, she ain't going to like it a little bit."

Cole was surprised when he asked Kate if he could go. "I 'spect so, son," she said, "I wouldn't want you staying here by yourself. Me and your grandmother have decided to make the trip, too."

"Now, Kate," Ned said when he heard what they had planned, "that's too tough a trip for ladies. You can't go!"

"Don't tell me what I can or can't do, Ned Armstrong. You seem to forget that we helped bring those five thousand head up from Waco when we started the ranch. That was five hundred miles through wild Indian country. It's only one hundred thirty miles to Dodge City and there ain't no Indians to worry about. Besides, we haven't been anywhere but Hidetown since '66'. We want to see what civilization looks like, and we want to do some shopping in a real store."

Ned could see that there was no way to win this argument, so he replied, "Okay, Kate, but I don't want to hear any complaining about dust, Biscuit's cooking, or the heat."

"You know we are just as tough as you men, maybe tougher. We intend to carry our part of the load," Kate said with fire in her eyes.

Ned smiled and said, "That red hair sure is pretty when you get your dandruff up."

Kate pretended to throw a cup which she was drying, and Ned ducked, knowing that she would, if provoked any further.

9

"Let's head 'em up and move 'em out!" Ned yelled early on the morning of September 11, 1879. Bell and Kate were mounted on their two roan mares and joined the other cowboys as they started the herd east down Red Deer Creek. Big Red took the lead along side of Ned, and the other steers followed behind him. He had made this trip several times before and knew exactly the gait to travel without spreading the herd over too great a distance. Once in awhile he would stop and look back as if to see that all of his herd was still following. Biscuit had moved out ahead with the chuck wagon, followed by a small freight wagon which Ned was bringing to carry the ladies' belongings. The extra wagon was Belle's idea because she and Kate had plans to purchase a wagon load of goods in Dodge City.

Two hours before sun down, camp was made on the south bank of the Canadian River and the herd was allowed to graze and fill with water while the cowboys washed the dust and sweat from their bodies in the clear river water.

The supper fare was steak, beans and hot biscuits. Cole and Chief were first in line as Belle and Kate began filling plates for the famished cowboys. Ned watched, smiling, leaning against a wheel of the chuck wagon while drinking a cup of strong hot coffee. Reminiscing, he thought to himself that the boys were not much younger than he had been when the first drive was made from Waco to the Llano Estacado, and how proud he had been to ride beside his good friend, Colonel Jim Cole.

That drive had taken six weeks on the trail, and they had been beset by storms, stampedes, drownings and Comancheros battles. Belle and Kate nearly lost their lives in stampede, but continued to carry their share of the load. He was proud of his two women.[1]

He and Kate were the last to fill their plates and sat together on the tongue of the chuck wagon. "A lot of water has passed under the bridge since we made that first cattle drive, hasn't it Kate?"

Kate smiled and replied, "It surely has, Ned. You and I were only seventeen years old, you were making eyes at me, and Colonel Cole and mother had just gotten married. It was a tough trip but one of the happiest times in my life."

"Looking at those two boys makes me realize how fortunate we have been. If only the Colonel could have lived to see his grandson grow up, everything would be perfect," Ned agreed.

The sun dropped below the western horizon and millions of stars could be seen in the dark clear sky. A large fire was lighting the area around the camp and Manuel was strumming his guitar and singing a Mexican ballad. Smokey pulled his harmonica from his shirt pocket and joined in. The rest of the crew, sat near their bedrolls, smoking their last cigarette for the day. The sound of the music drifted over the bedded herd as

1 Horns - Gerald McCathern

the night riders began their slow ride around the perimeter, quietly humming along with Manuel's music.

The two boys wasted no time climbing into their bed rolls and were soon asleep, dreaming about the excitement of the days to come.

....

Belle, Kate and Biscuit were the first up the next morning and had the coffee boiling as the camp began to come to life. Smokey and his wrangler had the horses penned in a rope corral and were busy roping the days mounts. Smokey moved through the herd quietly and would throw a hoolihan, an easy flip of the rope without slinging it over his head. The rope sailed through the air and dropped lightly over the horse's head without upsetting the others.

"Come and get it you lazy bunch of ranihans before I throw it out to the coyotes," Biscuit yelled.

When breakfast was completed, Ned asked Belle, "How about riding point with me today?"

Belle agreed, she never missed a chance to work side by side with Ned, it gave her a chance to visit about the ranch business, neighbors and news out of Hidetown. He was always so busy on the ranch that she seldom had an opportunity to visit at length with him.

"I hear there's a new covey of girls come to town last month," he said by way of conversation.

"Oh, maybe I can meet some of them the next time I go after supplies," she replied.

"I reckon," Ned agreed.

The Texas Panhandle was mighty scarce on women. Most of the ranchers were not married and Belle and Kate had very few female neighbors. Tom Bugbee's wife was the nearest, forty miles to the north. Molly Goodnight was eighty miles to the south. Other than those two, most of the female citizens were the painted ladies in Hidetown and Atascosa. Some folks referred to them as *soiled doves, saloon ladies, whores or prostitutes*. Kate preferred *'painted ladies'* and did not look down on them because of their profession. "Except by the grace of God, I could have become one of them," she would say, and always looked upon them with kindness and understanding. "Lord knows they serve a purpose, with men outnumbering women fifty to one in this wild frontier."

On several occasions, Kate had invited a few of the ladies of Hidetown to parties at the ranch and they had conducted themselves in a very respectable manner.

"Yes," Ned said, "and I expect several of them will be marrying ranchers and cowboys one of these days and will become respectable citizens." Even Sonny, Kate's brother, was keeping company with one of the girls in Hidetown.

Kate smiled, "Just so they keep their hands off of my man!"

Ned smiled, "You needn't worry about that, but what about your son -- have you noticed, he's nearly a man?"

Kate nodded, frowning, "I noticed," she replied.

The day passed slowly as the two of them rode point. They had to keep their pace slow so as not to rush the steers. On one occasion, they had gotten nearly five miles ahead of the herd, when they came upon Wolf Creek, a small spring fed stream. A clear blue pool, several feet deep tempted them, and soon they had shed their clothes and were cooling their bodies in the quiet waters.

Kate had weathered the harsh environment of the Texas

plains well, and her tall, supple body still had the sleekness of the seventeen year old that Ned had married fourteen years before. Looking upon her nakedness as she frolicked in the cool water, aroused his love for her.

He remembered the time, shortly after meeting her, when the three ruffians had surprised her while she was bathing in the Brazos River, and attempted to rape her. He had rode upon the scene and took on all three of them, like a tiger protecting her cubs. He had killed one of them, Kate shot another and the third they had overpowered and hauled to jail in Waco.[2]

He marveled as he watched her now, swimming in Wolf Creek, still as young and beautiful as she had been then. Taking her in his arms, he kissed her lips and said, "I love you, Kate." She wrapped her arms around his neck and returned the kiss with passion. "I know," she said, "but I still like to hear you say it."

Ned lifted her naked body in his strong arms and carried her to the sandy bank, where they lay in the sun and shared each others love. The sound of Biscuit shouting obscenities at his mules interrupted their passion and they quickly dressed, mounted and rode across the creek, looking at each other, as embarrassed as two teenagers caught in the act. Then they began laughing at their embarrassment, and laughed so hard they could hardly stay in the saddle.

Hearing their laughter, Biscuit was puzzled and wondered what two people could find so humorous in this God forsaken empty land, a hundred miles from nowhere.

....

Cole and Chief were kept busy the second day of the drive,

riding drag and chasing a few obstinate steers which were determined to leave the herd and return to the ranch. By evening, the steers finally surrendered to the demands of the two boys and reluctantly rejoined the herd.

"I'll swear, Pa," Cole told Ned as they sat around the fire eating their meal, "I thought about making steaks out of that big black steer. We had to rope him and drag him back into the herd a dozen times."

Ned smiled, "I guess I'd of had to deduct the price of him out of your wages if you had."

"What wages?" Cole asked. "That's the first time I've heard anything about wages."

Ned smiled as he answered, "I've been giving it a lot of thought and have come to the conclusion that since you boys have been working as hard as the other hands, you deserve to draw the same pay. Starting two days ago, you are going to receive thirty dollars a month, all you can eat and a couple of horses to ride."

Cole let out a yell, "Hey, Chief! Did you hear that? We're going to get paid for cowboying, just like all of Pa's hired hands."

Chief grinned, "What we going to do with all that money. Ain't nothing out here to spend it on, and when we get to go to Hidetown, we ain't allowed in the saloons to spend it on whiskey and girls."

Ned turned his back to hide his smile -- leave it up to Chief to come up with a reply like that. Sounds like his pa, Quanah, talking.

....

It seemed like every time the Ceebara herd hit the trail for Dodge City the weather turned bad. This drive was no different.

On the third day, they broke camp and started the herd north in a fog so thick you could cut it with a knife.

"How you going to know which way to go, Pa?" Cole asked.

"Didn't you notice," Ned replied, "every night Biscuit points the tongue of his chuck wagon toward the North Star, and it doesn't matter whether it is daylight or dark, cloudy or sunny, I can look at the chuck wagon and get my bearings. The fog will burn off after the sun has been up a couple of hours and I just keep the sun on my right shoulder and know that I'm traveling north."

Sure enough, the sun broke through the fog after a couple of hours and Cole could see the herd strung out behind him in a straight north-south line. Ned, on point, was due north of the lead steers. "I need to remember that," Cole thought, "some day I will be trail boss and won't have Pa along to lead the way."

The wind continued to blow from the southeast, piling moisture into the area and by mid-afternoon, thunder heads were stabbing their ominous fingers into the sky. A distant roar of thunder could be heard in the west and flashes of lightning could be seen, lighting up the dark fringes of the huge thunderhead.

Cole, who had been riding point with Ned, said, "Looks bad, don't it Pa."

"Yes, it does, Son. You ride on up and catch Biscuit and your grandmother. Tell them to locate a camp site. We're going to need to get the cattle bedded down early before that cloud reaches us."

Cole kicked Comanche in the sides with his spurs and disappeared over a small rise in the prairie. He could see the chuck wagon moving slowly about a mile ahead. Giving Com-

anche the reins, he closed the distance in a hurry. Riding up to
the chuck wagon he shouted, "Pa says to make camp soon. He
don't like the looks of that cloud coming up."

Biscuit nodded and waved, acknowledging he understood.
Ahead another mile he could see a line of trees indicating a
small stream. Speaking to Belle, who was setting the seat next to
him, he said, "That be the Kiowa Creek, up ahead. We'll make
camp there, plenty of wood and water."

Reaching the nearly dry creek bed, Biscuit crossed the team
and wagon to the north side and pulled to a stop on a small
knoll. Belle pointed to a group of large cottonwoods next to
the creek bank, "That would be a better spot, Biscuit. We
wouldn't have to tote water very far and would have all the
wood you need for your fire."

Belle made two mistakes, one, the chuck wagon was Biscuit's responsibility and no one, not even the trail boss's wife,
could tell him where to make camp. Two, she failed to realize
that the nearly dry stream bed could be a roaring river by morning if the thunderhead started releasing its moisture up stream.
The spot she suggested could be six feet below water and the
chuck wagon would be floating downstream with all of their
food supplies gone. Biscuit frowned at Belle without saying a
word, stepped down from the wagon seat and began unhooking
the mules.

An hour later Big Red arrived with his herd strung out for a
mile behind him. He crossed the Kiowa and did not stop until
he was high above the stream bed. He, too, had learned that
Ned always wanted the herd across the stream before it was bedded down for the night.

"Pa, I seen some men off to the east when I was trying to

catch up with the chuck wagon, maybe six or eight," Cole said when Ned rode in.

"I saw them, too, son. Probably just travelers. We best keep a sharp eye out tonight, though, they may be up to no good."

The storm hit while they were still eating their meal, with the sun dipping low on the western horizon, and the cattle began to get restless. The men threw their tin plates in the wrecking tub, pulled on their slickers and ran for their horses which were still saddled. Belle and Kate mounted with the men and rode into the wind-whipped rain. The cattle were already moving and the cowboys formed a line between them and the creek bed. If the cattle were going to run, they wanted them to run north. The herd seemed to settle down and stopped, turning their tails into the wind.

The sharp sound of a pistol shot started them moving again. Then several shots could be heard above the howling wind and the cattle began to run, stampeding to the west. Eight strange riders rode into the melee, firing their pistols and shouting. The cattle scattered with some running north, others turned back to the east, and the remainder heading toward the creek to the south.

There was nothing the Ceebara cowboys could do in the dark except ride the fringes and try to keep the herd from scattering too much. However, the strangers continued to fire their pistols and the stampede picked up speed.

Kate got separated from the main herd as she continued to try to head three or four hundred steers which were running west. Darkness had closed in and she could see several riders around her when lightning flashed. She assumed it to be Ceebara cowboys, but could not understand why they continued to fire their guns into the air.

"Stop shooting," she shouted into the wind, but the cowboys paid her no mind.

For two hours she followed the small herd until they finally slowed to a trot and then a walk. She still could not identify the riders who were with her. When she tried to circle ahead of the herd, a rider rode near and grabbed the reins of her bridle. A gruff voice shouted through the howling wind, "Hold up, little lady, we ain't turning this herd around."

Lightning crashed and she could see he was not a Ceebara cowboy. His face was covered with a mat of black whiskers and she could see a long scar, beginning just below his left eye along the side of his nose, through the corner of his mouth and ending on his lower jaw. His mouth was open and she could see that two front teeth were missing.

She tried to pull away from his grip when another dark form pulled up on her other side and grabbed a rein. He was shorter, barrel chested with a face full of red whiskers. Grinning, he shouted, "We don't aim to hurt you none, ma'am, so long as you do as we say."

They moved ahead of her, leading her horse by the reins. Holding the saddle horn, she shouted for help but no one heard.

....

The long night was spent in the saddle, searching for the scattered cattle. The storm blew through after a couple of hours, leaving a sky full of blinking stars. By three a.m. all hands had reported in to the chuck wagon where Biscuit had a roaring fire and hot coffee. All hands, that is, except Kate.

"Anybody seen Kate," Ned asked, worriedly, as he dismounted and started pulling the saddle from his exhausted horse. Smokey led a fresh one up from the remuda and took the saddle from Ned's hands.

"Better git you a cup of hot coffee, Mr. Ned," he said. "I'll finish saddling you a fresh one."

Ned walked to the fire, stooped, picked up the coffee pot, and filled a cup with the steaming brew. Shorty spoke from the dark, "I seen her trying to head a bunch which was running west, boss, but I got cut off from her and lost her."

"She was alright?" Ned asked.

"Yes, sir -- riding like a banshee, she was!" Shorty replied. "Beat all I ever seen the way that woman can ride."

"You boys get mounted and split up. You find any strays, head 'em back to Biscuit's fire. Cole, you and Chief come with me, we'll head west and see if we can pick up Kate's trail. If we're not back by noon, head 'em up the trail. We'll catch up later."

"I'm going with you, Ned," Belle said.

Ned started to object, but knew it would do no good. "Alright, Belle, let's go."

They mounted up and the darkness quickly swallowed them as they headed west out of camp.

....

The eight rustlers drove the small herd west only a short distance before turning to the north. The rain had slackened but the herd was moving in the direction of the departing storm. Soon they were back in the midst of the rain and their tracks were being obliterated by the down pour.

The two men leading Kate's horse took the point, followed closely by the herd which was being pushed by the other six men. They traveled in the rain for another four hours before the clouds broke and a pale moon shone through.

"It'll take them cowboys two days to gather up all their strays and they won't suspect that we got off with three hundred head," Red said.

Bart laughed, "By then we'll be in Dodge, have these cattle sold and be entertaining the ladies in the Longhorn Saloon."

"What you planning on doing with this woman, Bart?" Red asked.

"What you expect? Ain't but one thing a woman's good for," Bart replied. "We'll tie her up and leave her in my shack until we git the herd sold. I'll come back and the two of us will have us a party."

Red laughed.

Kate was listening to the discussion and said to herself, "If Ned don't catch you first, you bastard!"

....

Sun up found Ned, Belle and the two boys still riding west along the swollen Kiowa Creek. No cattle could be seen and the rain had washed away any tracks that might have been made. Ned didn't realize that three hundred head of their herd were stolen, nor that Kate had been taken captive. He was thinking her horse had probably fallen and he would find her afoot.

"I think we'd best circle to the north a couple of miles and head back toward camp. I don't believe she could have gotten this far west," he said.

Riding back east, they found no tracks and no Kate. Slim had started the herd north and they dissected it about five miles north of the Kiowa Creek. Ned, worried, rode up and asked, "Any sign of Kate, Slim?"

"No, sir, no sign. We scoured the area south and east of camp and picked up all the cattle we could find. Our tally shows we lost three hundred head."

"Three hundred head? Find any dead?" Ned asked.

"No, sir. No deads and no trail as to where they may have gone," Slim replied.

"I'll bet Kate is with them somewhere. We find the missing cattle we'll find Kate," a worried Ned replied.

Looking at Slim, Ned asked, "Was that some of our boys that started that shooting?"

"No, sir," Slim replied. "I asked them all, none of them did any shooting."

"Well, some one did. That may be where those three hundred head disappeared to. And Kate may be with them. They'll be going north -- no place but Dodge City to market rustled cattle. We need to hurry!" he said.

Biscuit gave some cold biscuits and bacon to Ned, Belle and the boys who remained in the saddle. Ned thought a bit, then said, "I think me and Belle and the boys will ride on ahead and see if we can pick up their trail. Kate's got to be somewhere. If she were thrown from her horse, the mare would have returned to the herd. She's still mounted and is either trying to keep the missing cattle in our line of march, or she's captive and no telling what they might be doing to her. Come on boys, we need to make tracks," he said as he spurred the buckskin into a lope.

They spread out, Belle remained in the middle, the boys on the east side and Ned rode the west flank, each keeping the others in sight. They had soon left the herd behind as they traveled in an easy trot. After riding about five miles, Ned saw Cole waving, and Chief was dismounted looking at the ground.

"Fresh tracks, Pa," Cole said as Ned slid the buckskin to a stop.

Chief continued to walk around, observing the tracks. "Looks like two or three hundred head, traveling north, Mr. Ned."

"What about horses, any tracks?" Ned asked.

"Yes, sir, eight or nine horses wearing shoes -- two on each side of the herd and two bringing up the rear. Looks like maybe three more out front but the cattle tracks have pretty well covered them," Chief said as he kneeled and scratched in the damp dirt.

Chief continued to walk and search then yelled and waved his hat. Ned loped up to where he was pointing at a lone track in the dirt. "That's Miss Kate's mare's track, Mr. Ned. I'd know it anywhere. One side of the shoe is bent where the hoof had been cracked. It's her, alright."

"Okay, boys. Looks like someone has taken a liking to Kate and about three hundred head of our cattle. They can't be too far ahead, we'll ride along easy like, and when we spot them, we'll hold back until dark, then slip in and take them by surprise," Ned said.

....

Near sundown, the rustlers were spotted about two miles ahead, making camp in a cottonwood grove along a river bottom.

"That's the Beaver River, boys," Ned said. "It will give us lots of cover to get close. We'll circle around and come in from the east, keeping the herd and camp upwind. I'd say we have a good chance of getting within thirty yards without being spotted."

They reached the small river bottom about a quarter of a mile downstream of the rustlers camp, dismounted and tied their horses to the willows which lined the river bank. Ned pulled his Colt and spun the cylinder, making certain it was fully loaded.

"Better get your rifle, Cole. You know I always taught you not to pull your gun unless you were ready to use it. Well, this is one time you need to be ready. These bushwhackers are holding your ma against her will, and no telling what they plan on doing if we don't stop them. If there is any shooting, I want you to shoot to kill. They got us outnumbered two to one, we can't afford to miss."

Chief, Cole and Belle removed their rifles from the saddle boots and chambered a cartridge, then followed Ned as he walked silently in the soft sand toward the camp.

The large fire could be seen in the darkness as they silently approached the camp. Ned motioned for Cole to take the right, Chief the left, and he and Belle took the middle as they crept forward. They were now close enough to hear the conversation of the group.

"You might as well eat your chow, woman," Red said. "Ain't no one going to be coming to rescue you. Your people are probably still searching for you along the Kiowa. Probably figure you got washed away when the creek rose."

"I wouldn't feed that slop to a hog," Kate replied. "It isn't fit for a dog to eat."

"Well, now ain't you the uppity one," Bart said. "You git hungry enough, you'll eat it and like it."

Ned counted the figures around the fire -- all eight men were standing, Kate was sitting next to the fire on a saddle.

"They're pretty sure of themselves," he whispered to Belle, "didn't even post a night watch."

Motioning to Cole, he held up two fingers and pointed to the right. Then motioning to Chief, he held up two fingers and pointed to the left. "Belle, you take the two next to the fire, I'll take the two who are closest to Kate. Make your shots count."

He held up his left hand, then dropped it. Their shots echoed into the darkness as four of the rustlers fell, blood gushing from wounds in the chest. Their second shots thundered before the remaining outlaws realized what was happening. They fell beside their buddies, coloring the sand red with their blood. Ned rushed forward, looking for any movement from the bodies scattered around the fire. There was none, so he turned his attention to Kate who sat tied next to the fire.

Belle reached Kate first and began cutting the ropes which had held her hands and feet. Ned holstered his gun and pulled Kate to her feet and held her tight in his arms."Kate, honey, I'm sorry we were so long in finding you."

"I wasn't worried, Ned. I knew you would come," Kate said as tears rolled down her cheeks.

One of the rustlers who was lying in a pool of blood next to the darkness which encircled the fire, slowly moved his hand to his side and removed his pistol from the holster. Pushing himself upright, he turned the pistol toward Ned.

Cole, standing several feet to the right of the rustler, was still looking over the situation. When he saw the rustler's pistol come up, he shouted, "Look out Pa," threw his rifle to his shoulder and fired without sighting. Bart's pistol fired a second after Cole's rifle, and his shot was pulled to the left and only grazed Ned's arm. Bart took Cole's rifle shot in the eye, his body was thrown backwards and he rolled into the darkness, dead with half his head blown away.

"Thanks son, he would have killed me for certain if you hadn't been watching," Ned said as he and the boys dragged the dead bodies away from the fire.

Kate related to Belle her experiences with the rustlers. "They didn't hurt me, mother, but they planned on having their way with me after we reached Dodge City. I'm so glad you came when you did."

Cole and Chief walked back to where the horses were tied and led them back to the camp, unsaddled and hobbled them, then joined the others around the campfire. "We'll bury them in the morning," Ned said, "meantime, let's see if we can get some sleep."

None of them got much sleep, thinking about the day's adventures and the eight dead men laying in the dark just a few yards away from the camp fire.

....

Big Red, leading the main herd reached the Beaver mid-afternoon the following day. "Make your camp, Biscuit," Ned ordered. "We'll rest up till morning. There's no more water until we reach the Cimmaron, which is going to be a hard days drive from here."

There was a lot of talk around the camp fire after the evening meal had been completed. Everyone wanted to hear Kate's story of how she had been taken prisoner and how Ned, Belle and the boys had rescued her. Hearing that they had shot the rustlers, killing them all, Slim said, "Served them right, mistreating Miss Kate that away." The other cowboys all voiced their agreement with Slim.

Each of the cowboys walked over to Cole and Chief, patted their backs and said what a good job they had done.

The drive from the Beaver to the Cimmaron was started by daylight the following morning, and Ned gave orders to push them hard. "There won't be any water until we reach the Cimmaron and we need to make it by dark," he said.

Big Red, realizing that Ned wanted the herd to hurry, kept his head up and his eyes on the horizon, sometimes breaking into a trot. The Cimmaron was reached just as the sun dropped below the western horizon. The cattle were allowed to drink their fill, then were bedded down while Biscuit, Kate and Belle prepared supper.

"We'll be in Kansas tomorrow, men," Ned said as they sat around the camp fire. "That means four days crossing jayhawker country."

"What's a jayhawker, Mr. Ned," Smokey asked.

"Bands of outlaws that prey on travelers and trail herds. They may try to make us pay a head tax before we get into Dodge, so keep your eyes open."

"Does this country belong to them, Mr. Ned?"

"No, it doesn't Smokey, but they usually run in large bunches and use their numbers to force people to pay."

10

Crossing the border into Kansas, they paralleled Crooked Creek which was running with only a small amount of water, but enough to satisfy the cattle when they made camp for the night. Following the creek to the north the next day, they camped on the big bend of the creek, where it turned sharply to the west. The next morning, Big Red sensed -- or maybe smelled -- Dodge City, eighteen miles to the northeast. and picked up his gait.

Fortunately, no jayhawkers were crossed and they made the Arkansas River before sun down. Big Red splashed across the river and headed for the stock yards as if he was home. He had been here so many times that he knew exactly what he was expected to do. Walking down the dirt street with shacks and adobe buildings on both sides, he kept his eyes straight ahead, walked into the stockyard pens and continued up the long alleyway to the end where workers were waiting to cut the herd into several side pens.

A half dozen cattle buyers were sitting on the top rail of the pens, looking the cattle over as they passed. "Best damned herd we've had all summer," one buyer was heard to say. "Yes," another replied, "they're carrying a lot of taller under them hides."

Vince Abercrombie, who had bought Ceebara herds since the very first one was delivered years ago, was the first to welcome Ned. "Good to see you, Ned," he said. "You're kinda late and I was wondering if you was going to make it this year."

"Howdy, Vince. Yeah, we been working all summer trying to separate herds on the plains. That big blizzard last winter mixed them up so bad it took us all summer to get 'em back to home pastures."

"Well, I'm glad you made it," Vince replied, "looks like the best herd you've ever brought in. What you reckon they'll weigh?"

""We've been cross breeding with shorthorn bulls and it has helped. I 'spect they're going to go over eleven hundred," Ned replied.

Vince agreed, "Maybe eleven fifty," he said. "Markets been up a little this year, haven't been as many herds coming in from South Texas."

"Sounds good to me," Ned said, "maybe there will be enough competition that you'll have to pay a fair price for a change."

Vince feigned disappointment, and replied, "Ned, you know damned well I always pay you top dollar and more than they are worth."

The two old friends laughed.

....

Word spread through Dodge City that the Ceebara herd had arrived. Two men who were playing cards in the Long Branch Saloon quickly threw their hands in, gathered their winnings and headed toward the door. They mounted their horses which were tied to the hitching rail and kicked them into a lope toward the stock pens.

"Ned, you old sonuvagun," they shouted as they dismounted and gave Ned a bear hug.

Ned returned the hug, pushed them away and looked at them, "Bat Masterson and Billy Dixon, danged if you ain't a sight for sore eyes. I figured they'd have hung and quartered you before now."

"Like hell," Billy Dixon said, "if there's any hanging to do, we'll do it. Bat's the high sheriff of this here county and I been kinda hanging around so's he'd have someone to play cards with."

"Sheriff, huh?" Ned said, sizing them up and down, "Looks like it might pay better than Colonel Mackenzie paid us when we was scouting for him during the Indian wars."[1]

Belle, Kate, Cole and Chief rode up and Bat and Billy removed their hats and Bat said, "Well, howdy Miss Belle -- Miss Kate. Danged if you ain't the purttiest trail hands I ever did see."

"You always did have a silver tongue, Bat Masterson," Belle said, "but we like it."

"I know you folks are wanting to get a room and a bath," Billy said. "When you get cleaned up I'm going to convince the sheriff to buy you the biggest steaks in Dodge City and we'll talk over old times."

....

After the cattle were penned, Ned called the trail hands together. "I'll make arrangement for rooms at the Dodge House Hotel. Two to the room, so you decide who you want to bunk with."

Curly interrupted, "I'll take one of them gals at the Lady Gay, boss!"

They all laughed and Ned continued, "Take your meals at the Dodge House restaurant, they'll be paid for. The first round of drinks at the Long Branch are on me, after that, you're on your own. Try to stay out of trouble."

"Pa, you said me and Chief was part of the crew, does that mean we get one of them free drinks at the Long Branch?" Cole asked.

Ned laughed, "I 'spect you'd best take that up with your ma."

Kate frowned, "Over my dead body," she said.

....

Billy Dixon was good to his word. He, Vince and Bat met Ned, Belle, Kate, Cole and Chief at the Dodge House restaurant. As they sat down around the huge table, a dirty buffalo hunter at an adjoining table said, " What the hell is going on, I ain't eating next to no damned redskin."

Chief was sitting next to Ned and looked with anger at the hunter. Ned pushed his chair back and stood, "Then I guess you'll have to eat outside, mister," he said, as he hitched his gun belt a little tighter.

Bat caught his arm and pulled him back, "I'll take care of this, Ned," he said as he stepped to the hunter's table. "Mister, you should consider it a privilege to eat in the same room with this Indian lad. He is royalty -- son of my friend, the great Comanche chief Quanah Parker, and the adopted son of all of us. Now you can do one of two things. Shut up and eat your dinner or take a walk with me over to the calaboose. I've got a cell over there that will fit you to a T, and you can eat jail house grub by yourself."

The hunter wasn't convinced, pushed back his chair, stood and faced Bat. "I don't care who he is, I ain't eating with no redskin."

As he reached for his gun, Bat swung his cane, hitting him up beside the head. The hunter went down like a hog in a slaughter house. Bat motioned to two men who were leaving, "Looks like this gent got too close to my cane. Pull him outside where he can get a little fresh air," he said.

The meal was finished and the talk turned to the trail drive. Bat insisted that Kate relate her experience with the rustlers. "Too much of that going on south of the Arkansas," Bat said. "I wish I could put a stop to it but that is out of my district, and I don't even have enough deputies to keep the peace in Dodge. I'll speak to the General out at the fort. Maybe he can spare a few soldiers to patrol that area."

A commotion was heard on the boardwalk as one of the Ceebara trail hands rushed into the restaurant. "Better come quick, boss," Rowdy shouted, "there's a fight going on in the Long Branch. Blood all over the place!"

Ned, Bat, Billy and the boys jumped to their feet and headed for the door. They hit the street running and covered the short distance to the saloon in a matter of seconds. As they approached the saloon, sounds of glass breaking and shouts and cursing could be heard.

They stepped through the swinging doors and ducked as an empty whiskey bottle sailed past their heads. Smokey was standing with his back to the bar, fists raised and blood streaming from his nose. Three men lay unconscious at his feet, three more were warily approaching the black man. One of the men had a long skinning knife in his hand, another had a broken beer bottle.

Shorty and two more of the Ceebara cowboys were struggling with five dirty buffalo hunters in the corner. Without hesitating, Cole and Chief rushed to Smokey's aid. Cole tackled the knife wielding hunter and they both hit the floor, the knife was knocked from the hunter's hand and clattered across the floor. Cole, sitting on the hunters stomach, was pounding his face with his balled fist.

Chief grabbed the long hair of one of the other hunters, pulled his head down and brought up his right fist in an upper cut to the chin. The hunter fell to his knees as Chief released the hair and brought his left around in a vicious smash to the surprised hunter's ear. The hunter fell face forward, unconscious.

Bat and Billy dragged the two boys to their feet and pushed them back toward Ned, then separated the knife wielding hunter and Smokey. Ned rushed to Shorty's aid and quickly had that situation under control. Bat's voice could be heard over the yells of the onlookers, "I 'spect this fight is over or else I'll throw the whole lot of you into the calaboose. Now, what's this ruckus all about?"

Smokey said nothing, still standing with his back to the bar. Shorty answered, "We all came in for that free drink you promised, boss, and these bastards decided that they were going to throw Smokey out, said they wasn't drinking with no nigger. Well, sir, we kinder took offense at their attitude, and told them where they could go. That's when one of them hit Smokey in the nose, and you should have seen what Smokey did. He had three of them on the floor before we could come to his aid. Then these other fellers decided they was going to help throw him out and we just decided that was too many against one man. I 'spect old Smokey could have taken care of all of them cause he was hurting them pretty bad."

Looking at the buffalo hunters who were beginning to regain consciousness, Bat said, "Now boys, you know how I hate this kind of lawlessness. You best understand that man you called *nigger* is a friend of mine. So I want you to treat him like he's a friend of yours -- else I'm going to let him take you on, one at a time, and I guarandamtee you, that he'll mop the floor with you!"

The buffalo hunters got to their feet and slowly walked to the door, mumbling under their breath. The cowboys all gathered around Smokey, patting his back and offering to buy him drinks. Smokey smiled and said, "Thanks, men, but I limits myself to one drink a night. I found out years ago that liquor always makes me want to fight."

They all laughed.

Ned, Bat and Billy turned and walked from the saloon, leaving the cowboys to enjoy their celebration. Ned forgot about Cole and Chief, and the two young cowboys, just turned thirteen, remained with their friends, wanting a chance to take their first drink of strong liquor just to see why all the cowboys seemed to love it.

The Ceebara crew gathered around them, ordered their drinks, and Shorty held up his glass, "A toast to two of the best danged cowboys and toughest fighters on the Ceebara range," he said. Cole and Chief nervously held up their drinks, then cautiously turned up the glasses and drank it down. They choked, coughed and spit as the other cowboys laughed at their embarrassment.

The two boys couldn't understand why anyone would like to drink something that was so disgusting, and refused to drink any more. However, the one drink set their heads to spinning and they couldn't refuse the advances of two of the younger, scantily clad dance hall girls.

The boys looked much older than their actual years, standing nearly six feet tall with muscles bulging under their broadcloth shirts. "My, you certainly showed that buffalo hunter a thing or two," the pretty red head said, as she placed her hand on Cole's shoulder and tickled his ear. "What's your name, cowboy?"

Cole blushed, "C-Cole," he stammered.

Chief was not as embarrassed as Cole, and when the dark haired beauty which had him by the arm began to pull him toward the stairs, he followed obediently.

"Well, Cole, my name is Cindy, now that you've had your drink, what say you and me go to my room and you tell me all about being a cowboy," the red head whispered in is ear.

Well, Cole could do that, he thought, because he really liked to talk about his work. He didn't realize all of the other things she was aiming to talk about and things that she was going to do to him as the door to her room closed.

A coal oil lamp burned dimly on a small table in the corner of the room, and a feather bed filled the middle of the room. A yellow cat, curled on the bed, bounded to the floor and jumped to a cane bottom chair in the corner of the room. Before he knew what was happening, Cindy curled her arms around his neck, pulled his head down and kissed him full on the lips.

He should have been scared, but the drink had given him a false sense of bravado, and he relaxed and returned the kiss. Her perfume was so sweet, that he thought he was going to drown in its fragrance.

She guided him to the bed and began unbuttoning his shirt. He thought he should resist but he seemed to be paralyzed. His shirt and then his pants fell to the floor.

He gazed in astonishment as she began unbuttoning her blouse and stepped out of her skirt. He didn't know whether to run or stay. Looking at the cat which sat licking its paws in the chair, he decided only the cat would know -- he didn't run.

He walked into her room a boy, one hour later, he walked out a man!

....

The next day, the cowboys had all disappeared. Some were sharing the beds of the saloon painted ladies. The others, nursing hangovers, were still in bed.

Cole and Chief, however, were up early, excited over their previous night experiences. They were already in the Dodge City Cafe when Ned, Belle and Kate joined them.

"I see it didn't take too long for you boys to get into trouble," Kate said as she examined Cole's black eye and Chief's bandaged hand.

Cole, embarrassed, said, "It wasn't our fault, ma. We was just helping out Smokey."

"And what other kind of trouble did you get into," Kate asked as she sat down.

Cole didn't know if she was aware of their rendezvous with the dance hall girls or not -- but he certainly didn't intend to bring up the subject. "Nothing, ma -- we just kinda stayed a-round talking with the other hands."

Kate feigned surprise, "Oh, and I'm certain those other boys wouldn't think of leading you into any kind trouble."

Cole and Chief dropped their heads and filled their mouths with pancakes and eggs. Ned turned his head to hide a smile.

Vince Abercrombie came in and took a chair at their table. After greeting everyone he said, "Ned, we've always been up front with each other. I know every damned cattle buyer in Dodge is going to want to buy your herd. You get the best offer you can and I'll give you a half a cent more."

"Fair enough, Vince. And me and the boys will load them on the box cars for you," Ned replied.

....

The steers weighed eleven hundred twenty pounds each and Vince paid eight and one half cents a pound, for a total of two hundred eighty five thousand, six hundred dollars. Ned took fifty thousand dollars in gold and had Vince deposit the remainder in Mr. Hoover's new Dodge City Bank.

Belle and Kate spent considerable time and money shopping in York, Hadder and Draper Mercantile, Jacob Collars Dry Goods, and Wright, Beverly and Company general mercantile. The wagon was overflowing with goods before Ned stopped them, explaining the wagon would hold no more.

Eddie Foy was in town, performing at the Masterson and Springer Comique Theater. Ned took Belle, Kate, Cole and Chief to see the comic, musical and dance routine of the well known performer. Miss Belle Lamont, a popular singer, joined Eddie in his routine. Foy enjoyed the wild and rowdy crowd of Texas cowboys and buffalo hunters. He became known as the

"Pet of Dodge City".

Foy was very gracious as Bat introduced Belle and Kate to him, kissing their hands and bowing. "It's such a pleasure to meet the queens of the Texas Panhandle," he said. "I have heard about the great Ceebara ranch and the Cole and Armstrong families. I plan on making a trip to Mobeetie for an engagement at the Lady Gay and hope to see you there."

Kate smiled and said, "We would love to have you pay us a visit at the ranch when you come."

Foy beamed, "That is my heart's desire, dear Kate -- to be able to ride and hunt on a real Texas ranch. I definitely will make an effort to come."

....

As the Ceebara crew were loading and preparing to leave for Texas, a new herd of cattle arrived. Ned and Vince were standing next to the stock pens when the trail boss stopped and spoke.

"Howdy, Vince," he said as he dismounted. "How's the market?"

"Howdy, Cody -- shake hands with Ned Armstrong. Ned, this is Cody Hartman , foreman on Senator Dorsey's Triangle Dot spread over south of the Rabbit Ears."

Ned shook Cody's hand and said, "Pleased to meet you, Cody. I met the Senator a couple of years ago when we were in town with the herd. Did he come along with you?"

Cody seemed a little nervous, "No -- he's back in Arkansas, or maybe Washington. I don't see much of him when Congress is in session."

"Pretty good looking bunch of steers," Vince said. "I'll be wanting a chance at them. How many did you bring."

"About a thousand head. You'll have your chance, just like all the rest of the thieves on Front Street," Cody said as he mounted and joined his cowboys as they began to cut the herd into different pens.

Ned watched the cattle as they passed, especially the brands. It seemed that the triangle had been blotched on most of them. "Kind of a strange feller, ain't he," Ned said.

"Yeah, that's putting it mildly but I guess the Senator has a lot of confidence in him. He takes care of all of the ranch business," Vince said. "In fact, the money for the cattle is deposited in an account to Dorsey and Hartman. Cody's allowed to draw on it just like he owned the cattle."

....

Bat and Billy stood by and waved as the Ceebara crew pulled out. "See you next year," Ned said as he spurred his big sorrel and took the lead out of town.

Big Red, the old lead steer, tied to the rear of Belle's wagon, bawled and tossed his head, anxious to get back with his herd at the ranch.

11

Colonel Goodnight was visiting with Miss Molly at the breakfast table. "I need to make a trip to Pueblo to arrange for more financing with John. That piece of ground up on Tule Canyon is available and I think we need it. I hear that the Matador has been casting their eyes toward it. I may as well take a herd up to Dodge, since I'll be going that way anyhow, and then take the train into Pueblo. I was wondering if you'd like to go along?"

"Lands, I'd love to go, Charles, but I just don't feel up to two weeks on the trail. I'll stay here and see after our boys," she replied as she took a sip of coffee.

"Alright, Mary," he refused to refer to her as Miss Molly, like her brother Leigh and the other cowboys were doing. "It'll take us a week to get a herd together. You make a list of things you'll be needing and I can pick them up in Pueblo."

Leigh and the cowboys were standing around the bunk house, waiting for the Colonel to give orders for the days activities when they spotted a group of riders coming up the canyon.

"What the hell?" Leigh said, "looks like a bunch of Indians. Better come look, Colonel."

Goodnight appeared in the doorway. "You boys check your

guns, but don't use them unless I give the word."

Leigh led the big blue roan out of the corral and Colonel Goodnight mounted and rode toward the approaching Indians.

Holding his hand up in the sign of peace, he stopped before the leader of the group. "What is your name," he asked.

"Quanah, or Mr. Parker -- whatever you wish," Quanah replied. "Don't you know that this canyon is mine?"

"Maybe one time," Goodnight replied, "but the great white chief claims it now and I am paying him for it."

Quanah had several old warriors and a few young ones, along with several squaws and children, numbering about eighty in all. "Are you killing buffaloes?" Quanah asked.

"No, we have plenty of cattle to eat. Buffaloes are no good," Goodnight responded.

"Buffaloes are all gone," Quanah said, motioning up and down the canyon.

"We drove the mangy bastards out the lower end of the canyon," the Colonel replied, pointing to the south.

"My people are hungry," Quanah said, "the soldiers promised us meat but did not bring it. We ate many of our horses and mules and now we have left the reservation to find buffalo."

Goodnight thought for a moment, then said, "I will treaty with you. You may camp here until you locate the buffalo, and I will give you two beeves a day. It is not good that the soldiers did not keep their promise and feed you. Many buffalo are there," pointing to the south, "when you find them, kill all you want and have your squaws make much pemmican and jerky and then return to the reservation. If the soldiers find you hear, they will surely kill you."[1]

---
[1] Charles Goodnight - J.E. Haley

Quanah nodded, "That is good -- we will do as you ask."

"After you have made your camp, come to my house as my guest and share my food. We will smoke the pipe and talk about the old days when this land was yours," Goodnight said.

Turning his roan gelding, he rode back to the bunk house and told the cowboys about the agreement. "Stay away from them, I don't want any trouble -- Quanah is a great man among his people, he will keep his word."

As the sun began to set behind the purple cliffs, Quanah, accompanied by three of his braves, dressed in his Chief's regalia, eagle feathers flowing from his head dress, appeared at the door of the ranch house. Sour Dough had built a huge fire in the front yard and Miss Molly had arranged several brightly colored blankets on the ground around the fire.

Goodnight directed them to be seated and the chuck wagon cook appeared with heaping platters of steaming steaks, passing them to the Indians. They took the meat in their hands and began to eat. When they had finished, Miss Molly appeared with several black cigars in her hand, giving them to the Colonel. Before passing them to his guests, Goodnight said, "Chief Quanah, this is my woman, Miss Molly. She has had your son, Bold Eagle in her home, has fed him and treated him as a son of her own and she is anxious to meet you."

Quanah stood, nodded and offered his hand in the white man's way of greeting. "It is good," he said, "my son is learning the white man's way with my friend, Ned Armstrong and his family on Red Deer Creek. I thank you for treating him kindly."

"Your son has learned much," Miss Molly said. "He is always welcome in my home, he and Ned's son, Cole."

"Yes," Quanah replied, "some day he will return to the reservation and help his people with what he has learned."

The Colonel passed out the cigars, and taking an ember from the fire, they all lit the smokes and began to puff. Quanah, holding his cigar as if it was a peace pipe, blew smoke to the east, the west, the north and the south, then said, "It is good that we can be friends. We will abide by your wishes and leave the canyon as soon as we have enough meat to carry back to the reservation."

Goodnight nodded, blew the smoke as Quanah had done, and said, "You are welcome at my lodge any time your tribe becomes hungry."

The Indians broke camp the next morning and moved south, seeking the small herd of buffalo that remained in the canyon.

Cole and Chief, unaware of Chief Quanah's visit to the JA, continued to dream about the hidden sheepmen's treasure, as they went about their work as cowboys on the Ceebara spread.

....

They were now receiving men's pay and were expected to do men's labor -- and the labor during the winter and spring of 1880-1881 was considerable. Mr. Glidden had introduced his newfangled barbed wire to the area and all of the ranches, including Ceebara, had begun to fence their holdings.

Fence building was not one of the most glamorous jobs on the ranch. Cowboys are a strange lot, they'll work from *can to can't* as long as they can do it from the back of a horse, but a job which requires them to do it afoot is downright embarrassing.

"Reckon you could help paint the barn," Ned asked Hondo, an old bow-legged cowboy one day when there wasn't much to do around the ranch. Sitting his horse, Baldy, and rolling a cigarette, Hondo replied, "I reckon, boss, if I can get old Baldy to stand still long enough." Hondo replied.

Since Cole and Chief were the two youngest cowboys, they were relegated the task of cutting and hauling the cedar posts for the fence building crew. They would harness the mules, hitch them to a wagon and head for the cedar breaks on the upper Washita River, taking enough grub to last three or four days, and trailing their two saddle horses behind. Once the wagon was full of posts, they would return to headquarters, unload the posts, spend the night, then return to the Washita for another load the next day.

It was lonely hard work, but good for their young bodies. Their muscles became as hard as the posts they were cutting. They were excellent shots with both pistol and rifle, and when they tired of swinging the axe, they would relax by practicing their quick draw. They left a lot of lead embedded in cedar trees and in the process, became as quick and accurate as any of the gun slingers in Hidetown.

"Pa always said not to draw my gun unless I meant to use it. I don't aim to, but if I have to, I sure don't want to be too slow or too cockeyed," Cole said as they threw a huge corner post into the wagon.

Chief nodded, smiling, replied, "I'd hate to be the one who tried to prove they was faster or straighter than you."

The gold in Palo Duro Canyon was still strong on their minds, even though Ned was reluctant to let them off. "Too much work to be done right now -- maybe later," he had said.

"Gosh, pa," Cole would reply, "If we don't get a chance to look soon, someone is going to find it before we do."

"Now, son -- what do you need with twenty-five thousand dollars? You'd just blow it on women and whiskey like all the other cowboys do with their money."

Cole had responded, "I ain't planning on doing that, pa, but at least I could hire someone to take my place on this fence building crew."

The sun was hot, the weather was dry, the boys were thirsty, and Ned wasn't around. "What say we take the day off and visit Hidetown," Cole said. "It ain't but fifteen miles to the south. Shorty says that a new covey of painted ladies came to town last week."

Chief threw his axe into the wagon and said, "You ain't waiting for me, white eyes," as he vaulted onto his pony's back.

....

The two boys rode into Hidetown two hours before sundown. Two dogs welcomed them, barking and nipping at their horses' heels. Comanche, Cole's chestnut gelding, backed his ears and kicked, catching one of the dogs in the ribs. The dog sailed through the air, fell and rolled in the sandy street. Howling, it headed for protection under a wagon with the other dog close behind.

Horses lined both sides of the street, tied to hitching rails, standing three legged and switching flies with their tails. Now and then, one of them would stomp in an effort to scare away an overly industrious deer fly which was sucking blood from the horses leg.

Several gunshots were heard, coming from the east end of the street. Three soused up cowboys, guns in the air, were riding hard, west down Main street, firing as they raced out of town. Cole and Chief laughed as they swayed in saddle, hardly able to remain on their horses.

Stopping in front of the Lady Gay saloon, the largest of the more than dozen of the town's most profitable enterprise, they dismounted and tied their horses to the hitching rail. Using their hats, they knocked some of the dust off their clothes. Several dirty, unshaven men, loitering in front of the saloon, eyed them suspiciously.

Hidetown, in 1881, was noted as the toughest town in the west, even tougher than Dodge City and Tombstone. Even though Wheeler County had been organized and elected a sheriff, it was still a wide open town. Tascosa, one hundred miles to the west, came in a close second, reason being that they were the only two towns in the entire Texas Panhandle and were populated by buffalo hunters, cowboys, gamblers, rustlers, outlaws, soldiers and prostitutes -- and little or no law.

In Hidetown alone, there was an estimated five hundred prostitutes vying their trade in the thirteen saloons along the quarter mile long Main Street. It was a place where gun shots could be heard hourly, and graves were dug daily, mostly as a result of arguments over the painted ladies -- not a place for the timid to take root. In Hidetown, boys became men at an early age -- if they lived long enough.

"They don't allow no redskins in this saloon," one of the buffalo hunters said as he blocked the doorway.

Cole, six feet tall and hard as nails, smiled, walked up to the drifter, and without speaking, slammed him in the ear with his balled up fist. The man fell as if he had been hit with an axe handle, and lay unconscious with his head resting in a muddy puddle. Placing his hand on the butt of his pistol, Cole looked at the other men and said , "we just changed the rules," turned and walked through the swinging doors of the saloon. Chief smiled and followed.

When their eyes had adjusted to the dim light in the saloon, Cole and Chief stepped up to the bar and ordered beer. The bar tender was new and did not recognize the two boys, not realizing they were from the Ceebara Ranch. Looking at Chief, he said, "Sorry, ain't no redskins allowed in here, I'll have to ask the Indian to leave."

"He's just as thirsty as I am and I'm buying, now give us two beers," Cole said as he looked straight into the bartenders eyes.

The bartender nodded to a huge man at the end of the bar, who stepped up to Cole and said, "You heard what the man said, I 'spect you best leave before I have to throw you out."

Cole was no coward, and had more courage than good sense. Stepping back he raised his fists and said, "You and who else?"

As the huge bouncer started to swing, a loud voice from behind Cole said, "Well, howdy, Cole. What you and Chief doing in town?"

Turning, Cole replied, "Well, howdy, Mr. Temple. We been cutting posts over on the Washita and got thirsty, decided we'd come in and rest a bit."

Temple Houston, youngest son of Sam Houston and the new District Attorney who the Governor had sent up from Navasota, placed his arms on the shoulders of the two boys, and said, "Now Pete, you wouldn't want to throw these two friends of mine out, would you, just about the time I was fixing to buy them a drink? Besides, you start throwing Ned Armstrong's son out of your establishment and you'll have all of the cowboys in the Texas Panhandle tearing this place apart."

"Sorry Mr. Houston," the bartender said, as he placed two beers on the bar. "I didn't know they was friends of yours. Ned's son? Who's the redskin? "

"Chief Quanah Parker's son -- old Quanah hears you been mistreating his son, he might take a liking to what little hair you've got left on that empty head."

Looking at Cole and Chief, Temple said, "Bring your beers and join me at my office, Cole, and tell me what's going on out at the ranch."

His *office,* it turned out, was a table in the corner of the saloon.

"Thanks Mr. Temple," Cole said as he and Chief followed Houston to his table. The boys had become acquainted with DA Houston when he had visited Ned at the ranch.

....

Temple Houston was new to the area, but folks were already recognizing him as a man to be reckoned with, not because he was Sam Houston's son, but because he was a self made man. Old Sam had died when Temple was only five years old, but he had told his young protege to study law and the Bible if he ever wanted to succeed in life.

Temple remembered the advice of his father, and the Father of Texas, and when he left home at age fourteen, he strapped on old Sam's pistol, stuck a new Winchester rifle in his saddle boot, packed Blackstone's Book of Law and the Holy Bible in his saddle bags and joined a cattle drive that was leaving south Texas for the grasslands of Montana.

Three months later, he drew his pay in Miles City, Montana, sold his horse and saddle and took a river boat down the Missouri to the Mississippi then to New Orleans. Looking up an old friend of Sam's who was a Louisiana Congressman, he accepted a job as the Congressman's Page in Washington, D.C. and spent a year listening to the politicians debate on Capitol Hill. It was there that he decided that law and politics was going to be his future.

Returning to Texas, he enrolled in the new Texas A and M college, attended for a year, transferred to Baylor University, and after only one year, passed his law exam and received his law degree before he was eighteen years old. He was practicing law in Navasota at age nineteen when Governor Roberts, an old friend of his late father, appointed him as District Attorney in the newly formed 35th Judicial District in the wild Texas Panhandle.[2]

Temple could out draw and out shoot any of the gun slingers in Hidetown and Tascosa and on several occasions proved his ability. He wore his pearl handled pistol in the court room and used it many times to restore order.

A flashy dresser, he wore a huge Mexican sombrero hat, leather fringed vest, and tight Mexican trousers when he was prosecuting criminals. He soon became the darling of the court room and people came from miles around to listen to his oratory.

He and Ned Armstrong had become very good friends, and he could see himself in Ned's young son, Cole. He was no older than Cole when he started making a name for himself, and realized that Cole was straining at the bit to get out on his own.

....

"Ain't much going on out at the ranch," Cole said as he sipped his beer. "Just cutting posts and stringing that new fan-

[2]Temple Houston. Lawyer With a Gun - Glenn Shirley

gled barbed wire around the place. Seems like a waste of time and money to me but Pa thinks that it might help to keep down some of the rustling."

"Well, something got to be done about the rustling. I've been trying to get the governor to send up a few Texas Rangers but he says the state's broke and can't afford it. We've finally got Wheeler County organized and elected a new sheriff but he's got so much crime in Mobeetie to look after he ain't going to have time to go chasing around forty thousand square miles looking for cattle thieves."

Cole was feeling mighty grown-up, sitting here in the Lady Gay, drinking beer and visiting with Mr. Temple. Chief, as always, sat quietly and listened to the conversation.

"Do you know about that sheep herders gold over in Palo Duro Canyon?" Cole asked.

"Yes, Colonel Goodnight was telling me about it. Said his cowboys was digging up half of the state of Texas looking for it, but no one has found anything yet," Temple replied. "Said he wished someone would find it so he could get a little work out of his men."

"If someone found it, reckon they could keep it?" Cole asked.

"Well, now, I guess legally it would belong to Mr. Goodnight since he owns the land. But I wouldn't worry too much about it -- I doubt seriously that any gold exists."

Cole smiled, reached in the pocket of his chaps and pulled out the twenty dollar gold coin which he and Chief had found, two years before. He lay it on the table in front of Temple. The DA picked it up and examined it. "Where'd you get it, Cole. Looks freshly minted?"

"Palo Duro Canyon," Cole smugly replied.

"Well, I be damned," Temple said, rolling the coin in his hand, " You think it might be a part of the treasure?"

"Yes, sir, I surely do," Cole replied, then told about Miss Molly's experience with old Coaley and his and Chief's run in with the old crow. "Miss Molly said that if we found the treasure, it was ours to keep."

"Well, if Miss Molly said it, then I expect it is so," Temple replied.

Two dirty, rough looking men, sitting at a table behind Temple, were listening closely to the conversation. When Cole had finished his beer, he stood and shook Temple's hand. "I 'spect we'd better be going. We got a big day tomorrow, cutting enough posts to finish loading our wagon. Pa's liable to fire us if we don't show up tomorrow night."

Temple laughed, "Tell Ned howdy for me and my love to Miss Belle and Miss Kate."

The two men followed them out of the Lady Gay, and remaining far enough behind, followed them back to their camp on the Washita.

Chief had a fire lit and was roasting a couple of steaks when "halo, the camp," was heard from the dark.

Cole moved to the shadows away from the fire and replied, "Come on in but keep your hands where I can see them."

The two men materialized from the dark, leading their horses with their hands outstretched before them.

"Howdy," the tall slim one said, "We was heading for Hidetown when we saw your fire and thought maybe you might spare a hot cup of coffee."

"Help yourself," Cole said, remaining in the shadows with

his hand resting on his Colt. "We might even share our steaks."

"That's mighty neighborly," the short, stocky one said as he pulled two tin cups out of his saddle bags. Dropping the reins, he bent over and picked up the steaming coffee pot.

After pouring the coffee, they both sat down next to the fire and began to sip the hot brew.

Cole stepped from the shadows, reached out his hand and said, "Cole Armstrong and this is my pard, Chief Parker."

"Slim Maynard, Cole," the slender one said, "and this is Rusty Johnson."

They shook hands around, and while Chief turned the steaks on the spit, Slim asked, "What you fellers doing out here?"

"Cutting fence posts for my pa who owns this ranch," Cole said.

"Owns it? Reckon he could use a couple of hands -- we came up with a trail herd to Dodge City from Fort Worth and was on our way back home. We left all our money with the bar keeps and whores in Dodge City. We could sure use a couple of months work."

"Well, we don't need any cowboys, but we could sure use some post cutters," Cole said, smiling.

"Cutting fence posts is our specialty," Rusty said, laughing.

"Alright, pull the riggings off your horses and we'll see what kind of post cutters you are tomorrow. Pa pays thirty a month and keep."

....

The next day, after cutting enough posts to finish out their load, the four of them left for headquarters. Ned looked the two men over and after Cole had recommended them, hired them to help with the post cutting.

The two drifters hated the job of post cutting but were hoping to learn more about the treasure before quitting. In fact, they planned to follow Cole and Chief, if and when they headed for the Palo Duro in their search.

They worked hard for two weeks and soon had enough posts stacked to last the fence building crew for a month. Cole and Chief were hoping that Ned would now let them off long enough to take a trip to the Palo Duro for their treasure hunt. Slim and Rusty should be able to keep enough posts for the fencers without their help.

Cole realized, however, that once enough posts were cut, there would be other pressing jobs which would prevent them from making their treasure hunt.

....

Their hopes rose a few days later when Colonel Goodnight rode into the Ceebara ranch headquarters on his big blue roan cow horse. Belle greeted him as he dismounted and tied the horse to the hitching rail in front of the veranda. "Howdy, Miss Belle," he responded. "We're taking an early drive to the railroad in Dodge City. Got about four thousand head over at the Canadian River crossing and I thought I'd come by and see you folks."

"Well, that's very nice of you, Colonel. You know you're always welcome. Come set awhile and have some cookies and buttermilk. Ned and the boys are down at the corrals breaking some colts. I'll send Kate down to tell them you're here."

Kate greeted Goodnight and said, "Just keep your seat, Colonel, and enjoy your cookies. Won't take me but a minute to fetch Ned."

"How's Miss Molly?" Belle asked as she poured herself a glass and sat down across the table from the Colonel.

"Fair to middling, I guess. She get's awful lonely though. No females to visit with, nothing but me and the cowboys for seventy miles and most of the time we're out working from daylight till dark."

"I know what you mean, Colonel, but Kate and me have each other and also the Garcia girls to visit with. I sure would like to pay a visit to Miss Molly but it's nigh onto seventy miles from here to your ranch house."

"Lord knows she would be grateful if you did, Miss Belle. I will be gone close to a month -- plan on making a trip to Pueblo on the train after I get the steers sold -- got some business that needs to be taken with Mr. Adair."

Ned, Cole and Chief came into the kitchen and shook hands with the Colonel. Looking at Chief, Goodnight said, "By the way, Chief, I saw your pa the other day. He rode into the canyon with some of his tribe hunting buffalo. We had a damned good visit."

Chief was surprised, then asked, "Is he well?"

"I 'spect so -- looked a little drawn around the gills, said they hadn't had enough to eat lately. Seems like the army hasn't lived up to the terms of the treaty and hasn't been feeding them."

Ned looked worried, "That's terrible, Colonel. If I had known about it, I would have driven some of my cattle over to the reservation.'

Goodnight nodded, "Well, that's taken care of now -- they've been eating my beef and have found that herd of shaggies down the lower end of the canyon. I figure they are going to carry enough home to last a spell."

Looking at the boys, he said, "Damned if you ain't growed a foot since you helped with the roundup down in the canyon. You must be thirteen years old by now. I expected you two boys to be back looking for that sheepherder's gold before now."

Cole smiled, feeling right grown up the way the Colonel was talking to him. "Fourteen, Mr. Goodnight, going on fifteen. Yes, sir, we sure been aiming to come back and look for that treasure, but Pa's been finding too much work for us to do a-round here."

Pulling the twenty dollar gold coin from his pocket, he said, "This is the gold piece that we traded that old crow a silver dollar for. I been saving it to remind us that some day we're going to locate the rest of them."

"Well, any time, boys, and good luck. If you find it, its yours. But my cowboys have made a dozen new canyons, digging up the ground looking for that gold. I 'spect as how you may be disappointed like the rest of them."

"No, sir, Mr. Goodnight. We know where the gold is, we just need time to go dig it up."

The Colonel laughed, "Well, sounds like you've got confidence. I hope you find it. Maybe you two can escort your ma and grandma when they come to see Miss Molly. You could spend a little time looking while they are visiting."

Ned looked surprised, and to Belle said, "First I've heard of a trip to the canyon. I ain't about to let you women make that trip by yourselves."

Belle replied, "Since when do you think you can tell us what to do, Ned Armstrong. We'll go if we're a mind to."

"I think that's a great idea, Colonel," Kate said. "If Ned

don't want us going alone, we'll take the boys along. They've already proved that they are as grown up as any of the cowboys we've got working here."

Cole blushed, wondering if his ma knew about the escapade he and Chief had with the whiskey and painted ladies in Dodge City.

The two boys looked at each other with smiles as big as a west Texas sunrise. '"When can we go, Ma," Cole asked.

"Well, seems to me we ain't got much to do around here. Your pa and the other boys are leaving in the morning and will be gone a week building fence in the west pasture. I suppose we could put together a few things and leave tomorrow."

"Yippee!" Cole shouted.

Ned and the Colonel visited for a couple of hours about the cattle business before Goodnight said he needed to get back to the herd before night. "Any thing you need from Dodge City, Ned? I'd be more than glad to pick it up for you."

"Yes, sir, there is. One of my wagons is ready for the junk pile. If you'd buy me a new one and a team to drag it, I'd be mighty thankful. Maybe you could get me some more of that new fangled barbed wire and steeples."

"Count it done, Ned. I'll have one of my boys drive it back for you," the Colonel replied.

....

Spring was busting out all over as Belle and Kate made plans for the seventy mile journey to the JA ranch headquarters to visit Miss Molly Goodnight. They planned on staying for at least a week and filled two traveling bags with extra clothes and toiletries. They were as excited about the trip as was Cole and Chief. The boys were loading a pack mule with food and equipment which they would need to spend a few days treasure hunting after taking Kate and Belle to the Goodnight headquarters.

"It's been so long since we made a trade with that old crow for this twenty dollar gold piece that someone may have already found the gold," Cole said as he held the coin up for Chief to inspect.

"I think the gold is still there," Chief replied. "Those three hunters that the Colonel hung in Tascosa should have discouraged anyone from trespassing on the JA looking for treasure."

"I hope you're right," Cole replied as he took another pull on the pack rope. The mule looked around and nipped at Cole's rear to tell him that the rope was tight enough.

Belle and Kate climbed into the buckboard and Cole and Chief mounted their horses and the small caravan set out for the Palo Duro. Evening found them camped at the line camp on the North Fork of the Red, a roaring camp fire lighting up the area.

"Tend the horses, Chief," Cole said, "I'm going to see if I can kill some fresh meat for supper. He walked a quarter of a mile downstream before finding a flock of turkeys, threw his rifle to his shoulder and fired, taking the head off a big Tom. It was soon roasting over the fire for their evening meal.

Half a mile back down the trail, a smaller camp fire was burning, hidden behind two large boulders. Slim and Rusty were eating beef jerky and cold beans.

"I hope this ain't no wild goose chase," Rusty said.

"It won't be -- Cole says he knows exactly where that gold is hidden. Once they find it, we'll shoot them and it will be our'n"

....

Miss Molly was fit to be tied when they pulled into the yard.

All of the men were away building fence at the south end of the canyon and she was alone with her chickens. Jumping up from her chair, she ran to meet them. "Oh, my land! Oh, my land!" she said over and over as she hugged Belle and Kate.

Pushing them back for a moment, she looked at them, wiped tears from her eyes and said, "I can't believe it, female company! Oh, Kate, this is such an enjoyable surprise. Come on in the house and tell me about your trip."

The ranch house had been completed and there was plenty of room for all of them. "Cole, you put Kate's bags in this bedroom and your grandmother's bag in the one across the hall. You and Chief can take the room at the end of the hall."

While they were unloading the wagon, she was busy in the kitchen and soon had biscuits in the oven and steak on the stove. Belle and Kate washed some of the trail dust off their faces and came in to help.

Sitting around the table after the meal was finished, Miss Molly asked Belle how long they could stay. "We plan on a week if that's alright with you," Kate replied.

"Alright? My land, I wish you would stay a month. You're the first company I've had since we finished the ranch house."

Belle laughed, "You'll be tired of us in a week."

Miss Molly shook her head vigorously, "Never, Belle -- you're welcome as long as you want to stay."

Listening to the ladies, Cole took another piece of pie, then said, "Me and Chief are just staying the night, Miss Molly. We're going to see if we can find old Coaley and convince him to show us where that gold is hidden."

"He's still around. I see him now and then but he hasn't brought any more coins to me and he still has my thimble."

They all laughed at the thought of the old crow trading a twenty dollar gold piece for a ten cent thimble.

12

The boys were on the trail before sun up, with their pack horse loaded with enough supplies to last a week. By the time the sun's rays lit up their trail they were turning into the Lighthouse canyon where the cougar had attacked Cole. They were so excited that they failed to see the two men who were cautiously following a half mile behind.

"I ain't seen no crows, Chief," Cole said as he looked upward at the canyon's rim.

"Maybe too early, Cole. Maybe they come soon," Chief observed.

An hour later, they stopped in the shadow of the huge rock formation where they had last observed old Coaley. Dismounting, they pulled their canteens from the saddle and took a long drink while searching the area with their eyes.

No crow!

"Maybe he's dead," Chief said. "He's been around a long time."

Cole thought for awhile, "No," he said, "Miss Molly said she sees him once in awhile. I bet he's still alive."

Cole walked to the flat rock where he had placed the silver

dollar two years before, and old Coaley had flown down and traded a gold piece for the silver. Removing another silver dollar from his pocket, he placed it on the rock.

"Come on, Chief, let's make camp down by the stream where we can watch this rock. Maybe the silver dollar will be good bait to bring him back."

They soon had camp made, gathered rocks for a fire place and wood for the fire. The small clear stream gurgled as it bounced across the rock strewn bottom, flowing toward the Red River three miles below.

Removing the saddles from their horses and supplies from the pack saddle, they stretched out on their bed rolls and contemplated their next move. Looking up toward the rim, Chief said, "That juniper tree up there on the rim is where the crow took your silver dollar. I bet there's a cave up there where the treasure is hidden."

"I think you're right, Chief, but how we going to get up there -- must be five hundred feet straight up," Cole replied.

"I remember when my tribe lived here in the canyon that me and my friends would ride our ponies up here, pretending we were chasing blue coats. You can't believe the number of soldiers we killed and scalped in our games," Chief said, smiling.

"Kinda like me and the Garcia boys when we would play cowboys and Indians on Red Deer Creek. The Indians never won," Cole laughed. Then seriously added, "I'm glad we didn't kill you, Chief, you're my best friend."

"And you are mine, Cole." Pausing, he looked westward up the canyon. "I remember there was a trail of some kind about another mile up toward the head of this canyon that we would use to get up on top, then we would walk along the rim and look at the big rock from up there," pointing to the juniper tree.

"Was it a trail large enough for a horse?"

"Maybe, but I think just a small game trail where deer would come down for water."

"Let's see if it is still there," Cole said, getting up from his bed roll.

Before they could make a move, the air was filled with the sound of hundreds of crows, caw-cawing down the canyon. Looking in that direction, they could see a huge flock of crows flying south. One of the crows broke away from the others, rising on the updrafts it circled and circled until it was overhead. Fixing its wings, it sailed to the dead limb on the juniper tree above them and landed.

"That's him, Chief, that's old Coaley!" Cole shouted excitedly as he looked through his binoculars.

"That's him, alright," Chief replied. "Be still and don't scare him, maybe he will see your silver dollar."

The crow fluttered its wings as it jumped from the branch and disappeared in the rocks for a few minutes. Suddenly it reappeared and returned to its perch on the branch.

Looking through the binoculars, Cole whispered, "He's got something shiny in his beak."

"Is it a coin?" Chief asked.

"No, it is small and silver looking." Cole replied.

The crow jumped from his perch, spread his wings and sailed away from the cliff. Flying over the boys, the updrafts pulled him high into the sky until he was a mere speck above the canyon's floor. He did not leave however, but continued to circle over them, as if scouting out the situation.

Suddenly, he folded his wings and dropped like a bullet. Fifty feet above the floor of the canyon, he once again spread his wings and sailed to the flat rock where the silver dollar lay. Bouncing around on the rock, he looked curiously at the coin, as if wondering if the coin was more valuable than the bright object he was clutching in his beak.

Deciding it was a good trade, he dropped the object, pecked at the coin until he could pick it up, then took flight again. Flying almost straight up, he landed on the juniper branch, five hundred feet above the boys. He sat watching, as if to tell the boys it was their move to see if they were satisfied with the trade.

"Let's look," Chief said as he picked himself up from his bed roll and started climbing the small talus slope to the flat rock. Cole was close behind.

There on the rock lay a small, silver looking object. Cole picked it up and laughed. "I'll be danged," he said. "It's Miss Molly's thimble!"

Looking up at the crow as it looked down on them, Chief said, "Thanks, grandfather crow, for showing us the location of the treasure!"

A quarter of a mile down canyon, another set of eyes were observing the crows activities through binoculars. Too far to see the coin in the crows beak, Slim said, "I don't know what's going on, Rusty, but they sure are taking a lot of interest in that old crow."

....

The caprock formation was about twenty feet thick at this point, and the juniper tree was growing just below the bottom of the white sandstone cap. There was a sheer, straight drop from the top of the formation to the crow's perch on the juniper branch.

"There ain't no way for us to climb up five hundred feet of canyon wall to the juniper -- we're going to need to get up on top and figure some way to get down the twenty feet to the tree," Cole said, still scouting out the situation through his binoculars. "It looks like a crack in the caprock over to the right of the juniper. Do you suppose rain may have carved out a cave that reaches behind the juniper?"

"Maybe -- it could be hidden from the top," Chief replied.

As he watched, the crow once again disappeared behind the tree, placed the silver coin with the rest of his treasure, then took flight and sailed to the east, joining the rest of the crows which had invaded Miss Molly's garden patch.

"Are you certain there is not a larger trail up from the head of this canyon?" Cole asked.

"Not certain, but I don't remember us taking our ponies to the top from there."

"Let's check it out," Cole said as they walked back to their camp site and began saddling their horses.

An hour later, they were picking their way along the rock strewn path, as the canyon's walls came closer and closer together. Suddenly the canyon widened and the walls were not as steep. "There, Cole," Chief said, pointing ahead, "is the game trail that we used getting to the top."

Dismounting, they tied their horses to a small hackberry tree, and began climbing the trail. "Pretty steep, but we could probably lead our horses up that part," Cole said as they rested on the talus slope. It appears the trail widens from here. Let's go back and scout further up the canyon. If we don't find anything better, we can come back tomorrow morning and give this one a try."

"Ugh," Chief said, humorously reverting back to a native Indian. "Red man don't like to work when the sun is high. This is the time to lay in the shade and dream about scalping White Man."

"You can't fool me, Redskin. Maybe lay in the shade and dream about that dark eyed, painted lady that you met in Dodge City. Indian would rather make love than war," Cole laughed as they began their descent back to the horses.

Finding nothing better, they turned the horses around and headed back to camp.

Sitting around their campfire after eating a cold supper of biscuits and jerky, they listened to the night sounds. A family of coyote pups began yipping from on top of the canyon and were interrupted by the sound of a cougar screaming in the distance.

"Probably the mate to the one we killed," Cole said. "We best stake the horses a little closer to the fire."

....

They were awake to watch the sun break upon the dark canyon walls the next morning, with breakfast complete and the horses saddled. Filling their canteens with fresh water from the stream, they mounted up and retraced their steps to the game trail. The pack mule, brayed his displeasure at being left behind, staked next to the stream.

The horses didn't like the idea of trying to climb the steep slope with the two boys leading them but eventually gave in. Slowly they traversed the slope until they reached the bottom of the talus slope, mounted and then followed the trail which ascended at a less steep angle. It wound through a jumble of huge boulders which had caved from the cap rock above, through a forest of small juniper trees, then to a crack in the cap rock which had been widened through eons of time by rain and ice. It was just wide enough for the horses to squeeze through.

Their horses were sweating and blowing when they finally topped out and could see the flat terrain of the grassy plain on top. Looking back down their trail, they could see the canyon floor and the small stream which flowed by their camp ground. A herd of white tailed deer were cautiously drinking from the stream.

Dismounting, they loosened the saddle girths and allowed the horses to rest. Looking down the canyon, they could see the huge tower of the Lighthouse formation stabbing its point to the sky. Using it as a guide, it would be easy to establish the location of the crows treasure.

Remounting, they rode anxiously across the now flat terrain, the grass so tall it was brushing their stirrups. Only a few scattered cedar and juniper trees dotted the prairie along the rim of the canyon. A covey of Bob White quail took flight under their horses feet and the loud drum of their wings caused the horses to shy, nearly loosing Chief who had been relaxed, looking at the view over the canyon's rim. Cole laughed, "What's the matter, Redskin -- need some glue on your butt?"

Chief shifted in the saddle and said, "Sometimes Indians make quick moves to dodge bullets, White Eyes!"

Cole laughed, pulled up and pointed. The top of the Lighthouse formation, exactly the same height as the prairie they were on, stood silently to their left. The covey of quail, wings fixed, sailed around the formation and disappeared.

Dismounting, they ground tied the horses and walked to the edge of the chasm. Carefully, they approached the edge and looked down but could not see directly below because of a slight overhang of the cliff . Lying on their stomachs, they crawled closer and spotted the juniper tree about thirty yards to their right.

There were several cracks in the rocks which reached twenty or thirty feet back into the prairie. One was probably two feet wide, and the dirt and grass had been washed away, leaving an opening which seemed to get larger as it descended deeper. The cave was dark but a dim light could be seen coming from the cliffs face.

Cole's heart was pounding as he inspected the cavern. "I'll bet my hat that this crack leads to the crows cave," he said.

"I'll get my catch rope and you can let me down into it," Chief said as he turned and walked to his horse.

Cole had scouted the area around the crack and was standing next to a large cedar tree growing six feet away from the crack. Taking the rope he made a wrap around the base of the tree and pulled one end to the crack. The loop at the end of the rope made a good foot hold for his boot. When he started to place the toe of his boot into it, Chief said, "Better let me do it, White Man. Indians are good at disappearing in rocks."

Cole laughed and said, "That's why I want to do it. You might disappear with all of our treasure."

Chief took the loose end of the rope, holding it tight as Cole stepped off into the blackness below. Releasing slack, Cole slowly disappeared below ground. Chief continued to release slack slowly until twenty feet of rope disappeared.

"You better reach bottom soon," Chief shouted. "We're-about out of rope."

"Another couple of feet," Cole replied, then "O.K., I'm at the bottom. I can see light. This part of the cave must be ten feet across but it gets smaller toward the cliff."

Chief crawled to the edge and stuck his head over the edge. "The crows tree is just below," he yelled.

Suddenly Cole screamed and two muffled gun shots echoed out of the cave.

"What's wrong!" Chief screamed.

"Rattle snakes," Cole answered. "Two of the biggest sonsofbitches I ever seen."

"Are you bit?"

"No, but I never knew that my fast draw was going to save my life this way. I was nearly on top of them before they rattled."

Cole and Chief had hunted rattlesnakes all their lives, and Cole was not easily upset by them, but to be trapped inside a small enclosure with two monsters had him shaken. Chief, on the other hand, was deathly afraid of snakes, having seen one of his small Indian friends die after being bitten.

....

"What was that?" Slim asked, looking at his friend.

"Sounded like a couple of gunshots," Rusty replied, stirring the coals of the campfire with a stick.

"I wonder what the hell they could be shooting at," Slim asked, then answered his own question as he picked up the coffee pot, "Probably trying to get some camp meat -- maybe a deer."

"Damn," Rusty said, "wish we had some camp meat, I'm getting tired of bacon and beans."

Blowing on the hot coffee in his tin cup, Slim replied,

"You're going to have to be satisfied with bacon and beans -- we can't be doing any shooting and alerting them that we are near."

....

"Break off one of those dead limbs on the cedar tree and drop it down. I can use it in front of me to poke around and see if there are more."

Chief did as he was told and Cole began to move forward toward the cliffs edge, pounding the floor with the limb. No more rattles were heard.

"Holy shit!" he shouted. "Here it is, Chief! A pile of gold that would choke an elephant -- My gosh! Would you look at that!"

"I can't look at that, White Man -- I'm stuck up here taking care of this end of this dumb rope."

Cole laughed, "O.K., Redskin, I'll come up and let you come down and have a look. Wait until I fill my pockets and you can haul me up."

"Do me a favor, White Eyes," Chief said. "Throw them two rattlesnakes out, I don't think me and them would like to be down there together."

"Hell's bells, Chief, they're dead."

"Sometimes white men lie," Chief replied.

Using the stick, Cole pushed the snakes to the ledge and dropped them over. Replacing his foot in the rope, he shouted, "O.K., see if you can pull me up."

Chief tried but was unsuccessful. "Hold on a minute," he shouted. "I'm going to get my horse." Tying the end of the lariat to the saddle horn, he slowly backed his horse until Cole's head appeared, then his shoulders. When Cole's belt buckle appeared, Chief stopped the horse, Cole released the rope and crawled out.

His pockets were bulging with the coins. He started emptying them on the ground and the sun sparkled off the bright gold. They both stood and looked with awe at twenty of the coins piled on the ground. Neither said a word, hardly able to believe what they had found.

"Can you believe it, Chief? That's just twenty coins -- there's probably another thousand down there!"

Chief relaxed and smiled. "Maybe enough to buy some ponies?"

"Sure -- what you need with ponies?"

Stone faced, he replied, "Need ponies to trade for squaw, dumb White Man," then started an Indian war dance around the small pile of coins, with his hand over his mouth, chanting an Indian song.

Cole laughed and joined him, mimicking the Indian war dance. Then they both fell to the ground and laughed until their sides hurt, releasing all of the pent up excitement.

Laying on the ground, Chief finally turned to Cole and asked, "What now?"

"You ready to go down and have a look," Cole asked.

"No -- just more gold and maybe more snakes. We wait," Chief replied.

Cole sat up, wiped the tears from his eyes and replied, "O.K., let's go back to camp, put the pack saddle on the mule, come back up, recover the gold, and head for Colonel Goodnight's headquarters.

13

The outlaws' camp was hidden below an overhanging rock and behind two large cedar trees. Slim was asleep on his bed roll and Rusty was scouring the canyon above with the binoculars. He was worried, it had been two hours since they had heard the gun shots. Suddenly, he saw movement high on the talus slope below the caprock.

Kicking Slim with his boot, he said, "Here they come -- don't appear to be carrying anything."

"Gimme the glass," Slim said.

He looked toward the point where Rusty was pointing and zoomed in on the two horseback riders. "You're right, guess they didn't find anything. I don't see any deer so they must have missed whatever they shot at."

"Guess they'll be eating beans and bacon, too," Rusty said, smiling.

....

They were too excited to sleep, and spent much of the night around the fire discussing their good fortune, and formulating plans for recovering the gold.

First light the next morning, they caught the mule and fitted the pack saddle on his back. Chief emptied the contents of a burlap bag in which some of their supplies were stored and tied it on his saddle. Leaving their bedrolls and camp supplies next to the stream, they mounted and headed up the trail. Their hearts raced as they realized that twenty-five thousand dollars in gold coins would soon be theirs!

....

Rusty was up, stirring his fire and making coffee. He heard the mule bray, picked up the binoculars and zoomed in on the two boy's campsite. They were busy placing the pack saddle on the mule's back. He kicked Slim's bed roll and whispered, "Get up! They're breaking camp!"

Slim rolled over, pushing the tarp which was covering his bedroll aside and sat up. Rubbing the sleep out of his eyes, he asked, "They're doing what?"

"They're breaking camp -- putting the pack saddle on the mule. We best get packed."

They had very little to pack, carrying all their belongings on the back of their saddles. Within a few minutes, they had caught up their two horses, saddled them, tied their bedrolls and chuck sacks on, and watched as Cole and Chief saddled their horses.

"I'll bet they found something yesterday and figure on picking it up today," Rusty said, watching through the binoculars.

"Probably," Slim replied, "but they may have decided this isn't the right place and will be coming back down this way. Douse the fire, just in case. We don't want them spotting us."

Rusty poured the remaining coffee on the fire and covered the ashes with dirt. Slim led the horses back under the overhanging cliff and hid them in the shadows.

"They're heading back up the canyon, the way they went yesterday," Rusty said, lowering the binoculars from his eyes.

"We need to stay as close behind them as possible. If they get up on top before we locate the trail up, they'll be able to spot us," Slim said, as he stepped into the saddle.

Rusty mounted his horse and they moved into the trail, keeping close in the shadow of the trees which lined the banks of the stream, out of sight of Cole and Chief.

....

The mule was stubborn about being led up the steep slope, so Cole, walking, took the lead rope, Chief walked behind with a green willow switch. When the mule balked, Chief whipped his hocks with the willow and he would jump forward a couple of steps before once again balking.

Once they had reached the talus slope and the mule was leading without prodding, they tied it to a cedar tree, walked back down the trail to their horses and led them up the steepest part of the trail. Untieing the mule, they mounted their horses and continued the climb to the top, disappearing around a bend in the trail and entering the juniper forest.

As soon as they disappeared into the juniper forest, the two outlaws followed, keeping in the shadows.

....

Once on top, they dismounted to let the horses blow and Cole said, "When we get all that gold in the pack saddle, that stubborn jackass is going to have a load going back down."

"You're right, Cole, but mules have good feet. I think he can make it. Besides, he'll go down hill better than he came up."

They rode through the trees along the rim and, reaching the cave, Chief dismounted and quickly removed the burlap bag from his saddle and dropped it down the hole. Cole secured his lariat around the cedar tree and placed the loop next to the crack. "I go down, Cole, I want to see what we have found," Chief said.

They were so excited in their preparations to recover the gold that they failed to see the two outlaws slipping quietly toward them in the shadows of the trees.

Cole slowly lowered Chief into the darkness below, "Watch for snakes," he joked.

"With both eyes and both feet," Chief responded nervously.

He let his eyes get used to the dark, retrieved the burlap sack, then slowly stepped toward the light at the caves entrance on the cliff's face. He let out an Indian war hoop when he spied the pile of gold.

It had been stored in several canvas bags, but the canvas had rotted away, leaving the gold scattered on the floor. There were other bright objects piled on top of the gold -- brass cartridge cases, pieces of a broken mirror and lids from tin cans. Old Coaley had been busy through the years, increasing the size of his treasure.

Chief placed about a hundred of the coins in his burlap bag, tied it to the rope and yelled at Cole, "O.K., White Eyes, pull it up!"

Soon Cole had emptied the bag into the pack saddle and lowered it back down. The process was continued until all of the coins had been recovered. Tying the rope to his saddle horn, he slowly backed his horse until Chief was pulled from the depths of the cave.

As they prepared to mount their horses, Chief whispered, "Look, Cole -- the crow!"

Old Coaley circled overhead, set his wings and landed softly on the dead branch of the juniper tree and gazed angrily at the two boys. Cole removed a silver dollar from his pocket and dropped it near the edge of the cliff's face. "Thanks, old friend," he said, "maybe this will be a small payment for your help."

The crow hopped from the limb, looked at the coin inquisitively, picked it up with his beak and flew back to the limb.

....

"Alright, Cole, I 'spect you boys better reach for the sky," a voice ordered from behind them. "Don't turn around. We've got two Winchesters aimed at your backs, and if you even act like you might try to pull leather, we'll blow a hole in you big enough for that mule to jump through."

Rusty spoke, "Just keep your hands high while I remove those irons from your belts."

"Is that you, Rusty," Cole asked.

"Yeah -- me and Slim," Rusty replied. "We didn't think you boys were ever going to locate that gold. We've been trailing you ever since you left Ceebara with your ma."

Relieving them of their guns, he threw them on the ground next to the cliff and said, "Bring those leather thongs out of my saddle bag, Slim. We need to tie them before they decide to do something stupid and we'll have to shoot them."

Slim laughed, "We certainly wouldn't want to do that after all the posts they let us cut. They've been right nice to us. We want to thank you for everything, including loading our gold on that mule, if you know what I mean. Now, Cole, you lower your hands and put them to your back -- easy!"

Cole did as he was told and Slim tied his hands behind his back with the leather thong. "Now, Chief -- let's see you cooperate as well as your friend. I never did like redskins, so if you act the least bit like your going to try something, I'm going to put a hole in you, take your scalp, and shove you off that cliff."

He laughed as Chief lowered his hands, placed them behind his back, and Slim tied them good and tight.

"O.K., you boys can turn around now," Rusty said.

They turned slowly and faced their captors.

"Why you doing this, Slim?" Cole asked, "We took you in when you needed a job, and thought you were our friends."

"The same reason you are doing it," Slim replied, "twenty-five thousand dollars -- and all we have to do is tie you to that tree and lead that mule out of here! Friendship ends when gold is concerned. Now then, you just step over to that tree and turn around."

Cole did as he was told and Slim soon had him bound tightly with his lariat, with his back to the hackberry tree.

"Alright, Chief," you're next.

Chief knew it was useless to resist, walked to the tree and turned his back to it. Using the other end of the lariat, Slim soon had him bound next to Cole.

Only then did they step to the mule and look into the pack saddle bags. The gold sparkled as they opened the pack and looked inside.

"Damned if that ain't a pretty sight," Rusty said, reaching in, picking up a handful of the coins and letting them slip slowly through his fingers. The coins tinkled as they fell back on the others. "I never realized there would be so many of them."

Getting a handful, Slim looked at them, stepped over to the tree and shoved them into Cole's pocket. "Just to show you there ain't no hard feelings, I'm paying you for finding the treasure for us."

Rusty laughed, "First thing I'm going to do is see how much whiskey and how many whores this gold will buy in Atascosa."

Stepping into their saddles, Slim said, "*Adios, amigos* -- I hope some of Colonel Goodnight's cowboys find you before a hungry cougar does," turned his horse west and rode off down the trail. Rusty followed close behind, leading the mule.

"Better watch your backs," Cole said, "we'll be coming after you."

....

Reaching the game trail which wound to the bottom of the canyon, the two outlaws bypassed it and continued west. Soon they were on open prairie, leaving the deep canyon behind. After riding only a short distance, they dissected a well used wagon trail, bearing northwest.

Stopping, Slim looked both ways, "I 'spect this is the road that the JA's use to go to Atascosa. I heard talk over at Hidetown that old man Goodnight had constructed a trail wide enough for wagons to get in and out of the canyon. "

"Well, I'm durned tired of bacon and beans," Slim said, removing a plug of tobacco from his pocket and biting off a chew. "Lets head for Atascosa where they've got food, whiskey and wild, wild women."

Rusty smiled, nodded in agreement and turned northwest toward the lawless community on the Canadian River.

....

"What we do now, White Eyes," Chief asked, "Wait on cougar to come and chew ropes in to?"

Cole smiled, "For lack of a better plan, I guess that's as good as any."

"That Slim tied these knots pretty tight, I can hardly move my hands," Chief said.

"Yeah, he didn't plan on us getting free any time soon. The bark on this hackberry tree is pretty rough, maybe we could wear this rope in to if we moved back and forth."

"We try," Chief replied, as he leaned to the right, then the left.

"Ouch!" Cole cried, "that tightened up on my arms. We need to move together."

They soon had a rhythm going -- back and forth, back and forth. However, because of the tightness of the rope, they could only move a short distance. After four hours, Chief said, "maybe this is bad plan, White Eyes -- I think I have better plan."

"O.K., Redskin, what''s your plan?"

"Rain dance!"

"Rain dance? Leave it up to a dumb Indian to think of something like that. It's bad enough being tied to this tree -- I certainly don't want to be wet!"

"Well, I see rain clouds building in west. If we do rain dance, and it rains, at least we can say that we did something right. Besides," Chief added, "If it rains, these leather thongs will get wet and stretch, and we can get our hands free."

"Danged if you ain't right, Chief -- I take it back, you're a pretty smart Indian. Tell you what, you do your rain dance and I'll pray to my God, maybe one of them will hear our prayers."

Darkness fell over the canyon -- stars shone brightly overhead, and a bright orange moon rose in the east. Lightning could be seen to the west and the distant sound of thunder could be heard. A cougar screamed nearby, and the boys' two horses, grazing nearby, moved closer to the tree, seeking protection from the cougar. Comanche nuzzled Cole's stomach, as if to say, "Let's get out of here, boss." Cole spoke to him, trying to calm him.

The cougar never appeared and the rain cloud disappeared. Morning arrived with a bright sun replacing the moon. Time was beginning to tell on the boys' attitudes, but Chief tried to remain confident that his rain dance would be successful. "I was just thinking, Cole," he said, "we pretty lucky -- If Slim and Rusty were Indians, they would have tied us to that red ant bed by the juniper tree."

"That's a comforting thought," Cole replied, chuckling. "Get that rain dance to going again, maybe that cloud will be closer tonight."

"Yeah, and maybe that cougar will be closer, also," Chief said as he moved his feet and began to sing to the rain God. Cole looked up and prayed, "Jesus, the Bible says that if we ask we shall receive -- I'm asking that you send us rain to soften these leather bindings so we can get after them thieving outlaws."

The day passed slowly, their throats became dry and their stomachs empty. Chief groaned, then said, "Cole, I think I just wet my pants."

"Don't feel individual -- I wet mine three hours ago," Cole replied, then laughed, "At least that rain dance has brought forth water."

The clouds appeared closer as the sun reached the western horizon. As darkness settled once again, a puff of cool wind hit the boys in the face, a flash of lightning crashed nearby and thunder reverberated off the canyon walls.

"It's raining," Cole shouted as large drops hit him in the face.

"Yes," Chief replied, "now we need to pray to the rain God that his lightning doesn't hit this tree."

....

Slim and Rusty splashed across the Canadian river and rode toward the lights of Atascosa. Lightning could be seen to the southeast. "Looks like our friends are going to get wet tonight," Rusty said.

"Yeah, if they're not already cougar bait, "Slim replied. "I wish we would have gone ahead and shot them, then we would know they couldn't follow us."

Riding up to the Exchange Hotel, they tied their horses to the hitching rail and walked inside. Placing a twenty dollar gold coin on the desk, Slim said, "Two rooms and two tubs full of hot water. We'll be back soon as we put our horses up in Mickey's livery stable.

Placing his change on the desk, the clerk said, "Don't get very many gold coins here, you boys must have come from the gold fields up north."

Smiling, Slim replied, "That's right, the gold fields," as he turned and walked out the door.

A lantern was burning dimly in the livery stable, and Mickey McCormick directed them to three stalls. "We'll be needing a tack room with a lock on it," Rusty said as he started removing the pack saddle from the mules back.

"Don't need to worry none," Mickey replied, "No one's ever stole anything out of my stable."

"Always the first time," Slim said, "a room with a lock and we want the key."

Mickey frowned and nodded his head, "That room over there, just one door, no windows -- I'll get you a lock."

He watched inquisitively as they carried the heavy pack saddle into the small room. "Sure looks heavy," he said. "What's in it?"

"Really not any of your damn business," Rusty said, "but if you must know, it's full of horse shoes and a small anvil. We plan on opening up a blacksmith shop in Hidetown."

Locking the door, the two men walked out and returned to the hotel where they found two tubs of steaming hot water in the hall next to their rooms.

....

Rain fell in sheets as the cloud dumped its contents on the two shivering boys, still tied to the hackberry tree. The leather thongs which secured their hands began to soak up the rain water and as they strained and pulled, eventually stretched enough that Cole was able to get his hands free.

After rubbing his wrists and getting circulation started, he untied the rope around his waist and stepped free. "How you doing, Chief?' he asked.

"Still tied, give me some help."

Cole pulled his pocket knife out of his chaps, opened the blade and quickly cut Chief free. They both walked around rubbing their wrists and trying to get their blood to circulate. "I don't know who's God brought the rain, but I thank him from the bottom of my heart," Cole said.

"maybe they both helped," Chief said. "maybe they be friends like me and you."

The two outlaws had been so excited after seeing the gold, they had left the boys' guns on the ground where Rusty had thrown them. Walking over, they picked them up, holstered them, caught up their horses, then rode to the game trail and slowly descended to the bottom.

Reaching their camp, they broke some dry branches from a cedar tree and built a fire. Soon they had coffee made, beans and bacon heated and were drying their bedrolls next to the blazing fire.

The small stream was now a rain swollen river as it rushed by their campground. "I think we best remain here until morning," Cole said. "The trail is muddy and slick and our horses could slip and break a leg. In the morning, we'll ride to Colonel Goodnight's ranch house, tell ma and grandma what has happened, then take off after those sidewinders."

Chief nodded as he dished some of the beans and bacon into two metal plates. "Maybe Miss Molly will have some cookies we can eat. Beans and bacon don't taste very good any more."

....

It was near noon when Cole and Chief rode into the Goodnight headquarters. Kate and Bell, seeing them coming, rushed out to meet them, "We thought something had happened when you didn't show up yesterday," Kate said as Cole dismounted.

"It did, Ma," he said as he tied his horse to the hitching rail. "We've got a lot to tell."

"Come on inside, Cole," Miss Molly said. "We were just fixing to eat dinner. You can tell us while you eat."

Cole and Chief followed them inside, washed and sat down at the huge table. Miss Molly brought steaks, potatoes, biscuits and gravy as Cole began his story.

"We found old Coaley," Miss Molly, he said, handing her the thimble, "and he showed us where the gold was hid. We got it out of the cave and loaded it on our mule, then those two men we hired to cut posts caught us unawares, tied us up and stole our mule and gold. That was two days ago -- we finally got loose and came back to tell you about it. We ain't staying long. If Miss Molly can let one of her boys take ya'll back to Ceebara, we've a mind to pick up their trail and get our gold back."

"Lord have mercy!" Belle said, "You really found the gold?"

"Yes, ma'am, we found it alright -- twelve hundred, twenty dollar gold coins. It was in a cave up by the Lighthouse formation. It was being guarded by two huge rattlesnakes. I nearly got bit before I killed the snakes," Cole said as he filled his mouth with steak.

Chief agreed, "We would still be tied to that tree if it hadn't rained. The rain soaked the leather thongs and Cole was able to get loose."

"I don't think you boys need to be going after those outlaws by yourself," Kate said. "You go back to Ceebara and get Ned and some of the boys to go with you."

"No ma'am, the longer we wait the farther away they're going to be. They've already got a three day head start -- we're going. That's our gold and we ain't aiming to let them get away with it. We heard them say they were headed for Atascosa."

"Alright, I'll pack you some food. You be careful and don't take any chances. Maybe you can get Casimiro Romero to help you. If you find them, they'll surely try to kill you before they'll give up that gold," Kate said.

"Don't worry, Ma -- we don't intend to let them get the drop on us again," Cole said.

14

They rode all night and splashed across the Canadian as dawn was breaking over the small community of Atascosa. A dog barked and a rooster crowed as they rode down Main street and stopped in front of Scotty Wilson's cafe. Another rooster, off to the left of the first, answered. Three horses were tied to the hitching rail and three cowboys were eating breakfast as the boys stepped inside.

"Howdy, Cole," Scotty greeted, "you look like you been rode hard and put up wet. Have a seat and I'll pour you some coffee."

"Thanks, Scotty," Cole replied, "we could sure use it -- been on the trail all night and we're plumb tuckered out."

Pouring the coffee, Scotty said, "I'll have you some eggs and venison ready in a minute."

The three cowboys left and after a few minutes Scotty reappeared with eggs, venison steaks and a heaping bowel of hot biscuits. He refilled their coffee cups and set down across the table. "What brings you into town so early, Cole?" he asked.

"You seen a couple of cowboys, one tall and slim and the other shorter with bright red hair -- they'd be trailing a mule with a pack saddle?" Cole asked.

"Come to think of it I did," Scotty replied. "Came in three or four days ago. I remember they paid for their grub with a twenty dollar gold piece. I don't think they stayed around very long, though -- I didn't see them at all, yesterday."

"Any idea which way they went?" Cole asked.

"Sorry, Cole, I don't, but you might ask over at the hotel. That's where they were staying -- why'd you ask, they steal some of your cows?"

"Something like that, Scotty," Cole said as he paid for their breakfast with one of the gold coins that Slim had stuffed in his pocket.

Scotty looked at it, then looked at Cole, then back to the coin in his hand. "That's just like the one those two cowboys used to pay for their grub," he said as he handed Cole his change.

"Yeah," Cole replied, sticking the change in his pocket as he walked out the door.

Scotty watched them leave with a look of bewilderment on his face.

The boys untied their horses and led them down the street to the hotel. A lone man stood behind the desk with a pencil in his hand, writing something. He looked up and inquired if he could help them.

"Yes, sir," Cole said. "We're looking for a couple of men who came into town three or four days ago -- one tall and slim and the other shorter with red hair. I understand they may have had a room here."

"Yes, but they've been gone a couple of days. Just stayed one night, brought a couple of girls and a bottle up to their room, spent the night and took off the next morning like they was afraid of something."

"Did you notice which way they went," Cole asked.

"Sure did -- they took the Las Vegas trail to the west. They was leading a mule that seemed to be carrying a pretty good load," the hostler said.

"Well, thanks," Cole said. "I reckon we'll take a couple of rooms, our horses are plumb rode into the ground. We could use a little sleep, too."

"Will you be needing baths?" the clerk asked, looking at their dust covered clothes.

"I 'spect so," Cole replied. "We need to put our horses up at Mickey's first. We'll probably sleep four or five hours then see if we can't catch up with our friends."

They returned thirty minutes later, took their baths and as the town began to awaken, they climbed into bed, exhausted and were soon asleep.

....

Cole and Chief slept until noon, walked to Scotty's, ate a good meal, then picked up their horses at Mickey's, and rode west out of town. The road paralleled the Canadian River passing through several Mexican Plazas until it reached Salinas Plaza, on the New Mexico - Texas border.

They rode warily into Salinas Plaza, located next to the large salt lake where Mexicans mined the salt and carried it to Santa Fe, Mora, Cimarron, and Fort Union for sale. Stopping at Montoya's saloon and restaurant, they dismounted and stretched. The sun was just disappearing below the hills to the west as they stepped inside the saloon and ordered beer.

"We're looking for two men, leading a pack mule. Did they

come through here?" Cole asked the bartender.

"Si, senor, they passed through here two days ago. As they drank tequila I heard them talking about Las Vegas. Perhaps that is where they were going."

"How far to the next town," Cole asked.

"Nothing between here and Trujillo, senor," the bartender replied. "That's maybe two days ride."

Not wishing to push their horses too hard, Cole decided they would spend the night in Salinas. The saloon owner agreed to stable their horses behind the saloon, and promised to have breakfast cooked by five o'clock the next morning.

....

Slim and Rusty were nursing a hangover in Las Vegas from too much celebrating the previous night. "I think we should stay in Las Vegas," Slim said. "I'm tired of running -- we don't need to worry, they're cougar bait by now. Besides, they're just a couple of kids."

Rusty was nervous and scared as he pulled his Colt and checked the chamber to make certain it was fully loaded. "Maybe -- but maybe not. They may be kids, but I remember when we were cutting posts and they would practice shooting. Remember how fast they could draw and how straight they could shoot when they were practicing. I don't hanker to have to brace up to them if they ain't dead."

"You're probably right," Slim said. "If they ain't dead, they'll sure as hell try to catch us. I'll bet that redskin could trail a horney toad across a bare rock. We'll ride out to Mora tomorrow. I want one more night with the girls here in Las Vegas before we leave."

The next day they retrieved their horses and the mule from

the livery stable and rode out of town. Their whiskey clouded eyes failed to see two men follow them out of town.

After riding for three hours, they stopped along a clear, blue stream, dismounted and built a small fire. Placing the coffee pot on the fire, Slim said, "My head is splitting. We did too much celebrating last night."

"It was worth it, though," Rusty replied, smiling. "Them Mexican girls really know how to please a man."

Pouring two cups of steaming coffee, they sat down in the shade of a huge pine tree. The two men who had been following rode up and spoke.

"Howdy, gents," the larger of the two said, "that coffee smells right good -- reckon you could spare a cup?"

Rusty looked at them warily, then replied, "I reckon."

Slim slowly placed his coffee cup in his left hand and lowered his right hand to his gun butt.

As the two men stepped to the ground, they suddenly reached for their guns. Too late, they realized that their robbery had failed. Slim's gun spit lead and the fat man fell with his pistol only half drawn, staring unbelieving at his mistake.

Rusty's pistol fired simultaneously, and the small man was knocked to the ground, his shot digging a hole in the sand next to his feet. Rusty stepped forward and saw that the man was still alive.

"Why'd you do it?" he asked.

"We saw you spreading that gold around in Las Vegas, and followed you out of town. It looked like that mule was loaded pretty heavy and we figured on taking him."

He coughed, spitting up blood, then said, "Looks like we made a mistake."

"I reckon," Rusty said as he shot him again, holstered his gun and picked up his coffee cup.

....

The boys were in the saddle, riding west out of Salinas, at daylight. Mid-morning, they crossed Ute Creek and, pushing their horses hard, reached the confluence of the Conchas and Canadian Rivers, where they made camp for the night. It was there that they came upon a large herd of sheep, being cared for by *Don* Casimiro Romero and four herders.

Casimiro welcomed them into his camp. "*Buenos Dias*, Senor Cole," he said. "I am greatly surprised to see you this far west of Ceebara."

"Howdy, *Don* Romero, neither did we expect to see you this far from Atascosa Plaza. I thought you grazed your sheep north and south of Atascosa."

"You are correct, Senor Cole -- but I am returning from Las Vegas where I purchased these three thousand sheep. We are taking them back to my Plaza at Atascosa." Pausing, he said, "And you, Senor Cole, what are you doing in New Mexico?"

"We are trailing a couple of *hombres* who took things that belong to us," Cole replied, being careful not to mention the gold. "A tall slim man and a smaller man with red hair. They should be leading a mule."

"I have seen these men, Senor Cole. As we were leaving Trujillo. two days ago, we met them heading for Las Vegas. I talked to them and they said they were going to the gold fields in the mountains above Cimarron, but intended to rest up in Las Vegas. They looked like very mean *hombres*."

"They are, Senor Romero. They tried to kill me and Chief, then stole our mule and belongings."

"Is there anything I can do to help?" Casimiro asked.

"Thanks, but no, Don Romero. We had thought them friends, but now that we know what they are, we will be more careful."

....

Cole decided to continue to the small New Mexican village of Trujillo, as the sun was still high in the sky. The trail had become easier, now that they were out of the Canadian River breaks. Rolling, cedar and mesquite covered hills replaced the deep canyons and gorges. Arriving after dark, they took a room in the stage way station, and after a meal of buffalo steaks and beans in the local saloon, fell exhausted into bed.

The next morning, after paying the livery stable for feeding and caring for their horses, they mounted up and headed for Las Vegas, thirty miles to the west. They could now see the Sangre de Christo mountains, rising purple in the distance.

Cole was excited, having never seen mountains before. Pointing, he said, "Look at that, Chief -- ain't that something." Chief, remembering the granite mountains of Oklahoma, wasn't too impressed. Looking at the mountains rising in the distance, he replied, "Looks like much work to get over them."

Cole laughed, "Danged sure more difficult than the flat prairies of Ceebara."

By mid-afternoon, they entered the bustling community which was nestled in a valley on the Callinas River. A train was blowing steam as it began to move down the rails toward Santa Fe. The whistle echoed eerily off the ridges surrounding the town and a flock of geese took flight from the rivers edge. Riding slowly down Main street, they watched on both sides of the street for their mule. Unable to see him, they stopped at Gomez's livery stable at the edge of town, dismounted and stepped inside. The smell of fresh cut hay and horse manure enveloped them as they examined the stalls. No mule was present.

"Can I help, you, Senor," a voice asked from the darkness of one of the stalls. An elderly Mexican, with a pitchfork in his hand stepped out, wiping the sweat from his brow.

Cole shook his hand and introduced himself and Chief. "Yes," he said, "we need to stable our horses for the night."

"I am Juan Gomez, senor. One dollar each for hay and oats. You can leave them, I will remove your saddles and rub them down. It looks like they have been ridden pretty hard."

"Too hard, senor," Cole replied, then asked. "Which is the best hotel?"

"The Palacio, next to Jose's saloon. It is small but clean and Angelina serves very good enchiladas in the dining room." Smiling, he added, "I know, because Angelina is the mother of my children."

"Thank you, Juan" Cole said, removing his saddle bags. He and Chief swung their bags over their shoulders and stepped out of the stable. Watching both sides of the street, they walked to the Palacio Hotel. Mexican music could be heard, coming from Jose's Saloon next door.

Cole paid for a room with two beds, and asked, "We're looking for our friends, a tall slim man and a shorter, red-haired man. Are they staying here?"

"No body answering that description," the clerk replied, as he gave Cole change for the twenty dollar gold piece.

After cleaning up, they left their saddle bags in the room and returned to the street. Walking next door to Jose's Cantina, they stepped inside and stopped just inside the doorway, allowed their eyes to get accustomed to the dim light. Even though it was still early, the room was full of drinkers and card players. Looking around, neither saw anyone who looked familiar. Pushing through the crowds to the bar, they ordered two beers, then, turning their backs to the bar, they once again surveyed the crowd. Slim and Rusty were not in the room.

Picking up their drinks, they moved to a nearby table and sat down. Immediately, a shapely Mexican beauty, displaying a lot of flesh, pulled up a chair and sat down next to Chief. "My name is Conchita, could I entice you to buy me a drink?" she asked in Spanish.

Chief knew only a few words in Spanish and looked to Cole for help. "She wants to know if you would buy her a beer," Cole interpreted. Smiling at the senorita, he said, "He's Indian, ma'am, and doesn't understand Spanish."

Turning to Chief, she said, "Oh, I thought your were Mexican. I speak English -- would you like to buy me a Tequila?'

"We're drinking beer, ma'am -- would that do?"

Laughing, she whispered, "Sure, a beer would be fine, but my boss would make less money than he would if you bought me a Tequila."

"Would a Tequila be worth some information," Cole asked.

"If I have it," she replied.

"Alright, bring us two more beers and a Tequila, and then we will find out if you have the right information."

Soon she returned with the drinks and rejoined them at their table. Taking a sip of her drink, she dabbed her lips with her handkerchief and asked, "Now, what kind of information do you need."

"We are looking for two men, a tall slim man and a short,

red haired man. They may have been spending a lot of gold," Cole said.

Nervously, she looked around, then whispered, "Yes, I have seen them. Two men -- I only know them by their first names, Slim and Rusty. They bought me many drinks two days ago, then paid me and another girl to join them in their room. They paid us with a twenty dollar gold piece -- *muchisimo dinero* for one night -- I think maybe they were bad men."

"You are right, Conchita, they are bad men. Is that the last time you have seen them?"

"Yes, they said they were leaving the next day for Mora," she replied.

"Thank you, Conchita, you have been a big help," Cole said and paid for the drinks, and added five silver dollars.

"For the information," he said.

"Oh, thank you!" she said, then looked disappointed when they pushed their chairs back, got up from the table and walked out into the sun drenched street.

Spotting a sign which read, *Abaceria,* Cole said, "There's a grocery store. We're plumb out of grub.We best pick up some coffee, bacon, and beans in case we have to make camp along the way."

After breakfast the next morning, they picked up their horses at Gomez's livery stable, and took the road northwest toward Mora.

15

Leigh Dyer, Miss Molly's brother, accompanied Belle and Kate back to Ceebara. The ladies were anxious to tell Ned about the robbery, knowing that he would send help.

"They found the gold?" Ned said, unbelieving, as Kate related the boys tale.

"That's right, Ned, and they were robbed by Slim and Rusty who took their pack mule which was loaded with twelve hundred twenty dollar gold coins," Kate replied.

"Where are the boys now?" Ned asked.

"I tried to stop them but Cole wouldn't hear to it. They took off on the outlaws trail, saying they were heading for Atascosa first,"

"When was that?" Ned asked.

"Three days ago," Belle said.

Frowning, Ned replied, "Three days -- if they caught up with the bushwhackers in Tascosa, and were successful in recovering the mule, they should have been home by now. I best see if they're in trouble."

Smokey, who had been listening to the conversation, said, "I'll get the horses saddled, Mr. Ned."

"Alright, Smokey -- we'll also need a mule and supplies -- we may be gone a spell."

"Just me and you, Mr. Ned?" Smokey asked.

"Yes, we should be able to take care of those sidewinders if the boys are in trouble. Just two horses and the mule."

Within an hour, Ned and Smokey rode out of the Ceebara ranch compound, trailing a pack mule, and took the trail to Atascosa.

....

Slim and Rusty rode into Mora an hour before sundown. However, shadows were already falling in the sleepy Mexican village, with the Sangre de Cristo range looming to the west. cutting off the sun's rays. Locating the livery stable, once again they demanded a tack room and a lock, unsaddled their horses and mule, and walked down the dusty street, looking for a room.

Like other frontier towns, Mora had its saloons and cantinas to satisfy the thirst of the miners, hunters, cowboys, and soldiers from nearby Fort Union -- and saloon ladies to satisfy their other desires. Located on the trail to Taos over the Sangre de Cristos, and on the trail to the gold fields around Elizabethtown, high in the mountains, it was a bustling frontier village.

A half dozen adobe buildings advertising food were scattered along the main street. One which appeared larger than the others also had a sign reading, *Hotelero*. They took a room, washed the trail dust from their bodies, then followed their noses to the cafe.

"I don't believe Cole and Chief are following us," Slim said, as they began shoving the highly spiced enchiladas into their mouths. "That damned mule slows us down enough that they should have caught us if they were able to free themselves."

"I think you're probably right," Rusty replied. "Cougar's wouldn't have let them live very long, probably got 'em the first night."

"Yeah, we can relax and start enjoying that gold. First thing we need to do is spend some of it on new boots and clothes," Slim said.

"First thing I'm going to do is buy me a heavy coat. This mountain air is a lot colder than the plains, and I've been freezing my ass off," Rusty said, spreading butter on a tortilla.

Slim laughed and said, "We'll do that tomorrow morning -- we got business to take care of in the saloon tonight."

....

"Well, there she is," Cole said, pointing to the lights of the Mexican village which was nestled on the banks of the Mora River. "Mora, one of the toughest towns in the west. I remember Kid talking about holing up here one time when things got too hot for him in Union County."

"What you suppose happened to Kid," Chief asked, pulling a plug of chewing tobacco from his pocket. "He hasn't been back to Ceebara in a long time." Pulling his knife from his chaps, he cut off a small chunk and gave the tobacco and knife to Cole.

Taking the knife and tobacco, Cole replied, "I don't know, he left and went back to work for a rancher in Lincoln. I hear he took the outlaw trail after those killings in the Lincoln County war. He may be dead -- if he's alive, he might even be here in Mora. I heard him tell pa he had a girl friend here."

Darkness had fallen as they followed the trail along the river into town. Dogs were barking, kids were shouting, and the smell of food cooking floated in the crisp mountain air. The two boys rode past the livery stable, watching both sides of the street, to the western end of town. A lantern was hung on a barn door and the dim light illuminated a sign -- *Cocheria*.

"That's another livery stable. We might as well leave our horses here," Cole said as he dismounted and led *Comanche* inside. Chief followed, leading his black and white paint, *Badger*.

"*Buenos dias*, I am Pedro," the Mexican boy said as he took the reins of Cole's horse.

"*Buenos dias*, Pedro," Cole replied. "how much for one night, hay and oats?"

"*Uno pesos, cada caballo*," the boy replied.

Cole gave him two silver dollars, "*Mucho gracias*," he said, "feed them well and rub them down," as they walked out the door and down the busy street.

Slim and Rusty had finished their meal and were crossing the darkened street toward loud music coming from a lighted cantina. Reaching the other side, still in the dark, they leaned against the hitching rail and began rolling smokes.

Rusty dropped his makings, pulled his pistol, whispered and pointed across the street, "Damn! There they are!"

Cole and Chief were walking toward the restaurant, anxious to get supper and unaware of the outlaws presence. Light from a lantern bounced off their faces.

Rusty quickly threw up his pistol and fired. The bullet creased Cole's hat and lodged in a wooden post next to his head. Instinctively, he and Chief pulled their pistols as they hit the dirt and rolled behind a water trough.

Unable to determine where the shot had come from, they

lay still and remained hidden. Slim and Rusty ducked into a dark alley and ran behind the buildings. "Why the hell did you shoot?" Slim asked. "They were too far away and in the dark. Now they'll know that we are here."

"I think I got Cole," Rusty said.

"Yeah, and I think you missed," Slim replied. "I saw him pulling leather as he fell."

They continued running toward the livery barn and Slim said, "We've got to get out of town fast. They will know we had to put up our horses and mule, and if they find the mule, they'll find the gold."

Rushing inside, Slim gathered the horses and mule while Rusty retrieved their tack from the locked room. Quickly they threw on the saddles, tightened the cinches, mounted and rushed from the barn. In the light of the moon, they saw a sign pointing down a wagon road, reading 'Cimarron -- 40 miles'. Turning their horses down the road, they kicked their horses into a lope. The darkness swallowed them up as they disappeared, seeking protection in another hell hole of the west.

....

Cole, still laying in the dirt next to the water trough, whispered, "What do you think, Chief -- are they gone?"

"Maybe," Chief replied. "Maybe it was not Slim and Rusty -- just one shot -- maybe it was just a stray bullet."

"I think you are probably right. If someone was trying to kill us, there would have been more than one shot. Let's ease up, stay in the shadows and walk to the cafe. Even if it was them, they won't try again with all the people around."

Chief nodded as they got to their feet, looking in the direction where the shot had originated. Seeing no one, they stepped quickly inside the cafe and chose a table in the rear corner, facing the door.

No one seemed interested in them as they ordered and then ate their meal. Finishing, Cole paid the bill and they stepped back outside. Cautiously, they made their way down the street, looking into each saloon as they passed. Reaching the end of the street, they crossed over and came back up the other side, repeating their surveillance into each of the saloons as they walked slowly by.

Nothing.

"They've disappeared, Chief, and it's too dangerous to keep prowling around in the dark. We best go to our room, get a good night's sleep, and see what we can locate in the morning," Cole said.

....

By daylight, they were back on the street, searching for clues. Finding an expended cartridge lying in the street in the vicinity where the gunman fired, Chief picked it up, "forty-four," he said, giving it to Cole.

"Yeah, same as Rusty was wearing. Let's go to the other livery stable and see if the mule is there," Cole said.

"*Buenos dias*, how can I help you?" the elderly Mexican asked.

"We're looking for a mule -- loaded pretty heavily," Cole said.

"There was one last night, senor, but this morning when I came it was gone -- also the two horses which were with the mule. The men did not pay me for their keep."

While Cole questioned the attendant, Chief followed the tracks out of the barn, down the street to the Cimarron sign, and down the road a short distance. Returning to the barn, he met Cole at the door.

"They took the Cimarron road out of town," he reported.

"Alright, let's eat a quick breakfast, get our horses and follow," Cole said.

....

Ned and Smokey rode sweating horses into Tascosa and stopped in front of Casimiro's *hacienda*, Casimiro was on the porch, smoking his pipe. "Welcome, Senor Ned," he said. "Come in and tell me why you are in town."

Following the Mexican Don inside, he asked, "Have you by chance seen Cole and Chief in town."

"No, I have not seen them in Tascosa but I did see them in New Mexico."

"New Mexico? What were they doing in New Mexico?"

Casimiro poured three cups of coffee and sat down before replying. "I was coming from Las Vegas with a flock of sheep which I had purchased and I met Cole and Chief near Trujillo. They said they were trailing two men who had stolen their mule."

"Did they say where they were going?"

"Si -- Las Vegas," Casimiro replied.

"When does the stage leave for Las Vegas?" Ned asked.

"If it has no trouble, it should pull in from Mobeetie about three this afternoon," Casimiro responded. "You and Smokey look exhausted. I have beds, why don't you sleep. I will get tickets and awaken you when the stage arrives. I will care for your horses until you return."

"*Gracias* -- You are too kind, my friend. I believe we will take your suggestion," Ned replied, "I'm surely tuckered out."

The stage arrived on time, Ned and Smokey loaded their saddlebags, as the stage pulled out, waved and shouted "*adios*" to Casimiro.

There were stage stations every thirty to thirty-five miles, where passengers were allowed to stretch, sometimes eat, and teams were changed. With fresh horses the stage could make the distance between stations in about five hours.

Thirty hours later, the stage pulled into Las Vegas as the sun was setting behind the Sangre de Cristo mountain range. Dirty and tired, Ned and Smokey stepped down, brushed off the dust and walked into the hotel.

"Help you?" the receptionist asked.

"Maybe, I'm looking for Cole Armstrong. I think he may have stayed with you a few days ago."

"He have an Indian boy with him?"

"That's him -- is he still here?"

"No, sir," looking at the register, he said, "checked out three days ago. Don't rightly know where he was going but you might find out over at Jose's Cantina next door."

They left the hotel and stepped into the nearby cantina, approached the bar and ordered beer.

"Come in on the stage?" the bartender asked.

"Yep," Ned replied. "Feller over at the hotel said you might help me locate my son."

"Be glad to if I can," the bartender replied, setting two foaming glasses on the bar.

"Cole Armstrong, fifteen years old, looks eighteen -- six feet, sandy hair, traveling with an Indian."

"Yeah, I seen them -- they was talking with Conchita. That's her over at that table visiting with those two miners. She might know where they went."

Carrying his beer, Ned stepped over to the table, removed his hat and said, "Pardon me, ma'am. Could I have a word with you."

"Can't you see she's busy," one of the miner's said, starting to get up.

"No offense, mister. Just wanted to know if she knew where Ned Armstrong and Chief Parker may have gone. Cole's my son." Ned said.

Conchita smiled and placed her hand on the miner's shoulder, pushing him back into his chair. "Sure, they left three days ago -- said they were going to Mora."

"I'm rightful obliged, ma'am," Ned said and placed a silver dollar in her hand, then turned back to the bar.

Speaking to the bartender, he asked, "Is there a stage out of here to Mora?"

"Yes, sir -- but it only runs two days a week. Next one is day after tomorrow."

"Where's the best place to rent a couple of horses?" Ned asked.

"Across the street to the end of the block -- Gomez's Livery," the bartender replied.

Ned thanked him and motioned to Smokey as he walked out the door.

Walking to the livery stable, Ned asked, "What do you think, Smokey. Probably five or six hours to Mora -- maybe longer than that in the dark. Think we should wait until morning?"

"No, sir, Mr. Ned -- them boys may be in a heap of trouble and I 'spects we better find them as soon as we can," Smokey replied.

"Alright -- we'll rent a couple of horses, grab a bite to eat at the restaurant and head out. We should be to Mora before sunup."

....

The horses were not much to look at but they were stout mountain ponies and didn't know when to quit. They apparently had been down this rough wagon road many times and needed little guidance in the dark from Ned and Smokey.

At four a.m., they pulled up to the hitching rail of the only building in town with a light burning. Stepping down stiffly from their saddles, Ned and Smokey opened the door to Consuelo's Restaurant and stepped in.

A huge Mexican woman was busy preparing tortillas for her early morning crowd. *"Buenos dias,"* she said, looking up from her work. "I'm Consuelo. I just opened."

"Buenos dias, Consuelo," Ned replied. "Are we too early for breakfast?"

"No, senor, just the first -- what can I make you?"

"About a gallon of coffee, first. Then we will have six dozen eggs and a whole hog fried."

Consuelo laughed and her huge stomach shook. "It will take awhile to cook all of that, but I have coffee ready and can prepare ham and six eggs very quickly. Tortillas will be done by the time the eggs are ready," she said as she poured the coffee.

"That will be fine," Ned said, blowing his coffee and taking a sip.

Smokey laughed and said, "Mr. Ned, I guess you aren't hungry. I could eat that whole hog by myself."

"Consuelo, I am looking for my son who probably rode in a couple of days ago. Tall, sandy haired, fifteen years old -- he was traveling with a friend, Indian lad."

"Yes, I remember them. Very polite boys. I think they may have left because I didn't see them at all yesterday."

"Who might know where they went," Ned asked as she set the ham, eggs and tortillas in front of them.

"Probably, Pedro at the livery, that's where they had their horses stabled."

They spent nearly an hour at the cafe until the village began to awaken. Two men, who looked as if they worked at a saw mill, came in and ordered breakfast. Ned and Smokey nodded to them as they were leaving.

Mounting up, they rode to the livery, two blocks down the winding street. The stable owner was washing his face in the horse trough as they rode up.

"Howdy," Ned said, "I hear you've been stabling a couple of horses -- big chestnut gelding and a black and white paint -- belong to my son and his friend. Are they around?"

"They was but they ain't no more. Left early this morning -- going toward Cimarron."

"Damnation, Smokey!" Ned said, "them boys are determined to get that gold or get themselves killed trying. What do you think -- need a bed and sleep?"

"No, sir, Mister Ned -- when I was in the cavalry I learned how to sleep in the saddle. Sometimes we would ride for a week without stopping for sleep. We just about caught them, I don't think we aught to sleep yet."

"Mister, we leased these horses from Gomez over in Las Vegas. They're about tuckered out. How about us leaving them and renting a couple from you. We can bring yours back and pick up Gomez's on the return trip."

"That would be fine. Two dollars a day rent on each of my horses, a buck a day each for taking care of Gomez's until you return."

He led out two large, muscular geldings and assisted Ned and Smokey in switching saddles.

"Well, let's go back by Consuelo's and have her make some sandwiches to carry along. We should be able to make Cimarron by dark if these nags don't play out."

Riding up to Consuelo's, they tied their horses next to a gray grulla. Ned looked at the gray and said, "Damned if I don't believe that's the Kid's horse, Smokey!"

"Yes, sir, Mister Ned, I sho believe you's right. I'd recognize that horse anywhere."

Opening the door to the restaurant, they looked around and sure enough, Kid sat eating breakfast at a table by himself, with his back to them. Stepping over, Ned slapped him on the back and said, "Alright, Kid, you're under arrest."

Without thinking, Kid reached for his gun, stopped and without turning around, said, "Ned, damn you, I nearly drawed on you!"

Ned and Smokey laughed, shook his hand, and Ned asked, "What are you doing in Mora. I thought you was back in Lincoln County."

"I was until Pat Garret got on my trail. He's chased me over all of New Mexico and half of Texas! What brings you this far west?"

"Chasing that no good son of mine. He and Chief located that sheepherders gold down in Palo Duro Canyon, and a couple of bushwhackers stole it from them. They've been chasing the bushwhackers and we've been trying to catch up with them.

By the time we learned about it, they had nearly a week head start on us."

"The hell you say,"Kid said, whispering. "Found that twenty-five thousand dollars worth of gold coins?"

"Apparently that's right. I haven't seen it but Kate and Bell said the boys located it in a cave near that Lighthouse formation down in the canyon."

"Where are the boys now?" Kid asked.

"Seems they left out of here this morning, headed toward Cimarron," Ned replied.

"How many men are they chasing?" Kid questioned.

"We don't know -- at least two, and they apparently are pretty tough hombres."

Kid thought for a minute, took a bite of ham, and said, "I'm going with you Ned. There's a lot of tough outlaws holed up in this area. No telling what Cole is liable to meet up with in Cimarron."

"I'm much obliged, Kid, but we can probably take care of it. My boys are pretty damn good shots -- and me and Smokey can hold our own."

"I'm going, Ned -- that's the end of it. Those two boys are like brothers to me. Remember, I taught Cole his fast draw. Now all I need to do is drop by my cabin and tell my senorita that I'll be gone for awhile, pick up my bedroll and I'll be ready."

"Alright, Kid, I'm going to have Consuelo make us some sandwiches while you finish your breakfast."

The three of them left the cafe, mounted up and headed toward the east end of town. Riding up to a small adobe house, Kid dismounted and said he would only be a minute. He soon reappeared, carrying his rifle, saddle bags and bed roll. Strapping them on, he mounted up and said, "We're burning daylight, let's go!"

16

Cimarron, nestled at the foot of the Sangre de Cristos, on the banks of the South Fork of the Canadian River, was a bustling cross roads village located at the mouth of Cimarron Canyon. The small river, flowing out of the canyon, was a cold, clear mountain stream, beginning high in the mountains and fed by melting snows.

The wagon road up Cimarron Canyon was used by freighters to carry supplies to the miners in the high country around Mount Baldy and Wheeler Peak.

The rolling, rather treeless prairie of northwestern New Mexico ended at the western side of the village of Cimarron, and the beautiful pine covered mountains began. The beauty of the setting belied the wild life which was practiced by those who called the village home.

The town was full of gold miners, cowboys, buffalo hunters, gamblers, gun slingers and outlaws. Each of them competing for the title of meanest man in the west.

Slim and Rusty arrived in the village late in the day, stabled their horses and mule and locked the pack saddle with its treasure of gold in the tack room, then headed for the nearest cantina. The nightly celebrations had already begun and the shouts of laughing painted ladies could be heard, intermingled with Mexican fandango music. shouts of drunken brawlers, and the sounds of an occasional gun shot.

Approaching the Golden Nugget Cantina, they had to step aside as two inebriated brawlers hurtled through the door and landed in the street, pounding and gouging each other. Slim and Rusty watched as both men drew knives and began slashing and cutting. One finally made a lung and stuck his knife up to the hilt in the other's chest. With blood gushing from the wound, the miner fell dead in the dusty street.

Turning, they stepped warily over the body and into the smoke filled cantina, pushed their way to the bar and ordered whiskey. The room reeked with the smell of whiskey, tobacco and sweat. Slim and Rusty had discussed the possibility of hiring some gunmen to help in putting a stop to the two boys who had been dogging their trail. There seemed to be plenty of hired guns in the Golden Nugget Cantina.

Noticing three men, guns slung low on their hips, sitting at a corner table. Slim and Rusty joined them.

"Mind if we buy you gents a drink?" Slim asked.

Looking them over from head to boot, the leader of the trio answered, "Sounds like a good offer -- what's it going to cost us?" A long, ugly scar from his eye to this chin glistened beneath a mat of black whiskers as he attempted a weak smile.

Pulling up two chairs, Slim and Rusty sat down. "Ain't going to cost you nothing," Rusty said. "My names Rusty Johnson and my pard is Slim Maynard. We've got a proposition if you're interested."

Sticking out his hand, the leader said, "Name's Hitch, these two boys is Jake and Turtle."

Rusty thought the name Turtle fit the gunman well, his head seemed to be spouting out of his broad round shoulders like the head of a turtle barely protruding from its shell.

Shaking hands around, Slim motioned to one of the scantily dressed waitresses and said, "Bring these gents another round of what their drinking," as he dropped a twenty dollar gold coin on the table. Hitch picked up the coin and examined it, turning it fondly in his fingers.

"Don't see many of these around," he said. "You fellers must be from the gold fields."

"I reckon," Rusty said, smiling at the thought.

The waitress brought the drinks, took the gold piece and gave Slim his change.

"What kind of proposition you talking about?" Hitch asked.

"We just need a little backing to make sure that a couple of fellers who are gunning for us ain't successful," Rusty replied, taking a sip of his whiskey.

"Sounds like dangerous work," Hitch said. "We charge pretty steep for dangerous work."

Smiling, Slim said, "We pay pretty good for dangerous work."

"I'm listening," Hitch said.

"Five of those twenty dollar gold pieces for each of you if you help us make certain that those two fellers ain't successful," Slim replied.

"One hundred dollars for each of us? Just who are these two fellers you need help with? They must be pretty tough."

"They think they're tough -- but they're just a couple of

overgrown kids wanting to make a name for themselves."

"Kids? What for you need help to take out a couple of kids?"

Chuckling, Rusty said, "We just want to make certain that when the shooting is over, they're dead and we ain't."

"Sounds like our kind of work," Hitch said. "When we going to start?"

"We think they will probably get into town tomorrow. All you got to do is hang around. When we call them out, just be ready to back us up," Slim said, handing each of the gunmen a gold coin. "That's down payment -- you get the rest when the job is done."

Pulling his Colt from its holster, Hitch twirled the chamber and sighted down the barrel at the door of the cantina as if he were sighting down an enemy. "We'll be right behind you," he said as he replaced the pistol into his holster.

....

Cole and Chief rode easily on the trail to Cimarron. "I think we'll catch them this time," Cole said. "They'll be waiting on us so we're going to need to be extra careful. We don't want them pulling down on us like they did in Mora."

"Yes," Chief replied, "We need to see them before they see us. That's the Indian way -- sneaky!"

Cole nodded and smiled, Chief had a way with words. He let his eyes roam from the trail. Pines, spruce and aspen dotted the hillsides. Grass was green and deep and buffalo, deer and elk could be seen in the distance.

"This would be a good country for a ranch, Chief," he said. "What do you think about us using our gold to start a spread here?"

Chief nodded in thought. "Partners?" he asked.

"You bet -- partners," Cole responded. "How about this -- C bar P ranch, -- Cole and Parker? I'll bet the land can be had free and we can use our gold to buy cattle."

"Maybe P and C will be better -- Parker and Cole -- and don't forget," Chief responded, smiling, "Ponies, White Eyes -- lots of ponies!"

Laughing, Cole said, "O.K., Redskin, lots of ponies!"

The sun was setting when they topped the ridge and looked down upon the small village of Cimarron. Smoke was rising across the floor of the valley and lights were winking from lamps and lanterns.

As they approached the outskirts of the village, dogs welcomed them, barking and nipping at the hooves of their horses. Kids shouting and playing in the street moved aside as they passed.

"*Buenos dias, muchacho*," Cole greeted a young boy who stood at the edge of the street, watching. "*Paradero le caballeriza.*"

Pointing, the boy shouted, "*Aqui' tiene.*"

"He says there is a livery stable ahead," Cole said.

Leaving their horses in the stable, they slipped through the crowds down the darkened street and quickly turned into the hotel. Laying their saddle bags on the desk, Cole asked for a room with two beds.

"Sorry -- you'll have to take two rooms if you want two beds -- two dollars a room," the clerk said. "We've got a bunch of drovers in town, and they took all of our doubles."

"That's fine,"Cole said, "we'll be needing baths."

"That'll be another fifty cents each. Baths down at the end

of the hall," he said, handing Cole a bar of soap and towels. "Fresh hot water is on the stove next to the tub."

The rooms were number five and six with a connecting door. After bathing, they returned to the lobby, located a rear door and stepped out into the darkened alley. Moving quietly and remaining in the dark next to the side of the hotel, they surveyed the street.

Several cantinas could be seen on both sides of the street, and the noise within each was getting louder as the whiskey and beer began to affect the rowdy crowd. Several gunshots echoed from the darkened street.

"Look, Cole, there they are, and those three men seem to be with them," Chief said, pointing to an adobe cantina across the street.

Slim and Rusty seemed to be giving orders to the three men standing near them, pointing up the street. "You're right, Chief -- hired guns! See how low slung they are wearing their guns. I bet my hat that Slim and Rusty have hired them to help ambush us."

The three men remained on the street and Slim and Rusty stepped into the cantina. Cole and Chief continued to watch as the three gunmen scattered, taking positions on each side of the street.

After what seemed like a couple of hours, Slim and Rusty returned to the street,, slightly inebriated, carrying a bottle and accompanied by two senoritas. As the boys watched, Rusty argued with Hitch for a few minutes, and finally agreed to have two more of his friends help with the ambush. Rusty pulled two more gold coins from his pocket, and said, "Suits me, Hitch. The deader we can make them, the happier I'll be." Turning, he steered Slim and the senoritas to another hotel down the street. The three gunmen disappeared inside the cantina.

"Looks like Slim and Rusty are heading for bed, and have given their hired help the rest of the night off," Cole said. "Let's see if we can't get into that cafe without being seen."

After eating hot biscuits, buffalo steaks, potatoes and gravy, the boys slipped out, walked to the alley and entered the hotel from the rear. The lobby was empty except for the receptionist who was leaned back in a chair, asleep.

Slipping quietly up the stairway, they entered their rooms and opened the connecting door. Cole joined Chief in his room and sitting on the side of the bed, they discussed their situation.

Not realizing that two more outlaws had joined the plot, Cole asked, "Do you think we can take all five of them?"

"Maybe -- Slim and Rusty don't know that we suspect the other three, which should help."

"Yep, if we can catch them off guard, maybe in the street, we would have a little edge. That scar faced hombre looks like a real gun slick, but the other two shouldn't be too fast. I'll take scar face and Slim -- you take the little guy and Rusty. We'll both try to get the guy with no neck last. He doesn't look like he's much of a gunfighter."

"Alright, but how we going to get them into the street?" Chief asked.

"We'll get down early and wait in that alley where we can see their hotel across the street. If I'm right, Slim probably gave them orders to be waiting when they come down in the morning. We'll have the gunmen spotted, and when Slim and Rusty leave the hotel, we'll step out and call them down. The three hired gunmen will probably pull leather first and we'll need to beat them to the draw. After the first shot, you fall to your left, I'll fall to my right. Then we'll turn our guns on Slim and Rusty."

Nodding, Chief said, "Yes, the way we practiced -- they should be surprised enough that they won't draw until the shooting starts, and we will have the advantage."

....

The sky had begun to lighten in the east when Ned, Smokey and Billy topped the ridge overlooking Cimarron. They tied their horses to the first hitching post and walked slowly down the street, looking both ways for a sign of Slim and Rusty or Cole and Chief.

Ned motioned and Billy moved to the right side of the street and Smokey to the left. Several men were leaving the hotels and heading toward the two restaurants. Ned motioned for Billy and Smokey to stop. No one paid any attention to them as Ned removed a plug of chewing tobacco and bit off a chunk. Billy took makings from his shirt pocket and began rolling a cigarette. Smokey was picking his teeth with a sharpened match stem. They all three were holding Winchesters in the crook of their arms.

Moving slowly, they continued down the street and stopped near the two hotels. Five men seemed to be loitering in the street on the other side of the hotels.

Suddenly, the door to one of the hotels opened and Slim and Rusty stepped into the street. Almost simultaneously, Cole and Chief stepped from the shadows across the street.

"Alright, Rusty," Cole yelled, "Your running days are over. Throw up your hands."

As Hitch reached for his gun, Cole's hand was a blur as his

Colt appeared in his hand, and spit fire. Hitch's feet flew out from under him and he fell backwards, firing into the sand of the street. A round hole sprayed blood from his forehead.

Chief's draw was only a heart beat behind Cole's, and the small gunman screamed as Chief's bullet hit him in the chest, spinning him around, still trying to get his gun from his holster. He fell dead, painting the sand red with his blood.

Ned, Billy and Smokey raised their rifles and fired. The remaining gunmen on each side of the street were knocked from their feet.

Slim and Rusty had their guns in their hands as Cole and Chief fell to the side, firing as they hit the ground.

Slim was able to get a shot off, but Cole was a second quicker and blood began to color the gold thief's chest. Cole felt his knee buckle as a sharp pain told him he was hit. He watched as Slim slowly fell to the ground, a look of astonishment on his face.

Chief's lead caught Rusty in the neck, and the red-head's shot went wild, cutting a hole in a nearby water trough.

Ned rushed to Cole's side, dropped his gun and raised Cole to a sitting position. "How bad is it, son," he screamed.

"Pa, what you doing here?" Cole asked, then smiled. "I sure am glad to see you, pa."

"Where are you hit, son," Ned asked again.

"Just my leg, pa. It ain't bad -- I think it just went through the muscle."

Ned cut the cloth of his trousers away and tied his bandana tightly around the wound to stop the flow of blood. "I'll get you to a doctor, son. You just set still."

Slim was trying to get up as Chief rushed to his side and

kicked the gun away from his hand. Pulling his Bowie knife, he grabbed a handful of hair and said, "Tell me what you did with our gold, or I scalp you!"

"No, Chief -- please -- I'll tell -- it's locked in a tack room at the livery stable -- get me a doc," he begged.

"Where's the key?" Chief asked.

"In -- my -- pocket," Slim mumbled.

Chief searched his pocket, found the key and released his hair. His head fell in the dirt, gasping as blood flowed from his mouth, he died.

Billy and Smokey, after seeing that all the gunmen were dead, rushed to Cole's side.

"Well I be danged," Cole said, "Kid and Smokey -- you're a site for sore eyes!"

"Howdy, Cole," Kid said. "I just came along to see if you could shoot as straight as I taught you -- you hurt bad?"

"Naw, Kid -- my pride is all."

"Your pride! My gosh, Cole, you tried to take on half the outlaws this side of Santa Fe. You're lucky to be alive."

"Yeah, but I thought me and Chief could take them all. There was more of them than we thought. We'd be buzzard bait for sure if you hadn't showed up."

Ned laughed, "Well, I can say one thing for you, son. You've got a heap of self confidence."

"They had our gold, Pa, and we aimed to get it."

The sheriff ran up and asked, "What the hell is going on, looks like there's been a war!"

"Not a war, sheriff. Those men you see lying dead in your street thought they could steal these boys' mule and supplies and found out that crime doesn't pay."

"You mean all this is over a stolen mule?" the sheriff exclaimed.

"Yes, sir -- I guess that about sums it up."

Walking around and looking at the seven dead men, the sheriff returned to Ned's side and said, "Well, I can tell you one thing -- five of those dead men are about the meanest snakes in New Mexico territory. They all are wanted by the law and there's a sizable bounty on their heads. I appreciate your help in putting an end to their careers."

"Why don't you collect that bounty and put it in your city funds to help pay for this mess we made," Ned replied. "Now, I'd appreciate it if you'd direct me to the nearest Doc and I'll see if I can get my boy patched up."

The sheriff glanced at Kid. "Say, ain't I seen you somewhere before?"

Kid smiled, "Not unless you've been down to Texas. I've been working for Mr. Armstrong for the past ten years."

....

After the doctor finished cleaning and bandaging Cole's leg, he gave him a crutch and they all went to the livery stable, unlocked the door and recovered the pack saddle.

Opening it, Ned, Smokey and Kid whistled, "Looks like you been robbing a Wells Fargo bank," Kid said, as he picked up a handful and let them fall through his fingers. "I can see why you was so determined to get that mule back."

"How much is there, Cole," Smokey asked.

"Well, it started out being twelve hundred gold coins -- I don't know how much Slim and Rusty spent but I 'spect there's still over eleven hundred.

....

They were all exhausted and spent the next three days resting. Cole's wound proved to be minor, and he soon was able to walk with a noticeable limp.

Ned congratulated the boys for their perseverance, even though he felt they had acted irrationally, taking on seven gunmen by themselves.

They were eating breakfast and discussing plans for returning home. "If we head east out of Cimarron, we can cut off several miles on the trail back to Ceebara," Ned said, "but we've got these rented horses we need to deliver back to Mora, and pick up the two we left there and take them back to Gonzalez in Las Vegas."

Kid, taking a sip of his coffee, said, "That's no problem, Ned. I can return the horses for you. I'll be riding back to Mora anyways."

"I'm much obliged, Kid," Ned replied. "I can buy a couple of horses here and see that these boys get back home without causing any more trouble."

"That'll be the day, Mr. Ned -- these two boys been causing trouble since they was eight years old!" Smokey said.

They all laughed.

17

Leading the pack laden mule, they rode out of Cimarron the following morning. Looking around, Cole commented, "This is a beautiful country, ain't it, Pa."

"It certainly is, son," Ned replied. "Good cattle country, too."

"That's what me and Chief were thinking. We thought we might like to use our gold to start a ranch up here. What do you think?"

"Seems to me that might be a good investment, son. But maybe you should wait until you get a little older."

"Yes, sir -- but I'll bet we could file on this land now and it wouldn't cost anything. If we wait till we're older, somebody else is going to get the best land."

"Tell you what, son -- when we get back home, we'll ride over to Hidetown and ask Temple if he can help. Maybe he can wire Santa Fe and find out if there is any free land available."

That seemed to satisfy Cole and he was quiet for awhile, looking at the grass, the streams, the buffalo and antelope as they rode eastward. The land was slightly rolling, covered with grass and very few trees, with numerous small creeks flowing from the mountains and cutting through the low spots. Many of them were dry, carrying water only when it rained. In many ways, this country was very similar to the Llano Estacado, except it had the beautiful blue and green mountains as a backdrop.

Reaching the head waters of the Canadian River, they made camp early in a small cottonwood grove. The water was clear and pure, being fed from high in the mountains by melting snow,

Smokey gathered some broken limbs beneath the trees and started a fire while Chief began unloading the mule and then staked the mule and horses in the tall grass next to the stream. Cole carried the coffee pot to the streams edge, filled it and walked back up the steep bank where the river had cut through an underlying formation of black rock. Picking up one of the rocks, Cole was surprised that it was full of tiny holes and was very light.

"What kind of rock is this, Pa," he asked, as he placed the coffee pot on the fire.

"It's pumice, son. That's rock that is made when volcanoes erupt. The molten lava flows out and when it cools, it has all of those little air bubbles. I reckon when these mountains were formed, the earth was pushed up and cracked open and this whole country was covered by lava. As it began to weather away through time, wind, rain, ice and snow made soil of it and grass and trees began to grow."

Pointing in the distance, he said, "See those peaks sticking up out there on the prairie -- kinda circular. They are really small volcano cones, where most of this lava came from. At one time, they were nothing but lava, but through time, grass and trees have started to cover them."

"I noticed a lot of these rocks on the trail from Las Vegas to Cimarron," Cole said.

"Same thing, Son -- you'll find them all along the foot hills of the Sangre de Cristo range, all the way from Santa Fe to Raton," Ned explained.

"Reckon this land belongs to anybody?" Cole asked.

Ned thought for awhile as he dumped some coffee grounds into the boiling pot. "Remember the time we was in Dodge City and we met that politician from Arkansas?"

"Yes, sir -- I remember his name was Dorsey. He said he had a ranch over west of the Rabbit Ears."

Ned smiled, "You've got a good memory, Son," he said. "This may be some of his ranch -- he told me that the provisional governor of New Mexico Territory had made a grant of over a million acres to him. Called it the *Una de Gato* Land Grant. I think he built his headquarters somewhere between Cimarron and the Rabbit Ears."

"*Una de Gato* -- what does that mean?"

"Something like, *place of the wildcat*," Ned said, trying to remember.

"Why they call it the Rabbit Ears?"

"You sure are full of questions, Son. I guess if you ever saw it you would understand. You know how a jack rabbit will hide in the grass, and sometimes all you can see are his two ears sticking up. Well, there's two lava peaks that stick up, pretty close together out on the flat prairie and can be seen for many miles. Travelers coming west on the Santa Fe Trail used the peaks as a land mark, and somebody decided they looked like rabbit ears sticking up in the grass."

Smokey soon had steaks and beans cooked and they relaxed around the fire. The horses could be heard, snipping grass as they grazed near the stream. The sun began to disappear behind the peaks of the Sangre de Cristos. A bob-white quail whistled down stream and another answered from some where out on the prairie.

Chief had been quiet, lost deep in thought, as he watched the sun disappear and the peaks change from green to a deep blue, then black as darkness climbed the slopes. "I think that is the home of the Sun God," he said, reverently."

Cole followed his eyes and watched the colors change as clouds above the mountains turned golden, reflecting the sun's rays. Looking higher into the clear deep blue of the sky as it began to darken, he could see the sparkle of thousands of stars. "I think you are right, Chief," he said, "and he sends all of his warriors to light our way at night."

Ned, stretched on his bed roll, broke their reverie by snoring loudly. The boys continued to lay on their backs, looking up and dreaming of the day they would have their own ranch in the shadow of these great mountains. A comet flashed across the sky, a good omen for the hopes of the two young boys.

....

They were up early and on the trail when the sun broke the eastern horizon. Riding across the flat prairie, they kept the small volcanic extrusions to their left. Several miles in the distance to the north, Cole spotted a well formed volcano cone protruding above all others.

"Pa, look yonder," he said as he pointed.

Ned nodded, "That's Capulin Mountain, Son. Actually it is not a mountain but an extinct volcano -- the largest in this area. Millions of years ago, this entire country was covered by molten lava as it flowed from Capulin. There was no grass, trees, birds or animals, just a large flat lake of hot, smoking black rock as far as the eye could see."

"That's hard to believe, Pa," Cole commented, looking down at the grass and at the herds of buffalo in the distance. "Seems like this grass has been here forever."

Ned cut a plug out of his chewing tobacco and placed it in his mouth before replying. "It keeps changing every year, Son. Every time it rains, some of the soil is washed away. When the wind blows, soil is displaced, and when it snows, ice gets in the cracks of the rocks, freezes and breaks the rocks into smaller pieces, and it soon is able to hold the roots of grass."

He spit before continuing, rolled the tobacco around in his jaw, and said, "If you could be around a million years from now, all of these volcano cones might be gone, trees would be growing where there is only grass today, and there might be canyons where there are small creeks."

Near noon, they topped a ridge and were surprised to see a huge log and rock ranch house, sitting on the prairie below a large mesa. Numerous buildings, barns and corrals were scattered about behind the main house.

As they approached, they could hardly believe their eyes. A large, cement pond was located in the front yard, filled to the brim with clear, blue water. Several people were lounging around the pool and in the water.

A large, bewhiskered gentleman, a towel draped over his shoulders, was resting on the edge of the pool with his feet dangling in the water. He arose as they approached, and in a booming voice, said, "Light off them horses and set awhile -- I'm Senator Stephen Dorsey."

Ned dismounted, took his hand, and said, "Ned Armstrong, Mr. Dorsey -- we met one time in Dodge City."

"Of course," Dorsey replied, "You and that one-armed Colonel from the Texas Panhandle, Jim Cole I believe was his name -- welcome to *Una de Gato* and the Triangle-Dot Ranch."

"Mr. Dorsey, I'd like for you to meet my son, Cole, his friend Chief Parker, and one of my cowboys, Smokey Brown."

"Parker? -- Parker? Where have I heard that name?" Looking into Chief"'s eyes as they shook hands, he said, "Why, you're Indian, boy -- Quanah Parker, that's where I heard it -- Chief Quanah."

"Yes, sir -- he's my father."

"Well, I be damned -- royalty, that's what you are -- damned royalty come to visit. It's a pleasure meeting you, boy!"

Dorsey shook hands with each of them as he motioned for a Mexican cowboy to take their horses. "Come on in the house and let me change into something more appropriate. Looks like you men could take a little refreshment. I want you to tell me all about what's going on in the Texas Panhandle."

Cole held onto the mule, saying, "He's a little wild and don't take too well to strangers. I best tie him up at the rail." He definitely didn't want the gold laden mule to be led out of his sight.

....

The Dorsey mansion was something to behold. The only house within forty miles in any direction, it was huge, stout and beautiful. Made of logs that had been freighted in from the mountains, stone chimneys and fire places made from the rock that capped the mesa, tile shingles from Santa Fe covering the roof, and interior beams that would withstand the strongest storms of the area.

The interior was arranged with a parlor, living room, several bed room suites, bath rooms, kitchen and a huge dining room. Each room was furnished with fine furniture which had been freighted in from his home in Arkansas. It had running water and carbide gas lights.

The basement was stocked with wines and liquors equal to the best restaurants in New York City or Washington, D.C.. The mansion had been built with the idea of entertaining influential guests from all over the world, who might be interested in investing in some of the Senator's business ventures -- ventures such as railroads, land, postal services, mining and meat packing houses.

Dorsey, an Arkansas politician who had served as the state's senator, was a good friend of General U.S. Grant, Rutherford Hayes, Chester Arthur, John Jacob Astor, and J.P. Morgan -- using those influential friends to build a fortune on political favors. Many of them had visited this mansion in the New Mexico wilderness to hunt buffalo, wolves and other exotic game of the area.

The senator was known far and wide for his hospitality. A separate building contained a billiard room, bar, a museum and sportsman's retreat with mounted heads of all the animals and birds of the area.

The house, facing south, looked out over a vast expanse of flat prairie where longhorn cattle could be seen grazing with scattered herds of buffalo. In the distance to the west could be seen the towering snow capped mountains of the Sangre de Cristo range.[1]

It was truly a mirage of civilization in an uncivilized part of

[1] New Mexico Museum

the west.

Senator Dorsey led them into the parlor, pointing to the leather covered couches and chairs, he said, "Make yourselves comfortable while I change into something more acceptable." To a maid, he said, "Rosey, bring these gentlemen whatever they wish," and disappeared into one of the bedrooms.

Rosey soon appeared with a tray and glasses, and several bottles of whiskey, liquors, wines and beer. She poured their choices then disappeared into the kitchen.

Even Ned was overwhelmed at the luxury of the home. Cole, Chief and Smokey were speechless, looking wide-eyed at the elegance of the home.

A newspaper lay on a table next to Ned's chair. Picking it up he noticed it was a couple of weeks old, *The Raton Guard*. He began reading an editorial which stated, *"There are rumors that Senator Dorsey is considering selling his ranch in Colfax County. We are glad to hear of it. If he sells out his possessions in the territory, there will be one less thief holding property among honest men."*[2]

Ned lay the paper aside as Dorsey returned, dressed in Mexican clothes which would have pleased the most prominent *Don* in Santa Fe. White silk shirt, gold and silver embroidered vest, brown buckskin bell bottom trousers which were split at the bottom and laced with bright red ribbons. Black belt with a huge silver buckle, and black, high heeled boots.

Rosey reappeared with a tumbler, half full of fine Scotch whiskey. "I see you gentlemen have been taken care of," he said as he sat down facing Ned, taking a swallow of the whiskey.

"Now, Mr. Armstrong, what business brings you to my humble abode?"

2 Raton Guard

Smiling, Ned said, "It is everything except humble, Mister Dorsey. My friends call me Ned, sir," and held up his drink in salute.

The senator returned the salute with his drink and replied, "And my friends call me Senator."

"We are returning from an adventure, Senator. An adventure which climaxed with seven men lying dead on the streets of Cimarron. It is a long story which I am certain would not interest you," Ned said.

"Seven men dead! Of course I would be interested, Ned. And I have all the time in the world to listen to your long story."

Omitting the part about the gold, Ned began with Slim and Rusty robbing Cole and Chief, taking their mule and trappings, and leaving them to die in Palo Duro Canyon.

Dorsey listened enraptured to the tale of the two boys escaping and following the trail first to Atascosa, then to Las Vegas, Mora and Cimarron.

"When I learned of their plight, Smokey and I took a stage to Las Vegas, followed their trail to Mora where we met my friend Billy Bonney who accompanied us to Cimarron. We arrived as the boys were preparing to take on the seven outlaws in a gun battle in the middle of the street."

Looking at Cole, he smiled and said, "I really don't think the boys needed our help, but we assisted them anyway."

"My hat is off to you, Cole, and to you Chief -- courage unmeasured!" and he raised his glass once again, saying, "Salute to the warriors!"

Pausing, he said, "Billy Bonney, you say -- *Billy the Kid?*

"Yes, sir. Kid worked for us for awhile on our ranch," Ned explained, "before he took the outlaw trail after his boss, Mr.

Tunstall was murdered in Lincoln County."

"Yes, I knew Mr. Tunstall and John Chisum well. Damned shame that things got out of hand -- seems to me that Bonney boy was just repaying that bunch of snakes for what they did to Tunstall."

Picking up a mahogany box filled with cigars, he Passed it around and they each took one. "So -- how is my friend, Colonel Goodnight?" he asked.

Ned looked surprised, "I didn't realize you and the Colonel were friends -- he's doing well -- in fact, he trailed a herd up to Dodge City only last week -- stopped by Ceebara and visited a spell on his way."

"Yes, I knew the Colonel when he was ranching in Pueblo, and I also have done business with his partner, John Adair, in Denver. You may not know, but the Goodnight Trail -- when he was delivering cattle to the army and miners in Colorado -- went across the *Una de Gato*, just east of my ranch house, then to Capulin peak. I look forward to paying a visit to his beautiful canyon some day."

Snapping his finger, Rosey reappeared, "Have Juanita set four more plates for my friends -- they are joining us for lunch."

"That's very kind of you, Senator -- but we really must be on our way."

"Nonsense -- you will not leave my home with an empty stomach. Besides, the meal is ready."

A beautiful lady came down the stairs and joined them. "Helen, I would like for you to meet Ned Armstrong, his son Cole, Chief Parker and Smokey Brown, from Texas. They will be sharing lunch with us. Men, this is my wife, Helen."

A tall cowboy came in a side door and Dorsey introduced him. "Ned, this is my foreman, Cody Hartman. Cody pretty well manages the cattle end of my business.

"We've met, Senator -- in Dodge City," Ned said.

Cody looked at them as if they were intruders, shook their hands and joined them as Helen led them into the dining room. They all took seats around the huge dining table, which was heaped with beef steaks, fresh bread and all kinds of fresh vegetables.

As they began to eat, the Senator once again spoke. "You mentioned Atascosa, Ned. You might be interested that the name has just been changed to Tascosa on the Post Office rolls -- Texas already had an Atascosa on the rolls, and when the citizens there applied for postal service, the name was changed to Tascosa."

"How did you know that," Ned asked.

Cutting his steak without looking up, Dorsey said, "Some of my friends and I have a contract with the Federal Postal System to deliver mail to all of the area west of Fort Smith to Santa Fe, north to Fort Dodge, and south to Fort Elliot and Tascosa. It's called the Star Route."

"That's very interesting, Senator. I knew that Hidetown had been changed to Mobeetie, but I didn't realize that Atascosa had been changed."

Cole and Chief were listening intently as they devoured their steaks. "You mean you deliver the mail all over that area," Cole asked.

Dorsey laughed, "Well, not personally. I have people hired to do the delivering, I just take care of the business end of it."

"Sounds like you have a lot of business, Senator. How big is your Triangle-Dot ranch," Cole asked.

"I don't rightly know, Cole. There are no fences, no survey has been made, but it covers an area about sixty miles square -- probably over a million acres of eastern Colfax County. I claim all the land from the Canadian River on the west to the Ute River on the east, and Capulin Mountain on the north to the town of Mosquero to the south."

Smiling, he looked at Cole, and added, "Some of my neighbors disagree with my boundaries."

"How many cattle you run," Cole asked.

Ned interrupted, "Now son, you're asking too many questions."

Dorsey laughed, "That's alright, Ned -- I'm glad he's interested. Last count we had twenty-nine thousand head."

"That's about the size of our spread," Cole said. "Grandpa Cole was given a million acre land grant by the Republic of Texas and we now have about twenty-five thousand head of grown cattle."

Dorsey stopped a forkful of food on the way to his mouth, looked at Cole and said, "That's interesting, Cole -- what's the name of your ranch?"

"Ceebara!" Cole replied proudly. "Our brand is C Bar A, after Grandpa Cole and Pa."

"Huh," Dorsey grunted, "A million acres and twenty-five thousand head. I didn't suppose there were ranches that large in the Panhandle."

"Yes, sir -- lots of them. There's the JA, LE, LX, Quarter Circle T and the Turkey Track -- all as large as Ceebara."

Cole had made his point, and the senator remained quiet as he finished his meal. Shaking his head, he mumbled, "A million acres," as he pushed back his chair and got up from the table.

Cole had one more question, "Senator Dorsey, how do you get all that water for the swimming pool and running water in the ranch house?"

Proudly, the Senator replied, "There's a large spring on top of the mesa, and we installed a pipe line to transport it here. Gravity develops pressure and keeps the water flowing year round."

"Ain't that something, Chief," Cole responded, placing another fork full of steak into his mouth.

"I 'spect we had better be going, Senator," Ned said as they finished the meal and walked outside. "I was hoping we would be able to make it to the Ute by nightfall."

Hartman, frowning, asked, "You're going east to the Ute? Best way to Tascosa would be south to the Canadian."

Ned couldn't understand why Hartman seemed to object to their heading east across the *Una de Gato*, but explained, "Closest route to Cccbara is north of Tascosa. We'll be taking that route which crosses the Ute north of Mosquero."

"You should be able to make it," Dorsey said, "no more than twenty miles."

"If you are ever in our part of the country, we'd be proud to have you pay us a visit," Ned said as he swung into the saddle.

Cole untied his mule and mounted his horse. "*Adios*, Senator Dorsey," he said, waving as they rode out of the Triangle - Dot compound and headed east.

Cody Hartman stood with hands laced behind his back and a frown upon his face as he watched them leave. As they disappeared around the mesa, he ran to the stable, called a Mexican cowboy and whispered something into his ear. The cowboy mounted a horse and followed the group at a safe distance.

....

Riding through several herds of longhorns after leaving the ranch house, Ned said, "Good looking cattle -- fat and slick. I 'spect this grass is good and stout."

"Yes, sir, Pa," that's what I was thinking. Almost as good as ours. In fact, I saw one old crooked horned steer in that last bunch that looked just like one that we worked last year."

Riding close to a cow with a young calf by her side, Cole shouted, "Pa, come look at this brand -- I swear it looks like a C Bar A under that Triangle - Dot."

Ned rode over, looked and said, "Danged if it don't. Let's throw a rope on her and examine it a little closer."

Cole released the mule, untied his rope and made a loop. "Come on Chief," he said, "You take the horns, I'll catch her feet."

The cow began to run and the two boys spurred their horses after her. Chief's lariat sailed through the air and fell softly around her horns. As he dallied his rope and circled, Cole let fly his lariat under her belly and snagged her rear feet, then pulled Comanche to a quick stop. Both ropes tightened and the cow fell to the grass. As they held her, Ned rode over, stepped off his horse and examined the brand.

"You're right, Son -- that Triangle - Dot is covering a C Bar A. Let her up and let's look at some of these other cattle.

Riding through the herd, Cole said, "that's an LE brand on that one!"

Chief shouted, "Here's an LX, Mister Ned."

"This one looks like an LS, Mister Ned," Smokey yelled.

Another C Bar A was spotted and Ned determined that all of

the cattle had been branded over with the Triangle - Dot brand.

"This wasn't a mistake, these cattle were rustled off of Panhandle ranches," Ned said. "Looks like this is where a lot of our missing cattle have been going."

"You mean Senator Dorsey has been stealing cattle," Cole asked.

"Looks like it, Son -- or maybe someone who works for him."

"What we going to do about it, Pa?" Cole asked as he recoiled his rope and tied it on his saddle horn.

"Nothing now," Ned said. "Soon as we get home, we'll call the other ranchers together and tell them what we've learned."

18

Rain clouds were building as they stopped and looked out over the wide, deep valley of the Ute. A thick sandstone formation formed a caprock and a steep cliff, several hundred feet thick, fell away to the flat prairie below.

They gazed in awe at the scene below, able to see for several miles across the New Mexico plain. Cattle grazing in the valley appeared as small ants. "Just like the caprock on the Llano Estacado," Chief said, as his eyes searched for a trail down.

Finally he pointed and said, "There, Mister Ned. I believe there is a break in the caprock where that large boulder has fallen. I'll check and see if a trail leads to the bottom." Spurring his horse, he disappeared around the boulder and was gone for several minutes. Reappearing, he waved, and they rode to where he was waiting.

"It's a pretty good trail. Looks like cattle have been using it to get to the creek below for water," he said.

By the time they had traversed the steep slope, rain had begun to fall. Stopping beneath a large overhang of the cliff, Ned said, "We'll make camp here. Gather some of that dry cedar and we'll start a fire."

The boys soon had a fire going and had caught enough

rain water to make coffee. Smokey pulled a slab of bacon and some canned beans from the pack saddle bags and began cooking. After the huge meal at the Dorsey ranch, no one was really very hungry.

Lightning flashed, thunder rolled and water gushed from the rocks above as they watched the rain swollen stream rush by. They had chosen a good place for camp and were able to keep warm and dry beneath the overhanging rocks. It was plain that other travelers had used the place at other times. Old ashes gave evidence of recent use -- some painted pottery chards spoke of cultures long gone from the area. The rock wall in the back held petroglyphs of running buffalo, bounding deer, and stick men with bows strung with arrows.

Sitting around the fire, they discussed their days adventures and the apparent stolen cattle. "I can't believe that the senator would have anything to do with rustling cattle," Ned said.

"Me neither," Cole responded, "Remember he said that Cody took care of the cattle business. Seems like he's got so many businesses going that he wouldn't have time to run a ranch."

"Maybe his best business is cattle rustling," Chief said, smiling.

"You wasn't too impressed with the senator, was you Chief?" Cole asked.

Shaking his head, Chief replied, "Maybe he likes himself too much."

Ned laughed and scratched his chin as he thought about the article in the newspaper, "I wonder why that newspaper article called him a thief -- I guess he could be behind the rustling. Well, we're not going to find the answer tonight. Let's see if we can't get some rest."

They rolled out their blankets and were soon asleep, dreaming about gold, gun battles and rustled cattle.

....

By morning, the heavy rain had ended but a slight mist was falling. The valley was shrouded in fog as they saddled their horses, put on their slickers and rode southeasterly down the wide valley, paralleling Ute Creek. Soon, they struck a well used wagon trail which bore more easterly, away from the creek.

Stopping, Ned pondered whether they should follow the wagon tracks or keep to the creek.

"When I was with the cavalry stationed at Fort Bascom, we used to patrol this area, Mr. Ned," Smokey said. "I remember this trail goes to Amistad Plaza which is only about ten miles from the Texas border."

"Good -- how far you figure from here to Amistad?"

"Hard days ride," Smokey answered.

"Lead out, Smokey -- we'll follow along behind," Ned said.

Riding steady without stopping for lunch, they rode into the small adobe village an hour after sunset. The town dogs welcomed them with their yapping and barking, and faces appeared in the doorways to see who was passing by.

A dim light shone from a small building which had a crude sign over the door reading *Cantina*. Two horses were tied to the hitching rail, standing three legged with heads drooped, swishing deer flies with their tails. Ned and the boys stepped down, stretched and tied their horses to the rail.

"I'm plumb tuckered out, Pa," Cole said as he removed his hat and began knocking some of the dust from his clothes.

"Maybe we can get a hot meal here and a sarsaparillas."

"Pa, you know we don't drink sarsaparillas any more -- we're beer men."

Ned laughed as he opened the door and walked in, "You tell that to your ma."

"You folks go ahead and eat," Smokey said. "I best stay out here and keep an eye on that mule."

"Alright, Smokey -- we'll order something for you."

The two men eyed them warily as they stepped to the bar and ordered beer. "We'd like something to eat, also," Cole said.

"Si, senor -- I have eggs and antelope steaks."

"Four orders, three eggs each," Cole said, taking a drink of the beer.

The two men were talking so low that Cole could only catch a word now and again. He did hear *'Triangle - Dot'* and *'Hartman'* and *'not particular'*.

When the two men left, he told Ned what he had heard. "What you make of it, Pa?" he asked.

"Well, sounds like Hartman may be buying stolen cattle from men like those two.. Probably puts a triangle dot brand on them, runs them on Triangle Dot range until the hair grows over, then trails them to Dodge City and sells them. The senator may not even know what is going on."

Chief was not convinced. A man of few words, frowning, he said, "He knows."

....

Three days later, they rode into the Ceebara compound, stopped at the barn and began removing their saddles. Belle and Kate rushed from the house and gave them all a big hug.

"We're so glad to see you -- we just about gave you up for dead," Belle said.

19

"Pa, can you keep our gold safe for us until we determine what we want to do with it," Cole asked.

"Sure, son -- I'll keep it in my office safe. As soon as we decide what to do about Senator Dorsey and our missing cattle, we will take a ride to Mobeetie and talk to Temple about his help in filing on some of that New Mexico grass."

Cole and Chief carried the gold inside and watched as Ned opened the large safe in his office and placed the gold inside. "Now I will have enough to pay my cowboys for a couple of years," he joked.

Seriously, Cole said, "No, sir, Pa. That gold is going to help start a ranch for me and Chief."

....

The sound of wagons approaching the ranch house caused a frenzy of activity. Ned closed the safe and locked it as Cole and Chief ran to the front door to see who it might be.

Riding his big blue roan gelding, Colonel Goodnight stopped and stiffly dismounted. "Howdy Cole," he said. "Is your pa around?"

"Yes, sir," Cole replied, then yelled, "Mr. Goodnight is here,

Pa."

Ned stepped from the door with hand outstretched, "Howdy, Colonel, this is certainly a surprise," he said as he took Colonel Goodnight's hand.

"On our way back to the JA from Dodge City, Ned." Motioning with his hand to the lead wagon, being pulled by a span of four young mules, he added, "Brought that wagon you asked me to buy for you, and a load of supplies. I hope you like the mules."

"I'd be a fool if I didn't, Colonel. Fine looking set. I'm much obliged to you."

Slim and Smokey walked up from the barn, "Slim, see to these wagons and teams and have Biscuit feed the Colonel's crew. make room in the bunk house, they'll be spending the night with us. Come on in Colonel, you'll be joining us for supper."

"Colonel, there's soap and water and towels on the back porch if you want to wash up," Kate said as she led the way through the house.

After eating, they all congregated in the parlor and Belle passed out cigars. The room began to fill with smoke as Ned asked, "How's the cattle price holding up, Colonel?"

"A little better than last year, Ned. Vince told me that there were not as many herds in yet, so I 'spect that helped a mite. My herd fetched nine cents and weighed in at a thousand fifty -- can't complain," Goodnight replied as he took a drag on the cigar. Looking at Belle, he added, holding out the cigar, "I must confess, Miss Belle, there's nothing I enjoy more than a good cigar after a good meal -- and you have blessed me with both. How was your visit with my Mary?"

"Wonderful, Colonel! We had a great time, visiting and relaxing. She took us on a tour of your beautiful canyon and showed off that bunch of short horn bulls you brought in from Colorado. I think Ned should be thinking about putting some more with our cattle. We could have stayed longer if Cole and Chief hadn't had their problem."

"What kind of problem did you have, Cole," the Colonel asked.

Cole looked at Ned -- Ned nodded, and Cole said, "Well, sir -- me and Chief went looking for that sheepman's gold and found it."

With a look of surprise on his face, Colonel Goodnight exclaimed, "You found it! -- you found the gold?"

"Yes, sir -- and then we lost it," Cole said and began to tell of their adventure. When he had finished, the Colonel shook his head in disbelief, "The two of you took on seven of the meanest men in the west. I'm damned proud of you Cole. Sounds to me like you earned every bit of that twenty-five thousand dollars."

"Well, sir," Cole replied, "I guess it was a mite foolhardy, but we thought there was only five of them. I guess it would have been a different story if Pa, Smokey and Kid hadn't showed up."

The Colonel laughed, "Only five, huh? I guess that would have evened up the odds."

"Miss Molly said if we found it we could keep it. Is that alright with you?"

"*Finder's -- keepers*, is what they say. Yes, it's yours to keep, Cole, with my blessings. Maybe my cowboys will stop digging up my grass and go back to work building fences," the Colonel replied, smiling.

Ned interrupted, "We came back through Dorsey's spread,

Colonel, had lunch with him at his Triangle - Dot ranch house and then headed south and east until we hit the Ute."

Goodnight interrupted, "The Dorsey spread -- how was that old sonovab-- 'scuse me Miss Belle -- sonuvagun? Still as ornery as ever?"

Ned laughed, "I guess you could say that -- he seemed to be pretty proud of himself -- bragging about all of his businesses. I'll say one thing for him, he has one of the finest ranch houses this side of Saint Looie. What we found most interesting though, was his herd."

"Pretty big, was it," the Colonel commented.

Ned took a puff, blew the smoke, and replied, "Wasn't so much the size as it was the brands. It's hard to believe, Colonel, but most of the cattle we saw west of the Ute were wearing doctored brands."

"What do you mean, doctored?"

"We noticed it looked like that Triangle -- Dot was covering some old brands. I had the boys rope one of the steers where we could examine it better, and damned if it didn't have a C Bar A brand under that Triangle. I ain't never sold any of my cattle to Dorsey. There were thousands of head grazing that area, and everyone we passed looked as if a running iron had been used, covering LE, LX, JA, Turkey Track, and C Bar A brands. Colonel, looks like we located most of those ten thousand head that were missing during our roundup last spring."

"The hell you say! I can't believe the Senator would steal."

"Maybe he did and maybe he didn't, Colonel. His ranch is so large and he is so busy, he probably never sees half the cattle that are on his range. Maybe his foreman or some of his cowboys have a business going on the side."

"Why would they stick the Triangle brand on them if the Senator wasn't involved," Goodnight asked.

"Maybe to legitimize them. With Dorsey running thirty thousand head on a couple million acres, it would be easy to keep another ten thousand head isolated in the canyons of the Ute and Canadian. Then after the hair is growed over, they could trail them to Dodge City, sell them in the Senator's name and pocket the money."

"That makes sense, Ned. What do you think we can do about it?"

"Well, sir -- we don't need to go off half-cocked and get a range war started with the Triangle Dot crowd. You remember last year you suggested we form an organization of Panhandle ranchers and hire our own rangers to try to catch some of the thieves -- seems to me we need to get Temple to draw up some legal papers, by-laws and everything, so we can deputize some of our cowboys, and ride over to New Mexico and round up our cattle."

"I 'spect you're right, Ned. Then if anyone objects, we can hang them legal," Goodnight replied. "Let's call a meeting of Panhandle ranchers in Mobeetie for two weeks from today. I'll get my trappings home, and inform all the ranchers around the Palo Duro, you get the ones along the Canadian notified."

"Alright, Colonel," Ned replied, "in the meantime I'll contact Temple and have him draw up some papers."

....

The meeting was held in a back room of the Lady Gay saloon, Temple Houston presiding. Besides Goodnight and Ned, there was Bill Lee of the LS, George Littlefield of the LIT, Alfred Rowe of the RO, Deacon Bates of the LX, Hank Cresswell of the

Bar CC, Tom Bugbee of the Quarter Circle T, McAnulty of the Turkey Track, Henry Campbell of the Matador, and Preacher Carhart of the Quarter Circle Heart.

"Gentlemen," Temple said, "and I use that term loosely.'

They all laughed, then Temple continued, "Before we get down to the business of incorporating an organization, I think you should listen to what Ned has to say. "

Ned took the floor and proceeded to relate the story of his discovery of Panhandle cattle on the Triangle Dot range.

"How many you suppose there are," Tom asked.

"I'm going to say several thousand, Tom. We saw a lot of cattle and the majority of them had doctored brands. Roughly, I'd say there could be as many as ten thousand head."

Mouths fell open in astonishment around the table. Major Littlefield spoke, "What are we waiting for? Let's get our cowboys together and go get 'em."

"Now wait a minute, Major," Temple said, "You need to do this legal -- there may be shooting and there may be people killed."

"Damned right there'll be people killed, if we find out who's behind this," Bill Lee said.

Temple continued, "Upon Ned's request, I have drawn up a very simple plan of organization so that any action taken will be legal -- basically, you will have a president, secretary and treasurer. Each of you will be a member of the board of directors, and you will have the authority to hire rangers to patrol and police your ranges until such time that enough counties are organized to elect law enforcement personnel. And you will have authority to take legal action against anyone caught rustling your livestock.

"It's going to require operating capital to run your organization. Seems to me the best way is to levy per head taxes on your cattle to finance the organization. Any objection?"

"How much?" Deacon asked.

"I'm thinking ten cents a head in the beginning -- probably less after the first year," Temple replied. "Is there any other duties that you would like for the organization to perform?"

"Once we hire rangers and appoint a Captain, will he have authority to deputize other people if need be?" Hank asked.

"I don't see any reason why not," Temple said. "The situation you face in recovering this herd over in New Mexico is going to require every cowboy you can spare to round them up and get them home. They will probably have a fight on their hands, and when they start shooting, they need to have some legal authority supporting their actions."

"I say let's sign the papers and get started before those cattle end up in Dodge City," McAnulty said.

"I make a motion we appoint Ned as temporary Ranger Captain, and decide when we're going. That alright with you, Ned?" Tom asked.

"If it's temporary," Ned replied. "But like Temple says, let's make it legal -- I don't care about getting hung for doing something that's illegal," then added, "Colonel Goodnight knows that area well. Colonel, you got anything you want to say?"

Goodnight nodded, "Back in '67, I blazed a trail across that area -- started at Fort Sumner with five thousand head and headed due north -- crossed the Canadian just north of Tucumcari Peak, then followed the Ute north to just east of Mosquero. If you've never been there, you'll be surprised at how steep that cliff is, getting out of the valley of the Ute to the plains on top -- maybe seven or eight hundred feet high, almost as bad as getting out of the Palo Duro."

He paused for a moment, thinking. "We located a narrow trail up the cliff just out of Mosquero plaza and moved the cattle to the top. That country from there all the way to the Rabbit Ears is pretty much like our country here -- flat with a few creeks, not many trees.

"I think we should head north out of Tascosa, swing over just west of the Rabbit Ears, spread out and start our drive south. That way we can keep east of Dorsey's headquarters and maybe prevent a fight. We can hold the herd at Mosquero, cut out our brands, take them down the cut in the cap to the floor of the Ute, then back to Tascosa."

They nodded in agreement. McAnulty suggested that Colonel Goodnight draw up some rough maps for each crew to follow.

The discussion swung back and forth but Temple soon had a document drawn up and everyone signed it. A date was set to gather in Tascosa in seven days, with each ranch bringing a chuck wagon and twenty or more armed cowboys.

....

Nearly two hundred cowboys invaded Tascosa the day before departure date and the town saloons and the painted ladies were kept busy throughout the night.

Ned passed out slips of paper to each of them the next morning, which stated that they had been deputized as members of the Panhandle Livestock Association posse which would be pursuing cattle rustlers into New Mexico Territory.

....

Following the Rita Blanca out of Tascosa, the huge caravan moved north across the unsettled area of the western Texas Panhandle. Crossing over into New Mexico Territory just south of the small village of Clayton, they spread out and started their drive south, remaining east of the Capulin volcano.

Colonel Goodnight, riding his blue roan, continued to ride back and forth along the line, keeping the crews scattered across the plains,

Ned took his Ceebara crew to the western edge of the drive, keeping a sharp eye out for any of the Triangle Dot cowboys that might be working the eastern edge of the ranch. Not until the third day of the drive did he spot any strange riders. Two Mexican cowboys approached his chuck wagon and looked suspiciously at the herd they had gathered.

"*Buenos dias*," Ned greeted as they rode up.

"*Buenos dias*," they replied. "What are you doing with *Una de Gato* cattle," they asked, angrily.

In reply, Ned motioned to Cole and Chief and said, "Catch that spotted steer."

Cole spurred Comanche as he removed his lariat, threw it over his head and caught the steer by the horns. Immediately, Chiefs rope landed below the steers belly and snagged the two hind feet. The steer fell as the ropes tightened.

Motioning to the two Mexican cowboys, Ned dismounted and pointed to the brand. They dismounted and approached the prostrate steer as Ned began to smooth the hair around the Triangle Dot brand. A blurred LX was covered with the new brand.

"These are our cattle," he said. "Thieves have stolen them and changed the brand. We are taking them back to Texas where they belong."

"No, senor," one of the Mexicans said," this is Senor Dorsey's cattle. You must leave them here."

Ned placed his hand on the butt of his pistol and replied, "We do not wish for trouble, but we are going to gather our cattle out of your herd and drive them back to Texas. You tell your *patron* that we do not intend to take *Una de Gato* cattle, only those which belong to us."

"I will tell Senor Hartman, our *patron*, and he is going to be very angry," the young Mexican said as he spurred his horse and headed west.

Cole and Chief released the steer and Ned instructed, "Tell all the hands to keep a sharp eye out and send a rider to inform the other team. We're probably going to have trouble."

20

Ned continued to push his herd to the south, gathering cattle as they went. The next day, he saw a lone rider approaching from the east, riding a large blue roan gelding.

"Howdy, Colonel," he greeted as Goodnight pulled his horse to a stop.

"Howdy, Ned -- I heard you had a little trouble with some of Dorsey's riders."

"No trouble, Colonel -- two riders -- I showed them the doctored brands and they said they were going to tell that Hartman feller that we are stealing his cattle. I 'spect we'll be having trouble before we get the herd over the line into Texas."

Goodnight spit a brown stream at a lizard, then said, "I 'spect so, Ned. The other herds are pretty well in line with yours and we should reach Mosquero tomorrow. Maybe we will get all the herds together before Hartman catches up to us."

"I hope so, Colonel, I'd hate to take on his entire crew with just twenty cowboys," Ned said, removing his hat and wiping the dust and sweat from his brow.

"I'll ride back down the line and send five men from each

crew over to join you, just in case he does try to stop you before you reach Mosquero," Goodnight said as he spurred his horse and headed east.

Several cowboys from the other crews joined the Ceebara crew before nightfall. A dry camp was made at dusk, night riders were dispatched and the herd was bedded down. Ned increased his guards, preparing for any trouble that might develop during the night.

Morning arrived with still no sign of the Triangle Dot bunch. A hasty breakfast was eaten and the herd once again was put on the trail toward Mosquero.

In the distance to the east, dust from the other herds could be seen, all bearing toward the common point of Mosquero. Ned's herd was the first to arrive, and he stopped them about a mile outside the small adobe village. All day long, other herds arrived and by nightfall, the last crew came in.

"How many you suppose we've got, Colonel?" Ned asked Goodnight.

"Roughly, I'd say eight thousand head, more or less," the Colonel replied. "I've asked the other owners to join us at your wagon, Ned, to plan any action we may need to take in case we are attacked."

"Sounds good, Colonel. How far to that cut in the cliff where we can get the cattle down into the valley of the Ute?"

"No more than five miles, but it will take quite awhile to push these cattle down. The trail is not very wide."

....

The meeting was held around the Ceebara chuck wagon, the men's grim faces reflecting the light of the campfire. Each man held a cup of Biscuit's coffee as Ned explained his plans.

"We need to make a skirmish line with half of our men remaining on the west side of the herd, in case we are attacked. The cattle will be taken down the cliff's face first. We'll keep the chuck wagon's on top -- they'll make good protection if we do get into a gun battle. If we are attacked before we get the herd down, all cowboys will form a line behind the chuck wagons, between the herd and the Triangle Dot boys. I will try to negotiate with Hartman or Dorsey, so remember, no firing until they fire first, then shoot to kill."

"Ned, I've got an old spotted steer in my herd that will follow my horse anywhere I go. Why don't we let him lead the herd down the cliff," Tom said.

"Alright, Tom, you see to it," Ned replied.

....

The next morning the herd was pushed to the cliff's edge and Tom led the spotted steer down the trail. Chief and Cole took positions on each side of the cut and kept the cattle moving down the trail. The rest of the herd began the descent, single file, while the cowboys formed a ring around the herd and continued to crowd them into the narrow opening. By noon, nearly half of the herd had reached bottom and were spreading out, grazing on the lush grass along the stream's edge.

Then it happened! A cloud of dust was spotted to the west, and a large group of riders materialized out of the dust. Ned, carrying a white flag, rode out to meet them. The other owners, flanked by fifty cowboys, lined up between the herd and the approaching riders.

When the riders spotted the skirmish line, with rifles glistening in the sunlight, they stopped. Cody Hartman rode out to meet Ned.

"What the hell do you think you're doing, Armstrong?" he asked.

"Seems like some of our cattle strayed and got mixed with yours," Ned responded. "We know you don't want them eating your grass, so we're taking them home."

"Like hell, you will -- those cattle are Triangle Dot cattle," Cody said.

"Why don't you send Senator Dorsey to talk to me -- I'm sure he wouldn't want our cattle eating his grass," Ned said, smiling.

"I make the decisions on this ranch, Armstrong. I don't have to ask the Senator about anything," Cody answered.

Ned removed a plug of chewing tobacco and a pocket knife from his chaps, opened the knife and cut a piece, placing it in his mouth. He offered the tobacco to Cody, who shook his head no. Ned chewed for a moment, spit, and said, "Come to think of it, I did notice a Triangle Dot covering most of my brands."

Pausing he said, "Across the border in Texas we've got a couple of laws, punishable by hanging -- the first is against any- one caught molesting a woman -- the second is against anyone caught stealing someone's cows. Now I don't know if you're guilty of the first but it is damned certain you're guilty of the second."

Cody's face turned red with anger, his hand moved ever so slightly toward the pistol on his hip, and he said, "You go to hell, Armstrong!"

Ned watched Cody's eyes closely, waiting for that blink which would indicate a decision to draw. "By the way," he said, "I'm certain you've heard of Bill Lee of the LS, George Littlefield of the LIT, Deacon Bates of the LX, Tom Bugbee of the Quarter

Circle T, Bob McAnulty of the Turkey Track, and Colonel Charles Goodnight of the JA. They are all lined up back there with a couple hundred of their men, and madder than hell. Seems they found a lot of their cattle with Triangle Dots covering their brands. They are frothing at the mouth and determined to hang whoever put a running iron on their cattle. Now, my advice to you is to go back and tell Senator Dorsey that some cattle mistakenly got branded with the Triangle Dot , and you gave us permission to cut them out and take them home."

Nervously, Cody said, "I don't have to tell the Senator a damned thing -- you go back and get your men and get off this ranch and don't try to take any of my cattle with you. If you're not moving out in thirty minutes, we are going to start throwing lead in your direction," Cody warned.

"So they're your cattle now, are they -- I'm betting the Senator doesn't know a blessed thing about your little sideline business," Ned said.

"Thirty minutes, Armstrong," Cody said angrily as he turned his horse and kicked it into a run back toward his men.

Ned loped back to his line of men and said, "Looks like we're in for a battle. Move back behind the chuck wagons and start shooting if they attack.

They dismounted and took positions under and behind the protection of the chuck wagons. After thirty minutes had passed, the Triangle Dot cowboys formed a skirmish line and rode pell mell in their direction, firing as they came.

Ned's men waited until they were in range and opened up, throwing a barrage of lead into their ranks. Several cowboys were knocked from their horses and the line broke, with most of those who had not been hit, turning and rushing back toward Mosquero.

The cattle, excited by the gunshots, began to circle, threatening to bolt. Colonel Goodnight shouted at the cowboys around the chuck wagons to mount up and help hold the herd. The cattle were soon brought under control and the exodus down the cliff's face continued.

An hour passed before the Triangle Dot crew returned. This time they attacked from the north end of the herd, bypassing the chuck wagons. The Texas cowboys met their charge once again with guns blazing, but the cattle stampeded and they were forced to give ground.

As the Triangle Dot cowboys rushed into the midst of the herd, firing their guns, the cattle broke into a thunderous run toward the cliff's edge. Frightened and blinded by the dust, they crashed over the cliff's edge and fell by the hundreds to the bottom, five hundred feet below.

The Texas cowboys reformed and placed a withering fire into the midst of the Triangle Dot crew, who turned and once again headed for Mosquero. leaving twenty of their men lying dead in the grass.

Ned watched as they disappeared to the west, this time not stopping in Mosquero. "Looks like they've had enough, let's see if we can get the herd back together and start them back down the trail."

Once the cattle were all to the bottom and the chuck wagons had been brought down, Cole and Chief rode to the spot where the cattle had fallen from the cliff. Several hundred head were piled dead where they had fallen. Surprisingly, a few were still alive but crippled. The boys pulled their pistols and shot the injured, putting them out of their misery.

Riding back to Ned's side, Cole reported, "Looks like there might have been six or seven hundred head, maybe more, that went over the cliff, Pa."

"Thanks, Son -- I guess we're lucky we didn't loose more than that. Let's get the herd moving, we're burning daylight here."

Camp was made three hours later on the banks of the Ute River, the chuck wagons were circled and all the men joined together for the evening meal. Everyone was excited and happy that not a one of the Texas boys had been killed, although eight were carrying slight wounds.

They sat around the campfire until late night, discussing and laughing about the days adventure.

....

For two days, they slowly drove the huge herd along the Ute River until reaching its' confluence with the Canadian. After resting for a day, allowing the cattle to graze and the men to clean up in the water of the Canadian, they continued their journey east, down the Tascosa -- Las Vegas stagecoach road. Reaching Tascosa three days later, they stopped at Bill Lee's LS ranch headquarters on the Alamocita Creek and made preparations for checking brands and separating the cattle.

Mr. Mac, Lee's foreman, took charge and soon had the herd situated in a small valley, west of the headquarters pens. Lee's corrals were large, but not large enough to hold the entire herd. Cowboys held the majority of the herd west of the corrals and brought in a few at a time, ran them through a chute, examined the brand closely, then cut them into separate pens.

For two days they examined brands, tallying a total of seven thousand five hundred ninety head. Most of the cattle came from ranches nearest the New Mexico line. The LS tallied fifteen hundred thirty head -- the LE, eleven hundred seventy -- the LIT, eleven hundred forty -- the LX, eleven hundred sixty -- the Ceebara, nine hundred twenty -- the Half Circle T, eight hundred -- the JA, one hundred fifty -- the Bar CC, one hundred -- and the Quarter Circle Heart, one hundred twenty.

The chuck wagons pulled out, each trailing their cattle behind as they headed for individual ranch headquarters. After three days, the Ceebara crew hit the west line of the ranch and released their herd along the Canadian River.

Belle, Kate and Maria were waiting anxiously as the chuck wagon pulled into the ranch compound and stopped next to the barn.

Kate rushed to Ned, threw her arms around his neck and said, "We were afraid you had run into trouble."

"We did Kate, but let's go to the house -- I need a drink and a good meal while we tell you about it," Ned replied.

Hugging Belle, Cole, beaming with excitement, said, "You ain't going to believe all that's happened to us since we left, Grandma."

****

Author's note: The incident at Mosquero is, of course, fictional. However, it is a matter of record that several noted outlaws such as Dutch Henry, Billy the Kid, and John Sellman were stealing cattle, trailing them into New Mexico Territory, holding them until the hair grew over the old brands, then trailing them to Las Vegas or Dodge City and selling them. Even LX ranch foreman, Outlaw Bill Moore, was rustling cattle, taking them across the border into New Mexico and holding them on grass around the Rabbit ears, possibly on Triangle Dot range.

21

Cody Hartman was steaming. The rustled herd he had been putting together for the past two years was gone. His plans to start a ranch of his own in Montana were gone with the herd. And he had lost a lot of his Mexican cowboys in the shoot out at Mosquero.

The Senator was still away in Washington, D.C., and he knew that when he returned he would learn of the doctored brands and the battle with the Texas ranchers. He didn't plan on waiting around and trying to explain how the stolen Texas cattle had been discovered on Triangle Dot range, with Triangle Dot brands.

True, he had purchased most of the herd from itinerant cowboys who had stolen small herds of the cattle, slipped them across the New Mexico line and sold them to him for only a few dollars a head, which they blew on whiskey and women in Tascosa.

But it was he and and his men who had blotched the brands and placed the Triangle Dot on them. He had taken special precaution to see that they remained on the east side of the huge *Una de Gato* land grant, and away from the eyes of his boss, Senator Dorsey. Some of them he had trailed to Dodge City and sold and deposited the sales receipts in a special account in the Dodge City Bank, making it appear that it was a joint account with the senator.

He was as guilty as sin of cattle rustling and knew that if he was caught, a cottonwood limb was reserved for his necktie party. But before leaving the country, he intended to repay Ned Armstrong for his interference, and then head for California.

Calling four of his men together, he laid out his plans. "I've got about a hundred thousand dollars stashed in that bank account in Dodge City. First thing we're going to do is pick it up, then we're going to Mobeetie and make Armstrong pay for what he did to my plans. He sells four or five thousand head a year and I'm betting that most of the cash from the sales is stashed at his headquarters in the Texas Panhandle. I'm going to get that money, and place a forty-five slug right between his eyes."

Pete, his foreman, rolling a cigarette, looked up surprised, "Hell's bells, Cody -- you saw what those Texans did to our boys at Mosquero, I don't hanker to have another run in with them."

"We don't have to have a run in with them if we play it right. I've got a plan where we can get his money without him ever knowing," the Triangle Dot manager said.

"How you plan on doing it, boss," Little Joe asked.

Cody smiled, "Fire will solve a lot of problems," he answered. "You boys git your stuff together and load a couple of pack mules. We're getting out of here and heading for Dodge City in the morning."

....

Riding hard for four days, they reached Dodge City and splashed across the Arkansas River. Riding down the Santa Fe Trail Street, they stopped in front of the Lady Gay saloon, dismounted stiffly, tied their horses and mules to the hitching rail, knocked some of the dust off their clothes with their hats and stepped inside.

Sheriff Bat Masterson and Billy Dixon were playing cards with three more men when they bellied up to the bar and ordered whiskey. Cody glanced nervously at Bat, wondering if the news of the gun battle at Mosquero had reached the ears of the sheriff.

He relaxed when Bat smiled and said, "Well howdy, Cody. Bring in another herd already?"

"No, sheriff -- me and the boys needed to pick up some supplies before winter sets in. Not much going on at the ranch, so I figured now was as good a time as any to get it done. Besides, I had a hankering to see Lillian one more time."

"Well, be glad to have you set in for a few hands. Me and Billy just about won all of the loose change that's floating around Dodge," Bat replied.

"Not right now, sheriff. Me and the boys need to get a room and clean up some. Maybe later," Cody said, relieved.

Afraid that someone would show up with news about the gun battle, Cody was anxious to put Dodge City behind him. They took a room at the Dodge House, bathed and walked down the street to the Alhambra.

"You boys take your pleasures tonight and meet me in the morning at Kelly's restaurant," he said, and added, "Keep your mouths shut."

The Alhambra always had a covey of the prettiest girls in

Dodge City, and Cody intended to have one more night on the town before leaving for Hidetown. Lillian Handie, Cody's favorite. met him at the door and ushered him to a table in the corner. After a few drinks, she and Cody disappeared to a back room, and remained for the balance of the night.

The following morning, after withdrawing the money from his bank account, they headed south down the Jones-Plummer trail toward Mobeetie.

....

Sheriff Masterson was working on his records in the jail when Vince Abercrombie walked in. "Morning Bat," he said as he stepped to the stove where a pot of coffee was boiling. Pouring himself a cup, he sat down.

"Howdy, Vince," Bat replied. Smiling he said, "Why don't you have a cup of coffee?"

Taking a sip, Vince responded, "Knew you wouldn't mind, Sheriff."

"What can I do for you," Bat asked.

"I thought you might be interested in some information I learned," the cattle buyer said.

"Always interested in information, as long as it don't cost anything."

Vince set his cup down and removed a black cigar from his vest pocket, passed it under his nose and sniffed. "You know Cody Hartman from the Triangle Dot?"

Bat nodded as he put down his pencil. "Yeah, I saw him last night. Said he was in town to pick up some supplies."

Vince stuck the cigar in his mouth and pulled a match from his pocket, and lit it. Blowing a plume of smoke, he said, "I just saw him over at the bank. Said he spent the night with Lillian

Handie."

Bat laughed, "I guess he looked like he'd been rode hard and put up wet."

Vince smiled and nodded, then said, "Strange thing, he withdrew over a hundred thousand dollars from the Senator's bank account."

Bat whistled. "How could he do that?"

"It's a joint account -- his name is on it with the Senator's. He seemed to be pretty nervous."

"A night with Lillian shouldn't make him nervous. Well, if his name is on the account, I guess he can do anything he wants to with it."

Vince blew another plume of smoke, "I know -- but something's got me puzzled. Fringer says that Hartman set up the account a couple of years ago and he is the only person to ever draw any funds from it."

"And you think there is something crooked going on?'

Vince thought for a moment before replying. "You remember that herd that I bought from Ned back in the summer."

Bat nodded.

"Me and Ned was visiting down by the stock pens when Cody shows up with a herd of Triangle Dot steers -- about a thousand head. Ned commented about the brands being sloppy, and I must admit they were. Looked like they had been made with a running iron. I tried to buy them but the Kansas City Packers outbid me. I didn't think much about it then, but looking back on it, that Triangle Dot brand could have been made over other brands.

"You saying the Senator is guilty of stealing cattle?"

"No -- but Cody might be."

Getting up from his desk, Bat said, "Maybe I better have a talk with him," as he took his gun belt from the peg and fastened it around his waist.

"May be hard to do -- I watched him and four of his men ride out of town, trailing a couple of pack mules a couple of hours ago."

"Well, I guess it ain't any of my business," Bat said. "Next time he shows up with a herd, give me a holler. We'll do a little brand inspecting."

....

The following morning a couple of cowboys rode in from Tascosa, tied their horses at the Lady Gay hitching rail and stepped inside. Sheriff Masterson and Billy Dixon were already at their table, playing two handed, waiting for someone to join them. The two cowboys carried their drinks to the table and sat down.

"Howdy, Sheriff -- mind if we set in?" the larger of the two asked.

"As long as you got the money. I need to warn you though, me and Billy are pretty lucky."

"Couldn't be more lucky than us. We was in on that big gun battle with the Triangle Dot cowboys and didn't get a scratch," the smaller one said.

"What gun battle was that?" Bat asked, looking surprised.

"You mean you ain't heard. Hell of a battle. Seems like that Triangle Dot bunch got caught stealing about ten thousand head of cattle from the ranches around Tascosa, and the ranchers found out about it. They took about two hundred of their hands over to New Mexico Territory to recover their cattle and that Triangle Dot bunch come at us with guns blazing. Several of them were killed, but we run 'em off without a one of us getting shot. Pretty lucky, I'd say."

"Was Ned Armstrong involved?" Bat asked.

"Yes, sir -- he and Colonel Goodnight was kinda head of the ranchers. We choused the cattle back over the line into Texas, separated them and drove them back to the proper ranches. Me and Shorty drew up our pay from the LS five days ago and struck out for Dodge," the big one said. "We felt like we needed a little rest and relaxation after that."

Getting up, Bat said, "Let's take a walk, Billy."

Leaving the Lady Gay, they walked across the railroad tracks to Front Street and entered the Alhambra Saloon. Lillian was talking to a cowboy at the bar.

Motioning to her, Bat set down at a table in the corner. "Buy you a drink?" he asked.

Lillian smiled and shook her head no, "Too early, Sheriff -- what's on your mind? I've got my permit paid up."

"Just some information, Lillian. I understand you spent the night with Cody Hartman a couple of days ago."

Lillian sat down, "Maybe -- what's it to you?"

"Did he say where he was going when he left town?"

"Matter of fact, he did. He was mad as hell and said he was going to Hidetown and kill Ned Armstrong. He'd been drinking pretty heavy, so I didn't think too much about it."

"Did he say anything about a gun battle they had over on the Triangle Dot?"

"No -- we had more important things to do," she replied, smiling.

Bat left a silver dollar on the table for her and he and Billy left.

Back at the jail, they discussed the news and what it could mean. "If he's heading for Ceebara, he could gun down Ned without anyone knowing he's even in the country," Billy said.

"Yeah, but I don't know what we can do about it, we could never catch him, he's got a days head start on us."

"We could take the stage -- they advertise forty hours from here to Mobeetie."

"That's right," Bat said. "Trailing a couple of pack mules, it will take them at least five days. We could get to Mobeetie, rent a couple of horses and make it to Ceebara before they arrive."

"The stage will be leaving in less than an hour. We better hurry if we want to be on it," Billy said.

....

Forty hours later, the stage pulled up to Mark Huselby's hotel in Mobeetie and Bat and Billy stepped down and hurried inside.

"Well, howdy, Bat -- Billy, I ain't seen either of you in a coon's age," Mark said as he stuck out his hand in greeting. "What you doing in Mobeetie? The buffler hereabouts have all been killed."

They shook hands and Bat told him about their suspicions. "Take my horses," Mark said, "They're tied out front. Me and the Missus were fixing to take a ride down to the creek. Reckon I need to put together a posses and follow you?"

"No need, Mark -- there's just five of them. We'll tell Ned and be ready when they get there," Bat said.

....

Cody and his gang, hidden from view, were looking down from the top of the cliff above the Ceebara ranch house. The sun was an hour from setting and several of the ranch crew were tending to chores. Ned, Cole and Chief were walking from the barn to the house. A strong wind was blowing, kicking up dust in the ranch yard.

Looking through his binoculars, Cody said, "There the sonuvabitch is. He don't know it but he's fixing to pay dearly for what he did to me. Little Joe, you get that can of coal oil out of the pack saddle and one of those saddle blankets. Ride about three miles west of the ridge, tie the blanket to your catch rope, soak it with coal oil, light it and drag it across the prairie. Soon as you get the grass to burning, high tail it back here.

"Pete, we'll slip down behind the corrals. Soon as we see the smoke, I'll yell, fire! When everyone leaves to fight the fire, we'll go inside and find my money.

....

The Ceebara family was sitting around the supper table when Kate broached the subject of the gold. "Well," she said, "now that you boys are rich, what you going to do with all that gold?"

Cole glanced at Chief, then at Ned and replied, "We're thinking about a ranch up by the Sangre de Cristos, Ma."

Ned knew that Belle and Kate would have no part of agreeing to such a plan. He looked at his plate and moved his steak and gravy around with his fork, smiling, as he waited for the response.

"A ranch!" Kate said.

"Sangre de Cristos?" Belle asked.

"Yes, ma'am," Cole responded. "Over in New Mexico Territory. You should see it, Ma -- the most beautiful country I've ever seen -- mountains, trees, streams and grass up to a horses knees. And lots of land can be had just for filing on it."

Kate dropped her fork with a clatter, "How do you think you could manage a ranch -- you're just a couple of kids -- babies! I won't hear to it!"

"Aw, Ma -- we ain't babies!" Cole protested.

Chief listened, then said smiling, "No, ma'am, Miss Kate -- we ain't babies. We're grown up warriors!"

Kate looked at Chief and scolded, "Warriors, my foot! Maybe in ten more years -- now you are children and I'll not have you running off to heaven knows where, thinking you're old enough to run a ranch and fight outlaws."

"Grandma, how old was you when you and Grandpa McCardle left Tennessee for Texas?" Cole asked. "I remember you telling me you was only fifteen when you ran away with Grandpa Mac, got married and came to Texas in a covered wagon. And I bet you didn't have twenty-five thousand dollars in gold to start that ranch down on the Brazos. Looks to me like you did alright."

Belle looked at her hands and said, "Yes, but that was different. People grew up quicker back then."

Cole knew he had them on the defense as he took a bite of biscuit and gravy, swallowed and continued. "And how old was Pa when he and Grandpa started Ceebara? Sixteen, that's how old! And he had already been in the war. We're fifteen and near about grown -- and we've been helping run Ceebara now for five or six years!"

"Humph!" Belle interrupted, "Running Ceebara? My, but you do have a good imagination. I'll grant you boys are good workers and know how to build fence and herd cows, but there's a lot more to running a ranch than using your hands and back -- it takes brains, and sometimes I think you don't have a brain in your head -- running off and having gun battles with outlaws."

"Grandma, you always said me and Chief were the two best cowboys on the ranch, and now you say we don't know how to think. I know we've got a lot to learn, but we can learn by experience."

Looking at Ned, he said, "Tell her, Pa -- tell her about that country and how we talked about starting a ranch up there."

Ned's face turned red, he coughed and glanced at Kate and Belle who were looking at him with fire in their eyes. "Now, Kate," he stammered. "maybe we should give it some thought. Maybe we could partner with the boys and help them get started. They wouldn't have to start too big -- maybe a few thousand acres and a thousand or so head. We could sell them the cattle on credit and they could use their gold to operate for a few years until they get on their feet."

"Who's going to look after them while they are doing all them great things," Belle asked, wiping tears from her eyes. "Who's going to do their cooking and house keeping and patching their clothes?"

"Maybe you could, Grandma," Cole replied. "Maybe you could go with us for awhile and help us get started. Ma and Pa could probably take care of Ceebara, and you could keep us in line and teach us how to run the business end of the ranch."

"And leave Kate here all by herself? I won't hear to it." Belle replied, with just a little interest in her voice.

"Sounds like a good idea to me, Belle. It's not really all that far," Ned said. "There's a stagecoach from Hidetown to Cimarron now -- just three days and you could be back home, or Kate could pay a visit with you."

"Yeah, Grandma," Cole pleaded, "It would be another adventure for you -- and not nearly as dangerous as when you and Grandpa Cole left Waco and trailed five thousand head of longhorns up to the Llano Estacado when it was still Indian country."

Chief smiled, "And you didn't get scalped, Miss Belle, even though pa and his warriors were very dangerous redskins," he said mischievously.

Kate got up from the table, wiped her eyes with her apron and rushed to her bedroom, slamming the door behind her. They could hear her sobbing.

"She'll get over it, Belle -- she's just like an old mother hen, she just doesn't want to see her chicks grow up and take off on their own -- afraid a chicken hawk might catch them."

Getting up, he picked up the coffee pot from the stove and poured them all a cup of fresh coffee, sat back down and said, "I think Cole has a great idea, Belle. At least think about it -- it would be a change and an adventure for you. If it didn't work, you could always be back home in three days."

Belle sipped at her coffee, gazing into her plate, thinking. "I've got to see about Kate," she said, getting up. "I'll think about it."

"Son, get those papers off the cabinet and bring them into my office. I need to put them into the safe before I forget it," Ned said as he pushed his chair back from the table.

Walking into the office, he kneeled before the huge safe and turned the dials. The safe door opened and Cole said, "Pa, let me see our gold."

Ned laughed, "It's still here. What's the matter, don't you trust me?"

"Yes, sir, I trust you. I just like to look at it."

22

"Fire!" Cody shouted from behind the bunk house.

Cowboys rushed outside to see who had shouted. To the west they could see the glow, as flames leaped skyward. Slim rushed to the house and ran inside without knocking.

"Better come look, boss. There's a prairie fire back to the west!"

Leaving the safe unlocked, with Cole's gold laying on the floor, Ned rushed outside. "Get the mules hitched to the fire wagon," he shouted. "Everybody mount up, we've got to stop it before it reaches headquarters."

When Kate and Belle began to pull on their boots, Ned said, "I wish ya'll wouldn't go -- we can take care of it."

"I'm going, Ned. No telling who might get hurt and need me to look after them. Mother, why don't you stay here and make coffee and sandwiches for the boys. You can bring them later if we have trouble getting control of the fire."

Belle didn't like it, but agreed to stay.

Ever since the first fire that raged across Ceebara range, Ned had kept one wagon loaded with all kinds of fire fighting equipment -- shovels, brooms, blankets, buckets and burn medicine. Two barrels of water were lashed to each side and one on the rear.

Within minutes, six mules were harnessed and hitched to the wagon. Smokey, on the seat, popped the whip, yelling, hee-yaw! as he guided the mules from the yard and toward the cut in the caprock. Mounted cowboys followed behind.

In the ranch house, Kate and Belle quickly dressed in their riding clothes, tied their hair up tight with bandanas, and ran from the building. Cole and Chief, riding their horses, led the two roan mares of the ladies to the porch and waited while Kate mounted. Together, they turned and loped from the yard, leaving Belle in the empty house as they followed the other cowboys toward the glow in the west.

....

Bat and Billy topped the ridge to the south of Red Deer Creek and watched as the inhabitants of the ranch abandoned headquarters and rushed to battle the blaze.

Pointing, Billy said, "There, Bat, behind the bunk house. I saw movement."

As they watched, four figures materialized from the shadows and moved cautiously toward the house. Another, leading four horses and two mules, rode down the trail from the top of the cliff and stopped at the corrals. Opening the gate, he led the animals inside the pen, then shut the gate. Running across the yard, he joined the others in the house.

"I don't know what they are up to," Bat said, "but if one of us covers the front and the other the back, we can pen them inside until Ned and the crew finish with the fire."

Looking to the caprock to the west, they could see the figures battling the blaze, and the fire had diminished considerably.

"They got to it in time," Billy said. "They'll have it under control soon."

Leaving their horses tied in the trees below the ranch house, they slipped silently toward the darkened buildings. Bat took the front and Billy the rear, picking positions so that they could cover anyone trying to escape.

Inside, Cody and his gang had surprised Belle as she was working in the kitchen. They tied her up, then found the opened safe and the Palo Duro gold on the floor. "Damn, would you look at that," Pete said, as he picked up a handful of the gold coins.

Cody was pulling packages of money out of the safe. "There must be three or four hundred thousand dollars," he said as he stuffed the bills into a burlap bag.

Little Joe laughed, "This beats stealing cows all to hell, boss," he said as he stuffed some of the gold coins into his pockets.

"What do we do now, boss?" Pete asked.

"I expect Armstrong is going to leave the crew up there on the ridge to put out any hot spots, and he and his woman will be returning soon. They ain't going to be expecting us, and when they come in, we'll pull down on them. I don't want anyone left to trail us when this is all over."

With their bags filled with cash, they filled their plates from the left over supper and walked out onto the veranda and watched as the ranch crew battled the blaze. "Just about got it out," Pete said, "They'll be coming back pretty soon."

....

Unknown to the outlaws, Bat and Billy watched from the shadows, with rifles and pistols loaded.

Bat, hidden next to the gate to the compound, levered a shell into his Winchester. He could see Billy waiting in the trees with his rifle pointed toward the house.

He heard the clatter of horses' hoofs in the distance and watched as five riders approached in the dark. When they were nearly upon him, he stepped from the shadows and shouted, "It's me, Ned -- Bat Masterson -- don't shoot."

Ned, Kate, Belle and the boys stopped just outside the gate, still hidden in the shadows of the cottonwoods. "What the hell you doing here, Bat?" Ned asked.

Rushing up to Ned's horse, Bat whispered. "Be quiet and get down, Ned. You've got company in the house. Billy's watching the back."

Ned was puzzled but didn't argue. Motioning to the others, they dismounted and gathered around Bat. Whispering, he quickly told Ned about Cody's plans to kill him. "They're waiting inside to ambush you. A couple of you needs to slip around to the back, and the rest of you need to join me in the front. "When we all get in place, we'll call them out."

Cole and Chief followed Bat, through the shadows to the front of the house. Belle and Kate joined Billy in the rear. Ned slipped to the barn and yelled, "O.K., Cody -- all of you come out with your hands up -- we've got you covered."

Cody shouted a reply, "I reckon you'll have to come in and get me, Armstrong, unless you want to be responsible for what happens to the woman."

"Belle, you alright?" Ned yelled.

"Don't listen to him, Ned. I'm O.K.," she replied.

"Cody!" This time it was Bat. "This is Sheriff Masterson, you're under arrest for cattle rustling. Come on out!"

"Alright, Sheriff --be right out," Cody replied, laughing shrilly.

Suddenly the front door opened, and Cody appeared, pushing Belle in front of him. He had a pistol pointed to her ear. "

"Now, Armstrong, here's what I want you to do," Cody said. "Our horses and mules are in the corral. Have those two boys lead them up here to the porch, then I want you to shuck your guns and back away from them."

Ned motioned to Cole and Chief, "Do as he says, boys," he ordered.

They ran to the corral, gathered the horses and began leading them across the yard. Cole whispered to Chief, "Watch me and do as I do," he said.

The other four outlaws materialized out of the dark room and stood behind Cody. He pushed Belle forward, and took a step toward Cole who was holding the reins to his horse.

Belle was staring into Cole's eyes, winked and nodded. As she did, she fell forward and Cole dropped to his knee, drawing so fast, the men on the porch failed to see the Colt appear in his hand.

The pistol barked and Cody fell on top of Belle. Chief's shot took out Pete before he could get a shot off at Cole. Behind them, Ned, Billy and Bat drew and fired as one. The other outlaws were knocked from their feet and rolled off he veranda onto the ground.

Cole quickly pulled Cody from the top of his grandmother, who was covered with blood, and helped her to sit. "Grandma? Grandma?" he shouted, "Are you shot?"

"I don't think so, Cole, but I think he may have broken my

ankle when he fell on me."

Ned rushed up, and examined her ankle. "I don't think its broken, Belle. Must have twisted it," he said as he helped her up.

Kate was crying as she took her mother's hand. "Oh, mother, I'm so sorry," she said.

"You've nothing to be sorry about Kate. Just be happy that your son is such a good shot with that pistol. Did you see him? He didn't have much to shoot at, with me in the way, but he hit that jasper square between the eyes."

Every body gathered around, congratulating Cole and Chief. Billy Dixon shook Chief's hand and said, "My friend, Quanah, would be proud of his young warrior if he were here. You are as brave as any warrior who ever rode these plains.'

Chief beamed.

While the men hauled the dead outlaws away from the house, Kate washed the blood from her mother's body and helped her to a chair. The ankle was already swelling and turning blue.

"Cole, I wish you would gather up that money and put it back in the safe. No need in it being scattered all over the place when our hands get back from fighting the fire," she said.

Leaving the outlaws lying outside the gate, Ned said, "We'll bury these sorry relics tomorrow, if the coyotes don't get them tonight. Let's get back and check on Belle."

They all gathered around the huge dining table. Ned got out a bottle of bourbon and poured each of them a drink, before saying, "A toast to my friends, Bat Masterson and Billy Dixon -- who once again, saved me and my family from a fate unthinkable."

They all held up their glasses and said, "Salute!"

"Now tell us how you showed up just in time to save our necks!"

Bat and Billy related how they had learned that Cody was coming to Mobeetie to murder Ned, and how they had ridden the stage, then Mark Huselby's horses, to reach the ranch. "Had it not been for the fire, we probably would not have made it in time."

"Cody was responsible for the fire, Bat. We found a burned blanket and lariat rope where he started it," Ned said. "He was hoping to get us all out of the house, then rob us. Maybe ambush us when we came back and kill us all."

"I think you're right, Ned. That's the way I'll make my report."

The next morning, Bat and Billy rode back to Mobeetie and caught the stage back to Dodge City.

23

"Kate, me and the boys are taking the wagon to Hidetown after a load of supplies. Better make a list of the things you need. You can go along if you wish," Ned said at the breakfast table a week later.

Kate had mellowed some about the idea of the boys striking out on their own, but still harbored some reservations. The idea of Belle going along removed some of her worries, but she could hardly think about what it would be like on Ceebara without her mother, they had always been together.

"Maybe I'll go with you, Ned -- I'd like to see what kind of new cloth Uncle Johnny has in stock. I need to make me a new dress," she said.

"I 'spect we'll be spending the night -- better take along some extra clothes," Ned said. "Cole, you and chief get the team harnessed and saddle a couple of horses, we need to leave in a couple of hours."

Cole and Chief rode their horses, trailing along behind the wagon as they splashed across Red Deer Creek and followed the wagon road south.

Ned pointed to a small herd of buffalo which were grazing along the Washita valley and said, "Ain't many of them left, Kate. Remember when we first came up from Waco in sixty-six, the prairie was covered with those shaggie beasts."

"I remember," Kate said. "Seems like a shame that they have all been killed."

"Yeah," Ned replied, "but some say that's progress. If the buffalo were still here there wouldn't be enough grass for our cattle. And now that sod busters are coming in, they couldn't grow their crops without having them trampled by the shaggies."

They rode awhile without speaking, thinking about the way the country had changed. Finally Ned said, "We haven't had a decent rain all spring -- and very little snow last winter. Notice how dry the grass is -- it usually is green as a gourd this time of year."

"I noticed," Kate said. "Reckon we'll have enough grass to run our herd next winter if it doesn't rain soon?"

"It's got me worried, Kate. I hadn't mentioned it because I kept hoping that the weather would change. If it stays dry much longer we may have to cull our herd and take some to market. I sure would hate to part with any of our cows -- there's not a one that isn't raising good calves, and most of them are bred to our new shorthorn bulls."

Kate didn't reply for several minutes, thinking, then said, "That country up west -- the Sangre de Cristos -- was it dry up there, too?"

"No, grass was green and it showered nearly every day. All of the low spots were standing in water," Ned replied as he slapped the mules with the reins to climb an exceptionally steep hill.

"Maybe we need to think about moving some of the cattle up there instead of selling them," she said, thoughtfully. "Seems like the boys are determined to strike out on their own. And they are good boys -- if mother is willing to go along, maybe she could keep them out of trouble."

Ned couldn't believe what he was hearing -- but Kate had always been a good thinker. Without showing too much enthusiasm, he replied, "That's a thought -- if we all filed on a piece of land each, maybe we could put together a good parcel. I understand that a lot of that country was divided up into large Spanish land grants years ago. That Dorsey spread is on the *Una de Gato* grant, and there's a *Maxwell* land grant that covers several thousand acres back in the mountains. Maybe we could find a grant that is for sale. I saw an article in the Raton newspaper that said Dorsey was thinking about selling a part of his ranch. It might be worth looking into."

"How could we find out," she asked without looking at him.

"Temple could probably find out -- I understand that he knows some of the politicians in Santa Fe. In fact, I heard him say that he was a friend of General Wallace, who is territorial governor of New Mexico."

"Well, why don't you ask Temple to get in touch with the governor in Santa Fe and see if anything is available," she said.

"Alright, Kate -- If Temple is in town, we'll pay him a visit today."

....

Hidetown, like the rest of the Texas Panhandle, was changing. No longer was it a disorganized group of buffalo hide hovels, but several rock and wooden businesses had been built on Main Street. Work had begun on a rock jail, the first in the Texas Panhandle. Main Street, such as it was, was only two blocks long and a majority of the businesses were still saloons and brothels.

Citizens of *Hidetown*, wanting a post office, had petitioned the state for service, and renamed the town *Sweetwater* after the Sweetwater Creek. However, since there was already a post office registered under the name of *Sweetwater* in Central Texas, the name was changed once again to *Mobeetie*, the Indian word for sweet water.

Fort Elliot, a mile west of the village, was home to over five hundred U.S. Cavalry, the black Buffalo Soldiers, who's principal duty was to patrol the area and keep recalcitrant Indians from returning to the plains from the reservation in Oklahoma Territory.

Fort Elliot even had a telegraph line that was a part of the communication system of forts surrounding the *Llano Estacado* -- and messages to all parts of the west could be sent and received in a matter of minutes.

Atascosa, eighty miles to the west, was also suffering growing pains, and the name was changed to *Tascosa* for postal purposes. Now a stagecoach line was servicing the area from Mobeetie to Tascosa and on to Las Vegas, New Mexico Territory.

Residents of Mobeetie had petitioned the state for formation of a county government and Wheeler County was organized, with the establishment of a county government consisting of a sheriff, judge and district attorney. Tascosa citizens were talking about getting Oldham County organized.

Twenty-one year old Temple Houston, youngest son of old Sam Houston, had been appointed District Attorney of the newly formed 35th Legislative District by the governor, The remaining 25 unorganized counties were attached to Wheeler County and DA Houston found himself the only legal authority over a forty thousand square mile   area which was inhabited by no more than a thousand people.

Houston had set up a temporary office in the back of Uncle Johnny Long's Mercantile store, where he conducted the legal business of the district. Lacking a court house, most trials were conducted in the Lady Gay Saloon.

"Well, howdy, Ned -- Miss Kate," Temple said as he stood and invited them into his office in the mercantile.

"Howdy, Temple," Ned replied as he pulled up a chair for Kate to sit in. Kate nodded politely.

The two boys came in and shook hands with Temple, and they all sat down around the rough desk.

"Well, tell me, what's going on over on Red Deer Creek. I've been intending to pay you a visit since you recovered your herd over in New Mexico, but I've been so damned busy trying to get the county organized that I just couldn't find time," Temple said. "Bat and Billy came through and told about the fire and the attempted robbery."

"Not much going on now, Temple, dry as hell," Ned answered, "We've been building fence, patrolling the Canadian for cattle bogged in quick sand, and building a set of corrals up on the *Llano*."

Looking at Cole, Temple smiled and asked, "You boys spent all that gold, yet?"

"No, sir -- we're saving it to buy us a ranch some day."

"That's a good idea. What about Colonel Goodnight -- he lay claim to the gold since it was found on his property?" Temple asked.

"No, sir. He said *'finders-keepers'* and we could keep the gold. He was proud someone had found it so his cowboys would stop searching for it."

"Well, I be damned! Now ain't that something," Temple said. "I'm proud of you boys!"

"That's what we want to visit with you about, Temple. The boys took a liking to that country up around Cimarron and think they would like to invest the gold in a ranch up there. I was hoping that you might help us find out what the homestead laws are in New Mexico Territory."

"I can probably do that, Ned. I know General Wallace, who is Territorial Governor. I'll ride out to the Fort and send him a wire."

"Ask about those Spanish Land Grants, too. Senator Dorsey's ranch is located on one of them, the *Una de Gato,* and he says there are several in that part of the territory that the government has taken over. Maybe we could file on one of them," Ned said.

Temple wrote on a pad, then asked, "Any particular area you are interested in?"

Cole spoke up, "Yes, sir -- from Fort Union to Cimarron, along the foot hills of the Sangre de Cristos."

"How long you going to be in town?"

"We plan on going back to the ranch tomorrow," Ned replied.

After thinking a moment, Temple said, "I'll see what I can find out let you know. It may take few days."

....

Returning to the ranch, Ned began to make plans to complete the fence between Ceebara and the LX.

"Cole, I think we've got enough posts cut. I wish you and Chief would go along with us to the west pasture and help with the fence building," Ned said as they were finishing breakfast.

Like most men of authority in the west, Ned refrained from using direct orders to his men -- he would politely say, *I wish you would* -- but Cole knew that *wish* meant, *this is what I want you to do*.

Cole nodded enthusiastically as he swallowed the last bite of biscuit. As far as he was concerned, anything would be better than cutting posts.

The new wagon was loaded with wire and the four mules were harnessed and hitched. The team of Belgium grays were harnessed and hitched to the big Conestoga which was loaded with posts. Biscuit had his chuck wagon filled with food and supplies, enough to last the crew of twenty a week, and the caravan headed west out of the Red Deer Valley.

Immediately, Ned began to see the results of the drought. He looked with concern, seeing that most of the playas were nearly dry and cattle were standing knee deep in mud, trying to get enough water to drink.

Slim rode up and said, "Looks bad, boss. There ain't enough water to last the week out, and it don't look like we're any closer to rain than we were last week."

Looking to the west, Ned watched the heat waves dance in the distance. "I think you're right, Slim. There's plenty of dry grass for them to eat, but they've got to have water. Let's leave the fence wagons here and chouse the cattle to the river."

Slim removed his hat and wiped the sweat from his brow, "We're just about on the break between the Red and Canadian Rivers. I'll take half of the boys and head south, getting the cattle moving toward the North Fork of the Red."

Ned nodded, "O.K., I'll take the rest of the crew and head north, pushing the cattle on this side to the Canadian."

Waving for Cole to come, Ned set his horse and cut a plug of tobacco and pushed it into his jaw. Cole loped up on Comanche, and asked, "What is it, Pa?"

"We're going to forget fence building for awhile. We've got to get these cattle to water. Get half of the men and unload the wire out of the wagon and replace it with half the grub out of the chuck wagon. Tell Biscuit to take the the chuck wagon and go along with Slim to the south. Tell Smokey I wish he would bring the other wagon and go along with us to the north. We'll spread out and make a drive to the Canadian."

Cole nodded and kicked Comanche into a lope. Chief joined him as he rode up to the chuck wagon and told Biscuit the plans. The cowboys began unloading the wire and soon had the wagon reloaded with food.

Spacing the cowboys one half mile apart, they began their drive. Every playa was virtually dry, and was covered with cattle, standing in mud up to their bellies. Shouting and whistling, the crew kept moving them off the plains and into the breaks of the Red and Canadian Rivers.

Once a drive was completed, they returned to the middle, moved five miles to the east, and started another drive. For four days they continued the process and finally had swept the west pasture clean of thirsty cattle. Both rivers had only a small amount of water flowing, but it was enough to keep the cattle satisfied.

....

Meeting back at the starting place, the cowboys reloaded the wire and began constructing the fence along the western Ceebara property line. They soon met up with the LX fence crew who were building from the river to the south.

Building a wire gate where the two fences met, they completed their job, satisfied that one side of the ranch would now keep the cattle from straying. Saying goodbye to the LX crew, they headed back to Red Deer Creek and found Temple waiting with Belle and Kate.

"Good news, Ned," Temple said. "I got hold of the governor and he said there was a small Spanish land grant which the government had taken over, just east of Fort Union. It runs along the foot of the mountains, north to Springer. Actually, it is an extension of the *Una de Gato* grant. Apparently it reaches back into the mountains eight or ten miles. Sounds just like what the boys are looking for."

"How many acres?" Ned asked.

"He didn't say, but estimated it to be about twenty miles square."

"How much will it cost," Cole asked, realizing his twenty-five thousand dollars wouldn't be enough to buy twenty square miles of ranch land.

"That's the good part about it, Cole. You can file on it, pay a couple of thousand dollars filing fee, and if you remain on it for a period of five years, it's yours, free and clear."

Cole and Chief were fit to be tied. They shouted and slapped each other on the back. "Ain't that great, ma?" he asked, enthusiastically.

Kate turned her head and brushed a tear from her eyes. She still couldn't bear to think of losing the two boys and her mother, all at once.

Ned shook Temple's hand and thanked him. "The news came just in time," he said. "We just got back from building fence on the plains and the lakes are dry and the grass is burning up. We pushed the cattle into the river bottoms but there won't be any grass left by winter unless we reduce the size of our herd."

"What do we need to do now, Mr. Temple," Cole asked.

"Governor Wallace assured me that he would put a hold on the land until you get your herd moved up. He said soon as you get located, ride into Santa Fe and he will have the papers ready for you to sign. What you intend to name that ranch, boys," Temple asked.

Cole smiled, "Well, I wanted to call it the C Bar P, and Chief wanted to call it the P Bar C, so we compromised and decided it would be the P D G Bar."

"Where did you come up with that brand," Ned asked.

Cole smiled, "Palo Duro Gold, Pa!"

Chief nodded and said, "And we're going to get us a bunch of them *golden* palomino ponies!"

Epilogue

Because of the 1881 drought in the Texas Panhandle, the P-D-G Bar ranch in New Mexico Territory was born. Ned sold Cole and Chief five thousand head of mama cows and one hundred good longhorn - shorthorn cross bulls, on credit, and they trailed them up the Canadian River to Springer, then released them along the foot hills of the Sangre de Cristo range, in Mora County.

Traveling to Santa Fe, they had met with Governor Wallace and signed the papers, taking possession of the old San Juan Spanish land grant. Their twenty-five thousand dollars in gold was deposited in the Santa Fe Bank and Trust,, and they then returned to their Palo Duro Gold ranch.

Belle came with them as did Smokey and two of the Garcia boys, Manuel and Pedro. A log and adobe ranch house was constructed, according to Belle's specifications, and before winter set in, they were enjoying the beautiful view of the mountain backdrop from their veranda, which surrounded the hacienda's exterior, and were watching their cattle, slick and fat, grazing in the valley below.

The ranch would grow, as would the boys, and they would continue to be confronted with cattle rustlers, gun slingers, outlaws and painted ladies.

Chief purchased a beautiful palomino stallion and several brood mares and began raising golden palominos, which became known throughout New Mexico as the best cow horses in the territory.

They soon learned that another new family was putting down roots in the area, the O'Gradys from Kentucky. The O'Grady boys, Trent, Terrel, and Trace had purchased a piece of land up near Mora and had brought their aged mother out from Kentucky to live with them. Ma O'Grady would become a good friend and companion of Belle's, and --- but wait, *that's another story*!

~

Books by Gerald McCathern

Fiction

Palo Duro Gold -- hb -- Historical Novel, Texas -- 1875 - 1881

Ceebara Series
Horns -- hb -- Historical Novel, Texas, 1865 -- 1875
Dry Bones -- hb -- Historical Novel -- Texas, 1875 -- 1881
Devil's Rope -- hb --Historical Novel -- Texas, 1881 -- 1887

Quarantine -- hb/sb -- Thriller/Terrorism -- Texas, 1996

Line of Succession -sb-Thriller/Conspiracy - 1965-1976

Nonfiction

Gentle Rebels -- hardback -- Farmer's Protest, 1979

From the White House to the Hoosegow -- softback
Farmer's Protest, 1978

To Kill the Goose -- hardback
"The importance of agriculture, 1986"

Order

Outlaw Books
419 Centre Street
Hereford, TX 79045

806-364-2838
gmccath@wtrt.net